John Creasey

writing as

Anthony Morton

A Rope For The Baron

CORGI BOOKS
A DIVISION OF TRANSWORLD PUBLISHERS LTD

A ROPE FOR THE BARON

A CORGI BOOK 0 552 09606 7

Originally published in Great Britain
by Hodder & Stoughton, Ltd.

PRINTING HISTORY
Hodder & Stoughton edition published 1949
Corgi edition published 1966
Corgi edition reissued 1974

This book is set in 10pt Times

Corgi Books are published by Transworld
Publishers Ltd.,
Cavendish House, 57–59 Uxbridge Road,
Ealing, London, W.5.

Made and printed in Great Britain by
Cox & Wyman Ltd., London, Reading and Fakenham

THE BARON
was a legend. He was surrounded
by an aura of glamour and romance –
the most brilliant, dare-devil cracksman
in the annals of crime!

A ROPE FOR THE BARON, one of
the Baron series, is by John Creasey
writing as Anthony Morton, of which
there are now over forty titles and
many have been published by Corgi
Books.
Born in 1908, John Creasey died in June
1973. Overall, his books have sold
nearly a hundred million copies and
have been translated into 28 languages.
As well as travelling extensively, he had a
particular interest in politics and was the
founder of *All Party Alliance*, which
advocates a new system of government
by the best candidates from all parties
and independents. He fought in five
parliamentary by-elections for the
movement.

Also by John Creasey

FIND THE BODY	A CLUTCH OF COPPERS
FIRST A MURDER	INVITATION TO ADVENTURE
RUN AWAY TO MURDER	DEATH ON THE MOVE
DON'T LET HIM KILL	REWARD FOR THE BARON
THE BLACK SPIDERS	ENGAGEMENT WITH DEATH
THE LONG SEARCH	WARN THE BARON
DEATH IN THE TREES	SHADOW OF DEATH
THE CRIMEHATERS	VERSUS THE BARON
DEATH IN A HURRY	DARK MYSTERY
DAY OF FEAR	THE TOFF TAKES SHARES
ELOPE TO DEATH	THE TOFF ON BOARD
ROGUE'S RANSOM	A KNIFE FOR THE TOFF
DEATH FROM BELOW	MEET THE BARON
SLEEPY DEATH	CLOSE THE DOOR ON MURDER
NO NEED TO DIE	THE TOFF IS BACK
THE SNATCH	A PUZZLE IN PEARLS
THE BIG CALL	TWO MEN MISSING
THE MAN WHO STAYED ALIVE	MURDER WITH MUSHROOMS
THE SPEAKER	A SCREAM OF MURDER
KILL OR BE KILLED	ACCUSE THE TOFF
GIVE ME MURDER	THE TOFF AMONG THE MILLIONS
WAIT FOR DEATH	KILL THE TOFF
COME HOME TO DEATH	THE GALLOWS ARE WAITING
BLACK FOR THE BARON	'WARE DANGER
MISSING OR DEAD	ATTACK THE BARON
A PROMISE OF DIAMONDS	THE SECRET MURDER
THE BARON RETURNS	HUNT THE TOFF
A BRANCH FOR THE BARON	THE BARON AT LARGE
BLAME FOR THE BARON	ALIAS THE BARON
TRAP THE BARON	MYSTERY MOTIVE
DEATH ON DEMAND	A RABBLE OF REBELS
SHADOW THE BARON	LET'S KILL UNCLE LIONEL
A TASTE OF TREASURE	CALL FOR THE BARON
TERROR BY DAY	MURDER MOST FOUL
DEATH IN DIAMONDS	DEATH IN FLAMES
MURDER TOO LATE	DEATH IN HIGH PLACES
DOUBLE FOR DEATH	THE BARON COMES BACK
A CASE FOR THE BARON	THE BARON AND THE BEGGAR
THE DARK CIRCLE	THE BARON RETURNS
THE BARON AGAIN	THE TOFF AT BUTLIN'S

and published by Corgi Books

A Rope For The Baron

CHAPTER I

WARNING

THE narrow road wound over the bleak country side, dark and forbidding in the autumn evening. Here and there lonely trees, bent from the constant lashing of wind off the rocky coast near by, stood forlorn and frail. Great rocks of yellow sandstone rose out of the ashy soil, and nothing grew between their cracks and crevices. To the west, the sun was sinking, half hidden by heavy grey clouds which spread slowly and menacingly over the sky. Premature darkness fell upon the moor, but the winding, sandy road stood out clearly against the dark earth. The driver of the powerful car moving along it did not slacken speed.

The wild country was undulating, the road uneven; the car rode uneasily. Now it went uphill, now down into a shallow valley; here a tiny stream flowed across the road. The car splashed through it, and brown-coloured water speckled the windshield, planting a blotch of mud immediately in front of the driver's eyes, blocking his view.

He slowed down.

'Freakish thing,' he murmured to himself.

The windshield wiper smeared the mud so that he could not see out at all. He turned off the wiper and stopped the car. Taking a cloth from the dashboard pocket, he got out to clean the windshield.

Wind rustled the fawn-coloured raincoat which hung straight from broad, square shoulders; he was tall and lean, and his clear, hazel eyes were narrowed with the strain of driving. His face was striking; in repose it might have been chiselled out of the native rock, handsome yet rugged. He moved without haste, yet each movement hinted at great physical strength.

His calm eyes took in every part of the scene—and stopped roving when he saw a man standing by some rocks; standing and staring.

- It was a little man, brown and wizened, who did not move. He was dressed in brown, and only just discernible against the rocks.

The driver pretended not to notice him, and wiped the glass; the mud was thick and clayey; surely the wheels hadn't thrown that up. As he worked, he glanced casually towards the rocks which were ten or twelve feet high. Beyond them, the turbulent clouds were fringed with purple and red, but in the centre black and ominous. Northwards, rain was falling in dark, wide streaks.

As he finished with the cloth, the man raised his arm and beckoned.

The motorist glanced around. No one else was in sight, there seemed no reason why the man should not come forward. As he made no move, however, the driver went slowly towards him, stepping off the road on to dark, ashy soil sparsely covered with coarse grass and tough, straggly heather. The ground sloped sharply downwards towards the rocks, between which the stream flowed silently, reflecting the sullen sky.

The motorist paused.

'Come—please,' called the stranger.

His voice was frail, sighing as the wind might sigh, and he beckoned again.

The motorist leapt over the stream, and his heels sank in the brown mud, probably the same as that which had struck the windshield.

Now the wizened man took a few steps forward.

'Good evening,' said the driver dryly. 'Did you throw that mud?'

'I wanted—to stop you.'

'Well, you succeeded. What do you want?'

A few grey hairs curled beneath a cloth cap. The man was clean-shaven, but a day's stubble made a grey mist on his tanned cheeks. He looked hardy and weather-beaten, but his eyes were moist and bloodshot; he was tired, ill. His features were small; a little button of a nose made him look

8

comical, but it was tragicomedy; he was like a man yearning for sleep.

'Well, what *did* you want me for?' the motorist asked patiently.

The little man seemed to find it an effort to speak. He opened his lips, paused, opened them again, and said in the sighing voice:

'You are going to Hallen House?'

'Yes.'

'Ah-h!' The bloodshot eyes widened. 'So I was right. I warn you—don't go.'

'I must go.'

'Don't go,' repeated the little man. 'You mustn't go; there is evil at that house. Men wait there to strike all visitors down. There is evil and death at Hallen House.'

A gust of wind blew down from the north, whistling and whining, stirring the surface of the stream and the grass and heather, blowing sand over the rocks, tipping the cap from the little man's head and revealing his bald pate. It died away, and stillness reigned, but in the distance the wind was whining as if carrying an echo: '. . . death at Hallen House!'

If this ruffled the driver's composure, there was no sign of it in his voice.

'Do you mean someone has died there recently?'

'There is death——' began the stranger.

His words had become a refrain, uttered without feeling. He looked dazedly at the motorist, pressing his hand to his forehead, pressing hard, as if the effort had sapped what little strength he had.

All was quiet except for a distant sound, quick and regular. Tap-tap-tap-tap-tap!—the rhythm of a horse and rider approaching along the road which led to Hallen House.

'You—hear that?' The little man's voice was tense; a new light sprang into his eyes. Fear?

'Yes, it's——'

'Don't go,' whispered the other urgently, 'don't go on; I have warned you.'

He turned round swiftly, evaded the motorist's grasp, and slipped through a narrow fissure in the rocks, quickly lost to sight in the brooding gloom.

Another gust of wind shrieked over the moor, drowning all other sound. As it died away, leaving an uncanny silence, the driver turned towards his car. He heard the clip-clop of hooves plainly now, but could not see the rider. He climbed up to the road and peered along it; even the Sunbeam-Talbot was enveloped in the gloom; the black clouds were almost overhead.

He stood by the open door, and in the distance saw a wall of rain approaching. The hoofbeats drew nearer, as if the rider was making a desperate attempt to reach cover before the storm.

Clippety, clippety; but still he could not see the rider, although the breakneck pace passed on to him a sense of urgency.

The wall of rain drew nearer.

The black heavens were split in a vivid white flash! Lightning clove the clouds in two and lit up the moors in its lurid glare. Not far away, a woman was bending forward over the neck of a galloping horse, but thunder rolled and belched over the earth, drowning the sound of hoofbeats.

The driver reached inside the car and switched on the headlights. The beams caught the horse and rider, who were now only fifty yards away, and the woman straightened up in the saddle. Another flash of lightning was followed by a great roll of thunder; horse and rider alike would be afraid and glad of company. Yes, the woman was pulling at the reins.

Would the horse obey? Or would it gallop past in fright?

No, it was still under control, slowing down with graceful strides, its head well up.

The woman was young and hatless, and her face showed vividly in the bright headlights. Her fair hair was streaming back in the wind, making her Diana, hunted and not hunting; beautiful in a stormy way; at one with the elements.

The driver went forward as she slowed to walking pace. Lightning dimmed the headlights and threw her beauty into sharp relief. As she opened her lips a deafening roll of thunder drowned her words. She did not look scared, but aloof from the fury of the storm as she pulled up the horse only a yard or so away from the car.

The rain would smash upon them at any moment now.

The motorist smiled up at her.

'You'd better take shelter.'

She made no attempt to dismount, but sat there staring at him, her eyes bright and tense, her lovely body rigid.

'Are you—John Mannering?'

'Yes.' Only a slight narrowing of his eyes showed his surprise.

'Don't go on,' she said fiercely. 'Don't go to Hallen House; you may never come back alive.'

Across Mannering's mind flashed a picture of the weary, wizened, little man on the rocks. This woman wasn't tired, and she spoke with passion. Her voice carried clearly until it was swallowed up by thunder.

As it roared and crackled overhead, man and girl stared at each other, made dumb by the cacophony overhead.

Out of the dying rumbles came the girl's voice.

'Did you hear me?'

'I've travelled two hundred miles to visit Hallen House.'

'If you'd travelled a thousand I would still tell you to go back. You may never return alive; you'll certainly be in grave danger. You mustn't go.'

'I'm going,' said Mannering quietly.

She sat glaring, as if furiously angry, and trying to will him to change his mind. Yet in increasing darkness, blotting out the day, he saw something in her eyes which matched the fear in the little man's. She was fighting that fear and holding hard on to her courage.

The thunder boomed; she raised her voice to make herself heard:

'You'll be a fool if you go, I've warned you, you may never come back.'

'At least tell me why.'

'I've no time to explain. Don't go!'

Her haste wasn't all due to the storm.

Some way behind her was a lighter misty patch, which crept nearer. The girl either sensed it or saw Mannering looking past her, and guessed why. She glanced round quickly. A car was approaching with its headlights on, but it was still some way off.

She leaned down and touched his arm.

'Your death will be on your own head. Don't go.'

She straightened up, pressed her heels into the horse's flanks and made it rear. A lull made her voice seem loud and strident.

'Don't be a fool, stay away from Hallen House. But if you do go on——'

She knew that he would.

'Yes?'

'Don't say you've seen me. Please!'

The thunder swallowed the last word as she rode away.

Lightning dimmed the glow from the oncoming car, but when the flash faded, Mannering saw the headlights clearly—bright twin orbs and the dark shape of the car beyond. The clip-clop-clip-clop of the disappearing rider faded slowly.

Tired old man and handsome girl, both appearing out of the blue on the wild moor, saying 'don't go,' but refusing a word of explanation; and both undoubtedly frightened.

Fear had driven the girl away—fear of someone in the oncoming car, and of being seen talking to him.

He leaned inside the car and dipped his headlights; the lights on the other car dipped in response. The thunder was shifting noisily south, and the lightning was less vivid; but he fancied he could still hear the galloping hooves. *Clippety —don't go. Clippety—don't go.*

The rain hadn't reached him yet.

The other car drew up, and a tall, loose-limbed young man jumped out. There was nothing sinister about him as he smiled and called:

'Hell's bells, what a day! I'm from Hallen House. You Mr. Mannering.?'

'Yes.'

'Glad I've caught you here,' bellowed the young man. 'Easily miss the way in the dark. Going to be a big storm. May last all night. You okay?'

Mannering nodded.

'Nothing wrong, is there?' asked the stranger. 'Holding you up, I mean.'

'No, I stopped to wipe my windshield.'

'Better than a broken big-end! Well, we'd better get on. Just follow me, then. I won't be a brace of shakes.'

The young man grinned; lightning lit up his white teeth and blue eyes, his fair hair and fresh complexion; he was handsome and powerful, with a swashbuckling air. In his car he reversed for a few yards and swung on to the moor. Mannering slid into his seat, waited until the other was moving along the road again, then he let in the clutch and followed.

They were a mile along a rough road when the rain swept down on them, and he saw the red light of the leading car

12

through a blur. Soon, water was splashing up from large puddles, streaking his windshield, but he continued to drive on to Hallen House.

CHAPTER II

HALLEN HOUSE

THE rain had passed when they reached the gates of the house, and the centre of the storm had moved south. A faint tinge of daylight from the west spread over the country-side, casting an eerie glow upon the trees which lined the steep drive and upon the house, which was on the brow of a hill, its battlemented roof stark against the leaden sky. He had a glimpse of grey stone walls, arched, narrow win-dows and the massive, pillared doorway. At the front was a circular drive, dotted with puddles; in the middle of the drive was a single cedar tree which spread out long, furry arms as if to clutch anyone who passed.

The young man pulled up beyond the entrance, enabling Mannering to stop immediately outside the front door. As Mannering got out, the young man hurried to him, giving another broad grin.

'All quiet and serene,' he declared heartily. 'You okay?'

'*I'm* all right.'

Was the heartiness forced?

'That's what the doctor ordered!' boomed the young man, and continued, 'One of the men will bring in your bag and take your car round. Won't keep you two shakes of a lamb's tail!' He dug his hand into his pocket and took out a ring of keys, selected one and inserted it in the lock of the door. He pushed the door open and stood aside with a flourish.

'Welcome to Hallen House, sir!'

'Thanks,' murmured Mannering, stepping inside a vast hall.

Two electric lights shone dimly from the great height of the ceiling. A huge circular staircase led up to a gallery and spacious landing. Downstairs, several heavy, arched doors were closed.

'Let's have some more light on,' said the young man. He pressed switches, and lights blazed on the walls from flame-shaped lamps tipped with red, which made a reddish glow on the ceiling. 'Brrr, it's cold! You certainly chose a nasty day to come, Mr. Mannering.'

'Yes, didn't I?'

'But now you're here it's all right,' said the young man. 'Mr. Bellamy's bursting to see you. I'm his secretary, Harrison.'

'Oh, yes,' said Mannering, politely. 'You wrote to me.'

'That's right,' agreed Harrison. 'I'm the amanuensis. Let's go into the warm.'

He gave Mannering a sharp, piercing look before leading the way to one of the doors. It opened into a large, panelled room, where a coal fire blazed, spreading a pleasant warmth. Several huge leather arm-chairs were drawn up by the fire, and on a small table, bottles and glasses sparkled in the firelight. Harrison pressed a switch, and concealed lighting spread a friendly radiance about the room.

'Whisky?'

'Thanks,' said Mannering.

'Good!' Harrison rubbed his hands together, then clapped them and looked at Mannering in consternation. 'What an oaf I am! I forgot to take your hat and coat. Sorry, old chap. Hand over.' He took the hat and coat hastily. 'Help yourself, I'll be back in a jiffy,' he boomed, and hurried out of the room, closing the door behind him.

Mannering stepped swiftly in his wake, opened the door an inch, and backed away. Now he could hear anything said in the hall.

'Are they back?' That was Harrison.

'No.' That was a woman's voice.

'Any news at all?'

'None.'

'I'll break Rundle's neck,' growled Harrison. 'But no harm's done: they didn't see Mannering. Take these, I mustn't leave him alone too long. Where's the old man?'

'He'll soon be down.'

'Let me know the moment there's any news,' said Harrison.

When the man returned to the room, Mannering was standing with his back to the fire, drinking a whisky and soda. He smiled pleasantly. Harrison did not appear to notice that the door had been opened. He slammed it behind him and came briskly to the table.

'It *is* cold for the time of the year, and Mr. Bellamy thought you'd be glad of a fire. If the moor's like this in autumn, what the devil's it going to be like in winter?'

'Is this your first year here?' asked Mannering.

'Oh, yes. We've only recently bought the place,' said Harrison. 'Lock, stock, and barrel! All we want is a moat and drawbridge, and it would be a feudal castle.' He poured himself out a stiff peg, put in a splash of soda, and tossed the drink down. 'Ah-h, nothing like whisky to warm the old cockles, is there? 'Nother?'

'No, I'm all right, thanks.' Mannering was conscious of his own tension and restraint, and hoped Harrison would put it down to a diffidence in new surroundings.

'Plenty of time,' said Harrison, and poured himself a second stiff drink. He sipped it this time, and took a cigarette-case from his pocket. 'Smoke?'

He gave Mannering another bold, piercing look as he proffered his case. Was it suspicious?

Mannering took a cigarette, and said: 'I never like thunderstorms.'

Harrison gave an explosive laugh, and his face cleared; that had reassured him. But Mannering saw beneath the surface. The cloak of *bonhomie* would drop from Harrison's shoulders in a flash, if he chose. He was undoubtedly a personality—and not quite so young as he had at first appeared; in the early thirties, Mannering judged. His curly hair was cut short at the sides, his face was lean and his cheeks were pleasantly tanned; a strong, well-built and healthy man, with fine ease of movement and a nonchalant manner. He had clear blue eyes, a short straight nose, short upper lip, and a wide, well-shaped mouth; a sensuous mouth.

He was taller than Mannering, who stood six feet; a powerful adversary.

Adversary?

Yes, the thought was in Mannering's mind, put there by the old man and the girl. But would he have thought of hostility but for those warnings?

'You'll want to see your room,' Harrison said at last. He seemed unable to keep still. 'Come on.'

They went up the great staircase, past oil paintings of full-length figures, along a wide passage, and into the huge, end room. A four-poster bed against the door-wall was lost in it; large furniture seemed dwarfed by an open fireplace and window.

'You've your own bathroom and what not,' Harrison said, pointing to a door in the corner. 'Make yourself at home. I'll see you downstairs.'

'Thanks very much.'

Harrison waved and went out.

Mannering washed, then took stock of the room. The furniture was massive and really old; the dark-brown carpet had a thick pile. His suitcase had been brought up, and so he put on a clean collar, anxious not to stay upstairs too long. For there was mystery here, even if there were no danger; and Harrison might give him a clue to the mystery.

Mystery and crime were part of his business.

Harrison was sitting alone in the big room. He looked up eagerly.

'Can't say how grateful we are to you,' he burst out. 'Coming this frightful journey. Benighted place. Live here for years and no one would know. Die here, if it came to that!'

Was that just a casual remark?

'With the moor as a burial ground,' murmured Mannering.

'Hold it!' protested Harrison. 'Creepy thought! Still, it is lonely. And Mr. Bellamy can't get about much, you now. Told you, didn't I. Paralysis. Goes about in a wheel-chair. Lucky thing it only affects his legs. All right otherwise. Got full possession of his faculties, I assure you. Brilliant man— absolutely brilliant! And he'll be grateful because you've come, Mr. Mannering.'

'Well, I want to buy what he has to sell.'

'Oh, yes,' said Harrison. 'Business—but I hope it will also be a pleasure. How's life at Quinn's?' He did not wait for an answer. 'You've a wonderful little shop. Been told that you do more business there than at half the bigger places in London. Fascinating. Had a look round there myself a year ago. Must have a fortune in stock.'

'It is quite valuable,' agreed Mannering.

Harrison started to laugh. 'Ha! Quite valuable! You will have your little joke, Mr. Mannering. Don't mind admitting

17

that I've never seen a collection like it, although I've lived among antiques and *objets d'art* all my life. Brought up among them—that's how I came to suit Mr. Bellamy. I'm glad I can hold the job down—you'd be amazed if you knew what I'm doing.

'Would I?' asked Mannering.

'You would. Cataloguing the contents of this place—and Mr. Bellamy's collection. Stupendous! Fascinating! I——'

Someone tapped at the door.

'Oh, sorry,' said Harrison, jumping up. 'That might be a message from Mr. Bellamy.' He strode out of the room and closed the door with a snap.

It was too risky to open it again, but Mannering crossed the room and listened intently.

'. . . serve her damned well right,' Harrison was saying. 'Where is she?'

'Gone to her room.' That was the woman who had spoken before. 'Do you want to see her?'

'I'm going to see her all right.'

There was menace in the words.

The voices stopped, and footsteps rang out clearly. Mannering opened the door an inch or two, and looked into the hall. Two dim lamps were on, and the light from this room made a bright oblong on the floor. He slipped out, closing the door, and stood quite still, able now to hear two sets of footsteps—those of Harrison, who was near the landing, and of the woman, who had gone into another room on the ground floor. Slowly all sound faded, and the house was silent except for the heavy ticking of a huge clock near him. *Tick-tock-tick-tock.* It reminded him of the girl riding across the moor. *Tick-tock. Clip-clop.* . . . 'Don't go!'

He could just see Harrison's shadow on the landing, and suddenly heard a tapping sound; a knock at the girl's door?

He mustn't stay here too long.

'*Stella!*' Harrison's voice boomed out impatiently. 'Let me in!'

Mannering heard a rustle of movement, and looked towards the stairs, alarmed lest he were being spied on. There was no cause for alarm, but for astonishment. A shadowy figure was creeping down, hand on the rail, glancing behind her; a girl—*the* girl! She reached the hall and, without noticing him, hurried to the door of the room which he had just left.

'Stella, old dear.' Harrison began to wheedle; at least he believed that the girl was still in her room.

The girl opened the door and slipped into the room. As she closed the door behind her, Mannering heard an exclamation of dismay. When he went in, she was staring towards the far corner. She heard him, and swung round; her face was a mask of fear.

'Oh!'

'All's well,' murmured Mannering.

He closed the door and leaned against it. Behind the girl the fire blazed, filling the room with light and shadow. Her yellow, woollen jumper clung to her fine figure; her hair was plastered about her head and forehead, and stuck to her cheeks. She was trembling, perhaps from both shock and cold.

'So—you've come.'

'I told you I was coming, and I'm very glad I'm here.'

'*You must go away!*' she said hoarsely.

'Now don't let's go over that again,' said Mannering.

Her eyes were feverishly bright; despite her appearance and her agitation, her beauty shone through. She was nearly as tall as he, but above all those things, he saw her as a woman in desperate straits.

'I'd like to help you,' he said.

'I—I don't need help! You do. They're going to——'

'*Stella!*'

The door burst open, Mannering moved hastily, and Harrison strode in. *Had he heard those last words?* Mannering scanned his face, trying to judge. 'Stella,' Harrison repeated more quietly, and the girl raised her head as if in a gesture of defiance. 'Why on earth did you go out in the rain? You'll catch your death. And why did you come in here?'

'To—to get warm.'

'A hot bath is what you need,' said Harrison, heartily. 'Then a hot toddy and bed!'

He looked over his shoulder, and a woman came into the room.

She was short and stocky, dressed in a long dark-blue frock, which looked like a uniform. Her jet-black hair was plaited and coiled tightly about her head. Her face was pale, her lips a faint pink mark against the whiteness. Mannering noticed all those things, but her eyes held his attention; these were round, light grey, and curiously dull and lifeless, as if they were without sight.

19

The girl's lips tightened, and she sent the woman a look of hatred.

'Oh, Mrs. Dent,' said Harrison, 'run a hot bath for Miss Bellamy at once, will you? Go upstairs with Mrs. Dent, old girl,' he said to Stella. He was desperately anxious to make this appear normal, and not to arouse in Mannering any suspicions of his behaviour, and he over-elaborated.

Would she defy him again?

No, she hadn't the strength of will. She walked past him, head high, yet unable to conceal her fear both of the man and the woman. She did not look at Mannering again as she entered the hall, followed by the older woman.

Mannering turned to the table and picked up his glass casually. Some remark was called for.

'She looks chilled through and through.'

'She is. Mannering——' For the first .time Harrison dropped the 'Mr.' 'Did she say anything to you?'

'She was about to when you came in,' said Mannering. 'I'd advised her to change her clothes, and she'—he shrugged his shoulders—'rather let off at me. She didn't want help or advice, I gathered.'

Harrison's explosive little laugh burst out.

'Ha! No—she wouldn't want help, she's an independent little devil. Strong-willed?' He tapped his forehead significantly. 'Up to a point. Mr. Bellamy's niece,' he declared. 'She was never very strong. This house upsets her. If I were the old man, I'd have her put away somewhere. Or have someone here to look after her. But she won't worry us any more.' He sauntered over to the door and picked up his half-finished whisky. 'Ready for another?'

'Thanks.'

'Mr. Bellamy won't keep you long,' said Harrison. 'We'll have the preliminary chat before dinner. Dinner's an event here! The old man's something of a gourmet. Makes your mouth water, doesn't it?'

Mannering smiled. 'It sounds attractive.'

'We knew you'd appreciate it,' said Harrison, and finished his drink. 'Won't mind if we don't change tonight, will you? Changing is a bit of an ordeal for Mr. Bellamy, and he only gets into a bow tie on great occasions. Ha! Not that this isn't a great occasion—family occasions, I really meant! I was saying, before I went out, he's a remarkable man. Brilliant. And wealthy. There can't be many men left in the

20

country as wealthy as Silas Bellamy. Although you haven't many paupers among your customers at Quinn's, have you?'

'Not many,' murmured Mannering.

'I'll bet you haven't! It isn't often we put anything on the market,' Harrison went on, 'but when we saw your advertisement in *Apollo*, we answered it. I *think* the old man was as anxious to see you as he was to sell the emeralds. Oh, he'll sell 'em all right—he's a man of his word, but he'll think a talk with you worth as much as the money. You've got a buyer, I suppose?'

'At a price,' said Mannering cautiously.

'Oh, the boss won't sting you,' Harrison assured him. 'He's fair—too fair, I sometimes think. Too soft-hearted. I suppose his own affliction makes him——'

Harrison broke off and turned round, although Mannering had heard nothing. The door opened, and Harrison hurried across and pulled it wide.

A man in a wheel-chair came slowly into the room.

CHAPTER III

SILAS BELLAMY

IT was all wrong.

No man who looked as big and healthy as Bellamy, should be tied to a wheel-chair, his withered legs hidden by a black rug. He wore a dark-grey coat and waistcoat, across which stretched a gold albert, and he was perfectly tailored. He had a fine face and plentiful grey hair, parted in the middle and waving back. His smile of greeting radiated good will as he turned a wheel of his chair with his left hand, and held his right out towards Mannering.

'Well, Mr. Mannering, I'm delighted to see you—really delighted!'

'Nice of you,' said Mannering, smiling in turn.

Bellamy's handclasp was strong, his hand cool. His voice held a faint American accent.

'Not at all, Mr. Mannering, nice of you to travel such a distance at the whim of a helpless old man.' Bellamy looked no more than fifty-five. 'I just had a desire to see you, sir, to meet you in the flesh; I've heard so much about you and Quinn's. There aren't many shops famous throughout the world, Mr. Mannering, but Quinn's is one.' He glanced at Mannering's glass. 'Come on, now, you aren't drinking. Fill Mr. Mannering's glass, Jim.'

Harrison sprang to obey.

'Now sit down, Mr. Mannering—I can see you better when we're on the level. I don't mind admitting, sir, that wherever I've been I've heard of the reputation of Quinn's.

New York, Cairo, Bombay, Paris, Buenos Aires—but you don't need me to tell you what you know already. It's a fine little place you've got, and one of these days I'm going to see it, or my name's not Silas Bellamy.'

'Which,' said Harrison, coming forward with the glass, 'it is.'

'If you've travelled so far, I can't understand why you haven't been to London,' Mannering remarked.

'Well now, there's quite a story behind that,' said Bellamy. 'I wasn't always like this. I could get about when I was younger, but I didn't go to London. For some peculiar reason I couldn't make London—three times I was on the point of going when I was recalled. I lived and worked in New York, Mr. Mannering. And the fates played a cruel trick on me, they kept me away from what you folk call the largest city in the world.' When Mannering made no answer, he chuckled. 'Mr. Mannering, I've taken quite a liking to you already—forgive an old man for being frank. Most English people would shout: "so it is" when I said that about London.'

Mannering laughed. 'I know it is.'

'Well, that's a good one—that's what I like—a man who *knows*. Joking apart, Mr. Mannering, I'm proud to have you under my roof. I hope you'll enjoy my hospitality for more than one night. Yes, yes, I know that's what was arranged, but sometimes the best of us change our plans, don't we?'

Was it imagination, or was there a threat in the words? The emphasis on the desire to bring Mannering down here; the hint that he might stay longer than he expected; the curious way that Harrison had said, 'which . . . it is,' when his employer had said 'or my name's not Bellamy.'

'I'm sorry you arrived late, and it's dark now,' Bellamy said. 'I was looking forward to showing you over this old house tonight, Mr. Mannering, but that will have to wait until the morning. You couldn't see much of it, could you?'

'Very little,' said Mannering, 'but it's imposing.'

'I always dreamed of owning a house like this,' Bellamy said, 'a long, long while before I was rich enough to hope for it. A real English castle! And I guess that's what it is. Why, parts of this building are over six hundred years old, Mr. Mannering. The chapel is in its original state. Some of the furniture goes back to the twelfth century—you'll see that's true when you've had a good look round. It makes me feel like a piece of old England myself when I realise I own this place.'

'And you do,' Harrison drawled.

'Surely! Now, Mr. Mannering, you're a business man and a good one, or Quinn's wouldn't have the reputation it has. And as a business man, you want to get business done. That suits me. Jim——'

Harrison went to a Jacobean dresser in a corner, while Bellamy watched smilingly. Harrison opened a cupboard and took out a black leather jewel-case. He brought it to Bellamy, who held it in one hand, weighed it up and down slowly, then opened it.

The lambent green beauty of emeralds stole into the room, glistening on a pad of black velvet. There were three stones; the largest, in the centre, was shaped like a heart; those on either side were oval-shaped, and all were beautifully cut.

Bellamy handed the case to Mannering, who took it without comment and stepped nearer the light. He did not need to use his glass or to inspect them closely to see that these were the Lake Emeralds.

He was here to buy them for a dealer who said he had been seeking them for years. They had last been heard of in the United States; but no one had admitted possession until Bellamy had answered his advertisement for them. Precious stones like these gave rise to many crimes.

Had Bellamy a right to them?

Both men were watching him. Cat and mouse?

He looked up.

'Very few men would like to part with these, Mr. Bellamy.'

'I'm not saying I *want* to part,' said Bellamy, 'but I reckon you wouldn't want to buy them for someone else if that someone didn't want them mighty bad. It's a small sacrifice for getting you to come down here, and if we get the business over, we can enjoy ourselves. What *about* the price?'

'Three thousand pounds,' Mannering said, and did not miss the emphasis on 'getting you to come down here.'

'They're worth all of six!'

'Yes, I think they are, but three is my limit.'

'Five?' Bellamy said.

'I can commit myself to three, but no more.'

Bellamy looked at Harrison with a comical gesture.

'Well, Jim, he's hard—but they didn't cost me that much, did they? Three thousand pounds—all right, Mr. Mannering!

Put them in your pocket, you can give me a cheque before you leave. Satisfied with your visit *now*?'

'I'll give you the cheque right away,' said Mannering.

'Sure, suit yourself,' said Bellamy.

Mannering wrote out the cheque on the arm of his chair— a cheque for £3,000 to pay for jewels worth £10,000! He took the slip of paper to the fire to dry, conscious of the exchange of glances between the two men, needing no more telling that much was wrong. He had been prepared to pay £8,000, had offered an absurdly low figure to test Bellamy— and it hadn't been easy to keep a poker face during the brief, too easy haggling.

No man in his senses would sell these for £3,000.

Did it mean that they knew he would never take them away from the house?

Bellamy gave him a receipt with a flourish.

'Now we can enjoy our dinner. I wish everyone would close a deal as quickly as that.'

Dinner was served in the next room, a vast, high-ceilinged chamber. Of two chandeliers, only one was lighted, so that the far end of the room was left in cavernous darkness. Mannering could just discern the shape of pictures hanging on the walls, and tall chairs, a vast sideboard, laden with silver. The table was long and narrow, with a dozen chairs standing close to it. Bellamy sat in his wheel-chair, Harrison on one side of him, Mannering on the other. The light glistened on polished oak and gleaming silver. Lace table-mats made delicate white patterns on the wood. Harrison poured the wines—a dry sherry with the soup, a red Rhine wine with the fish; afterwards, champagne. A soft-footed butler waited on them. The meal was superb. Bellamy ate with a keen appetite; Harrison wolfed his food. Bellamy did most of the talking, and Mannering had only to say a word here and there, usually in answer to questions flung carelessly at him. He could not throw off the restraint which he had felt from the moment he had seen Harrison; before, he had blamed it on the strange encounters. He didn't now, for Bellamy and Harrison would have behaved like this in any case. He felt that they weren't interested in him, didn't care why he was so quiet; they had him here and that satisfied them.

But the Lake Emeralds nestled against his side. He could afford to smile.

Stella wasn't mentioned.

'I think we'll have liqueurs in the other room,' Bellamy said at last. 'We'll be more comfortable.'

Harrison jumped up to open the door, and Bellamy wheeled his chair swiftly into the hall. Mannering followed slowly. Neither of them had troubled to wait for him, but treated him with that remarkable casualness; almost indifference.

The butler appeared in the hall as Harrison opened the door of the smaller room.

'What is it, Holmes?' asked Bellamy.

'I'm sorry to interrupt you, sir, but Mr. Lark has called,' said the butler. 'I told him you were engaged, but he——'

'Sure, I'll see him. You won't mind, Mr. Mannering? Lark is a man who does some buying for me in London. Wonderful eye for a good thing—eh, Jim? He can pick out winners every time—our kind of winners, you understand, not horses!' He grinned, and Harrison gave his staccato laugh. 'But you know the game. If we paid the highest price for everything, we'd never have a penny to call our own. Send him in here, Holmes.'

'Very good, sir.' Holmes bent a curious, dark gaze on Mannering as he went silently out.

The fire was blazing; brandy glasses were warming in the hearth; liqueur bottles were on the small table, where an array of glasses twinkled and gleamed. Nothing had altered here, yet he was filled with great disquiet. They were mocking him; lying to him elaborately. 'Mr. Lark had called.' Who would just *call* at such a place as this? Miles from the nearest village, on a wild stormy night—yet Mr. Lark had 'called.'

'I can recommend the Courvoisier,' Bellamy said, and touched a box of cigars. 'And try one of these, Mr. Mannering. They're real Havana, the very best.'

'Thanks.' Monosyllables were all they wanted from him.

'We shan't be long with Lark,' Bellamy said; 'ten minutes or so. You just relax.'

But the visitor's coming had excited him and he couldn't hide it; the visit was not just a casual one. Had it anything to do with Mannering?

The door opened again.

'Mr. Lark, sir.'

A little brown-clay man entered, and at first glance

Mannering thought of the man on the moor; but this one was younger and even thinner, and his suit was a different shade of brown. His highly polished shoes shone as he walked across the room, perky and self-confident. He was dressed 'to kill,' with square shoulders, an exaggerated waist, wide trousers, and a huge blue- and-white spotted bow tie. His thin, fair hair was brushed sleekly over his small, bony head. His ears stuck out. He was grotesquely thin.

'Mr. Lark' approached Bellamy with his hands outstretched and a shrill:

'Well, Guv'nor, what a treat to see yer looking so well!'

He beamed with delight.

Luckily, the other two were looking at Lark and missed the flash of stupefaction which showed in Mannering's eyes. The caller saw but took no notice of Mannering; and none of them knew that Mannering's heart was thumping with a strange excitement.

His thoughts went back years; to the time when he had last seen this perky little man—who was one of the cleverest cracksmen in England.

Years ago——

A man bitter against a woman and society, restless, impatient with the pleasant easy gait of life, stirred by an inner compulsion to fling down the gauntlet and challenge the world.

John Mannering—who loved precious stones.

Their colour and brilliance fascinated him, drew him towards them, lusting for possession and not their value. He could remember now the day when he first planned to steal. The man then and Mannering now were not the same; he could look back dispassionately, feeling none of the old desire for the lovely illicit baubles, but his heart still quickened at the memory of the first daring, dangerous escapade; the incomparable thrill of success, and the wild exhilaration of escaping from the police.

About him there grew a legend.

The Baron was born.

The restlessness was stilled as the police hunted him, not then dreaming who he was, and the newspapers went wild about his daring. And irony of ironies, as John Mannering, he was consulted by the police because of his knowledge of jewels!

27

That phase hadn't lasted long, but in it he learned the cracksman's craft, as skilled as any; and, disguised, he consorted with rogues and vagabonds and found them to be people, and liked many of them as men—such as Lark.

Out of the first wild days had grown a different Baron.

The newspapers dubbed him Robin Hood, friend of the poor; the police recognised him as an ally against the uglier, vicious crimes of violence and blackmail, an aura of romanticism surrounded the Baron. . . .

And one detective, Bristow by name, learned who he was, but could not prove it. A strange friendship was born, guarded by suspicion and fostered by pitting their wits against each other.

Through all this—Lorna.

A tumultuous love for a woman who had soothed the last trace of bitterness away. Marriage! Happiness marred only by the intrusion of the past into their lives; and by the longing, deep within him, to fling aside restraints and safety and do wild, crazy things.

Sometimes he thought that Lorna knew him better than he knew himself, and did not make him fight against the urge but let him go, and sometimes helped him.

Now? Today?

The Baron was never talked about, although he lingered in many people's memory, and John Mannering had won for himself a reputation as a detective with an unrivalled knowledge of jewel thieves and their ways.

Lark was a jewel thief.

The police knew it, but he was always too smart for them. Mannering had seen him in a public house, sanctuary for 'honest' rogues, and knew his reputation well. A nice, little man with a plump, pretty wife, a ready wit and full of generous impulses—who would return jewels of sentimental value to their owners with an impudent flourish. A brilliant screwsman—whom Bellamy greeted as an old friend.

'Lor' lumme, Guv'nor, I coulda died larfin',' cried Lark. 'Looked him straight in the eye I did, and what do you think I said? I said, looking him straight in the eye, "Mister, that there's a valuable work of art, I don't mind admitting it," I said, "in my opinion it's a very fine picture, a very fine picture indeed." Strewth! You shoulda seen his eyes. Neely popped out and hit me on the nose they did. "Reely!"

he said, "and may I make so bold as to ask 'ow much it's worth to you?" "Mister," I said, touching him on the shoulder like I'm touching you—"mister," I said, "I'd be prepared to pay a hundred pounds for that work of art, *a hundred pounds*."

'Cor lumme,' gasped Lark, 'he looked as if he would drop through the floor! Couldn't wrap it up fast enough for me. Larf! I haven't larfed so much since the Gold Rush, I ain't reely.'

Bellamy chuckled.

'Very good, Lark, very good indeed.'

'I'll say it was good,' said Lark smugly. 'Worth every penny of five thousand. Mind you, I coulda got it for a fiver, but that wouldn't've been fair.'

'You always want to be fair,' said Bellamy gravely.

'That's me all over. The guy who sold me that picture 'adn't seen a hundred nicker all the same time in his natural. Next time I go there I'll be like a long-lost brother. Not that he'll pick up anything more like that, Guv'nor, you can't expect two miracles in a lifetime.'

'I'd expect anything from you,' purred Bellamy. 'What do you think of that for astuteness, Mr. Mannering?'

'I should say there was a fair profit in it,' murmured Mannering dryly.

'Wot?' exclaimed Lark. 'Fair—cor lumme, that's good, that is. Fair profit—'ear him, Guv'nor!'

Lark laughed so heartily that his whisky and soda spilt over the side of the glass. Mannering sat back, scorched by the blazing fire, cupping a brandy glass in his hands. Now and again he sniffed the bouquet and sipped. Harrison sprawled back in an easy chair opposite him, fair hair ruffled and cheeks red. He had been drinking heavily, and his eyes were glittering; but he was not by any means drunk. The 'ten minutes' had spread to an hour, and Lark showed no sign of leaving. He had not been easy on the whisky, but Bellamy appeared to be amused by the little crook.

'That's one o' the best I've heard for a long time,' said Lark again. 'In the trade, Mister?'

'Er—yes, in a way,' said Mannering.

Bellamy chuckled.

'Lark, you've dropped a brick. Mr. Mannering is one of the best-known men in the—er—trade. If he hadn't heard your story, he might have bought that Genoese panel you're telling us about. It would look very well in the window of Quinn's, wouldn't it?'

'I might buy it even now,' murmured Mannering, looking thoughtfully at Lark.

Lark's manner changed at mention of Quinn's. Now he sat very still, holding his glass carefully in front of him, and although he appeared to be looking at Harrison, he was in fact studying Mannering. The others were conscious of the change; Bellamy seemed even more deeply amused. Harrison said: 'Ha!' in that curious snort, the beginning of a laugh that never matured.

'Did you say Mr. Mannering of Quinn's?' asked Lark, after a long pause.

'That's right,' said Bellamy.

'Well, I never,' said Lark. 'Well, I never!'

He was uneasy for the next five minutes, and soon jumped up, saying that he must go.

Mannering heard the bark of a motor-cycle engine and then its staccato roar as Lark made off into the dark night.

CHAPTER IV

NIGHT AT THE HOUSE

MANNERING pondered over possible reasons for the little crook's change of manner, while he listened to Bellamy and Harrison talking animatedly about paintings on wood. Lark undoubtedly knew that the owner of Quinn's had been consulted occasionally by the police, and had helped many men behind bars; enough to make any thief uneasy. But that wasn't all. Strange rumours floated about that part of the East End where crooks foregathered, and news was spread furtively. That part of London was a whispering gallery of secrets.

Some crooks believed that Mannering was the Baron. Lark might be one of them.

There was plenty to worry about, without that. He had accepted the passive role which Bellamy and Harrison had allotted to him, for it gave him time to think. Thinking brought one all-important question: why had they brought him here? Certainly not to sell him the emeralds at a giveaway price, although he would not have come but for his old customer's eagerness to get the gems.

He knew the game too well to take Bellamy on his face value, and had made some inquiries. Bellamy was well known in the world of fine art; a cosmopolitan with a mysterious background—which was not unusual in the jewel business—whose reputation was quite sound. The first warning of trouble had been the mud splashing against his windshield.

There was one good thing; Lorna hadn't been able to come here with him.

He thought fleetingly of her, and smiled grimly at what she would think of this. At least, he wasn't to blame for it.

Bellamy's voice broke through his thoughts.

'You look amused, Mr. Mannering.'

Lorna faded.

'I am! I'm thinking of Lark's deal with the panel. Likeable little rogue, isn't he? I like a man who pays a hundred when he could get what he wants for a fiver. By George, it's warm in here,' Mannering said, pushing his chair back. 'You know how to build a fire. No fuel troubles?'

'We overcame them. But you're right, it is hot.' Bellamy looked at his wrist-watch. 'Well, I'll be jiggered! It's nearly half-past ten; I didn't realise it was so late. I reckon to get to bed early, Mr. Mannering, but you stay down here as long as you like. Show Mr. Mannering some of our little oddments, Jim.'

'I think I'll get to bed, I can see the oddments in the morning,' said Mannering. 'I've had a long drive, you know.'

'Surely—I'm sorry if we've kept you up,' said Bellamy, with solicitude. 'You take Mr. Mannering to his room, Jim.'

'Oh, I can find my way.'

'No, no—Jim will take you. Good night, Mr. Mannering. I hope you sleep well.'

But if Mannering stayed awake through a restless night, it would amuse him.

Harrison uncoiled himself from his chair and led the way out of the room. He strode through the dimly lighted hall to the staircase, with Mannering a little way behind. Mannering's mind was alert, noticing everything. The huge grandfather clock which was ticking on with its curious hollow sound; the heavy furniture and chairs stood against the walls; a large Indian carpet lost in the vast hall. There was no covering on the stone floor near the front of the stairs, where Harrison's footsteps rang out clearly. The soft pile of the stair-carpet; the carved, highly polished balustrade; the square landing, with two wide passages at right-angles to each other—he noted all these.

Harrison had gone along the passage leading to Mannering's room when he had tapped at Stella Bellamy's door.

Which was her room?

His was the third—and last—along the passage. The first door was ajar, and he saw a man's clothes flung carelessly over the end of a double bed. Firelight flickered about the walls. That was Harrison's; then, presumably, the girl was in the middle room. As they passed the door, Mannering saw that the key was on the outside. Was she locked in?

'Here we are,' said Harrison. 'You'll be as snug as a bug in a rug here, Mannering! Wonderful rooms, aren't they? Have a look at the plaster-work on the ceiling—superb!' He was back at the over-hearty stage. 'Anything else you want, now? Hot water bottle? Another drink—but you'll find *that* in the wardrobe, door on the right. They brought your case up, didn't they?'

'Yes, thanks,' said Mannering. 'I—oh, confound it!' He looked angry with himself.

'What?' Harrison, his hand on the switch, seemed suddenly huge, shadowy, and sinister. 'Forgotten something?'

'There's a small case in my car that I'll need up here,' said Mannering. 'Tell me where the garage is——'

'I'll send for it.'

'I'd better get it myself. I know just where to put my hand on it.'

That didn't please, but Harrison led the way downstairs again, and turned into a long, stone-floored passage opposite the front door. Two oil lamps in brackets gave a dim, flickering light, and a cold draught swept along. At the end, they entered a small, square hall. A short, thick-set man was standing by another door, and on a chair near him was a heavy service revolver.

Harrison glanced at Mannering.

'Precautions against burglars.' Crisp, abrupt, none-of-your-business.

'So I notice,' said Mannering dryly.

'Open the door,' said Harrison to the guard.

Mannering stepped into the grounds, and the wind shrieked down on him. He shivered. Was it because of the sudden cold or because of the armed man standing by the door? Were all the doors guarded? Probably. Against burglars? Or to prevent *him* from getting out?

Four cars stood abreast in the huge garage—a Rolls Phantom 111, a Bentley, the Austin in which Harrison had met Mannering, and the Sunbeam-Talbot. A motor-cycle was propped up in a corner. Harrison stood by the door as Mannering went to his car, put on the roof-light, and pulled a small, heavy attache case from underneath the driving seat. He was soon back with Harrison.

'Got everything this time?'

'Yes, thanks.'

Harrison was silently annoyed on the way back, said 'Good night' brusquely at Mannering's door, and strode off. Downstairs, Mannering heard him talking to a man who had not been in the hall when they had come up. Another guard?

Mannering closed and locked his door.

He crossed to the glowing fire and looked at himself in a huge overmantel mirror. Lorna knew that expression, had been the first to point it out. About his eyes and mouth there was a difference, a hint of the excitement he felt stealing over him.

He laughed.

What would Harrison say if he knew what tools were in the case? What would Lark say if he saw equipment with which he could break open any lock?

Mannering put the case in the wardrobe, then went to the door, unlocked it and left it ajar. He must miss nothing. As he undressed, he listened intently for any sound. He was in dressing-gown and slippers when he heard footsteps approaching. He reached the door in a flash, and peered into the passage.

Harrison was opening Stella's door; he disappeared.

He came out again after a few moments, turned the key in the lock and dropped the key into his pocket. He glanced towards Mannering's door, noticed nothing amiss, and went to his own room.

So Stella was locked in.

Mannering went to the big window and pulled the heavy red velvet curtains aside. They ran smoothly on their runners. He could hear the wind howling more clearly now. It was pitch-dark, but as he stood staring into the night, a light appeared not far away. It showed the face of a man who was lighting a cigarette in a little shed. The light went out; above the howl of the wind, Mannering heard footsteps below him.

Would they take such precautions to keep him in the house?

Silas Bellamy's bedroom was a small room for that sized

house. It was on the ground floor, off a passage which led from the hall, and Holmes was helping him to undress when Harrison came in. Harrison lit a cigarette and tossed the match into the fire, as Holmes murmured:

'Is there anything else, sir?'

'No—good night, Holmes.'

'Good night, sir. Good night, Mr. Harrison.'

Harrison nodded, and watched the butler closely as he went out. Bellamy sat in an easy chair in front of the fire, with the black rug over his knees, a glass of brandy by his side, the stub of a cigar between his lips.

Harrison smoothed down his hair.

'And what do you make of Mr. Mannering?' asked Bellamy softly.

'He won't give us any trouble.'

'I wonder if you've under-estimated him,' murmured Bellamy. 'He has been very quiet—but very watchful. Are you sure Stella didn't say anything to warn him?'

'She didn't say enough.'

'A little might be enough for some men,' Bellamy said. 'Have you seen Stella?'

'She's asleep.'

'You've locked her in, I hope.'

Harrison tapped his pocket. 'Yes, and the key's here. We needn't worry about Mannering, he'll crack once we put on the pressure. I wish we'd started right away.'

'But we aren't quite ready, my friend. Lark is still down here. I'd rather he was in London before we do very much. And we want Mannering to help us willingly at first. He will be easily persuaded to stay over tomorrow night, I think. If he refuses, we can show our hand. But I think he is pretty astute, Jim; and senses that something is the matter. You're quite sure that Stella——'

'If she'd said much, I'd have got it out of her,' boasted Harrison, 'and if I hadn't, Mrs. Dent would have. She might have caught up with Mannering if it hadn't been for the storm, mind you. But—she *might* give us trouble. I wouldn't put it past her to go to the police if she could get far enough.'

'Oh, come now,' said Bellamy gently, 'Stella wouldn't do that. She is far too fond of her uncle, don't forget her devotion to him. And I feel sure that Rundle won't be silly—but I wish we could catch Rundle.'

'He'll die out on the moor,' Harrison said callously. 'One night of it in his condition will finish him. But I'd like to wring his neck! If it hadn't been for him, Stella wouldn't have got out.' He kicked at a piece of coal in the fireplace, and sparks showered upwards. 'It *would* happen today. Think they knew Mannering was coming, and went to warn him?'

'You know I think that's possible. But the storm was a god-send! All the doors are being closely watched, aren't they?'

'And the main windows, you needn't worry about Mannering getting away. Not that I think he'll try,' Harrison added, tossing the end of the cigarette into the fire. 'He's just a dumb wit.'

'Well, we won't talk about it any more tonight,' decided Bellamy. 'Help me into bed, Jim, will you?'

Half an hour later, restless because of Bellamy's opinion of Mannering, Harrison went quietly along the passage and stopped outside the visitor's room. He could hear nothing. He tried the handle; the door was not locked, so he peered inside. In the red glow from the dying fire he could see Mannering lying in bed, and could hear his steady, regular breathing. He tiptoed into the room and stood looking down. Mannering did not stir.

Harrison grinned in the darkness, and went out, closing the door softly.

A clock struck three; its sonorous notes boomed loudly through the quiet house. Downstairs in the hall a guard lit another cigarette and took a drink from a whisky flask. In the back hall, the guard paced to and fro. Outside, three men, muffled in heavy sheepskin coats and thick scarves, walked round the house, watching doors and windows. They smoked continuously and occasionally stopped for a drink or to exchange a joke with one another.

Upstairs, Mannering opened his eyes, and wondered why he was awake.

Memory seeped back, and with it, that feeling of excitement. He had much to do.

He threw back the bedclothes and got out of bed. He put on his dressing-gown, tying the sash tightly, pushed his feet into slippers which lay near the hearth and were still warm,

36

and went to the wardrobe. Everything in the room was visible in the last flickers of firelight.

The wardrobe door squeaked.

He took out the tool-case, and carried it to the bed. Then he switched on a flashlight, and a pool of pale light revealed the assortment of tools. He selected three—a skeleton key, a small screwdriver, and a sharp knife—slipped them into his pocket, closed the case and put it under the bed.

There was no sound in the house.

He went into the passage and waited outside the door with his hand on the handle. The faint *tick-tock* of the clock downstairs murmured through the quiet. A man coughed. Mannering moved along to the middle of the passage, where it was carpeted, and reached the landing. In the hall, a lamp burned on a table near a guard who was sitting in front of the main door.

Beside the lamp lay a revolver.

Mannering turned back, passed Harrison's room, and stopped at Stella's door. It was light enough for his trained eyes to see all he wanted. As he touched the lock, a surge of excitement made his heart beat faster. When that calmed down, he examined the lock more closely. It was exactly the same type as that on his own door, and should not be difficult to open. He inserted the skeleton key; the click of metal on metal was very faint, yet sounded loud to his strained ears.

He twisted cautiously.

The years rolled away. Here was the Baron, standing in the darkness, deft hands working at the lock, every nerve taut. The work itself was almost mechanical, years of intensive practice had served him well, and he had never lost the touch. The tension came from listening for the man in the hall, and the regular, irritating beat of the clock. Now and again the guard stirred or coughed. Mannering worked through that, twisting and turning the key.

The man stood up and walked across the hall.

One moment his footsteps rang out clearly; the next they were muffled by the carpet. Had he heard a sound? Was he coming up here? Mannering paused in his work, waiting for the reassuring clatter of boots on the stone floor at the foot of the stairs. The footsteps were audible enough, but still muffled.

A sharper noise came.

37

Mannering drew back from the door and peered towards the landing.

No, all was safe; a chair creaked as the guard sat down again. Another match flared.

So he had only wanted to stretch his legs; he would probably settle for a while now. Mannering turned back to the door.

He hadn't oiled the key because traces of oil might show on the door. But little squeaking noises as metal scraped on metal still sounded very loud. Was it audible in Harrison's room?

Nonsense!

Ah! The lock was turning.

The pressure on the key nearly made it slip in his fingers, but he kept his grip. He must not let the lock click back sharply, or it would be heard downstairs.

A gentle click came as the lock turned.

He withdrew the key and slipped it into his pocket, peering towards the landing. Satisfied that he had not been heard, he opened the door silently. He stepped into the dark room, closed the door softly behind him, and stood waiting until his eyes became accustomed to the deeper darkness here. Soon, he could make out the bed against the left wall—against Harrison's wall; that was a pity. He could not make out the figure of the girl, but could see the huge wardrobe opposite the bed, the dressing-table, the dark curtains, still partly drawn.

He took out the flashlight, wrapped a handkerchief over it, to dim the light, and switched it on.

The faint glow showed the thick carpet, a chair which stood between him and the bed, and Stella Bellamy, who lay on her side, facing him, one arm over the bedclothes. He stepped nearer. She was wearing a nightdress or pyjamas with long, muslin sleeves, fastened at the wrist. She did not appear to have touched her hair since he had seen her; it was dry and fluffy and spread over the white pillow like pale gold. He could see her features clearly. In repose, she had lost her fear but none of her loveliness. She looked young— much younger than he had thought. She was breathing evenly, and her lips moved only slightly.

Her arm moved across the bedclothes and came to rest a few inches nearer to him.

He went closer to the bed. If she cried out when he touched

her, it might bring disaster; one of the risks. He *must* hear
her story. He rested his right hand lightly on her shoulder.
She did not stir. He pressed gently, and whispered:

'Wake up.'

She started, flinging her arm across the bedclothes but
she did not wake.

He patted her cheek gently.

'Wake up, Stella, wake up!'

She drew in a sharp breath; her eyes flickered but did not
open. He could see the way the muscles in her throat and
cheeks tensed. She was awake, but had made no sound.

'It's Mannering. Don't worry, just wake up.'

She opened her eyes and stared at him, without blinking.
The peacefulness of repose had gone; fear had taken possession again. He shone the torch on his own face, and she
eased herself up on her pillows, without speaking, staring at
him.

'Can Harrison hear?' Mannering asked softly.

'I—don't—think so.'

Her voice was so faint that he only just caught the words.
He turned the torch back, so that he could see her; she was
moistening her lips. Her eyes were calmer; alarm had gone,
and her presence of mind was welcome but not unexpected.
He remembered Harrison's careless gesture when he had
touched his forehead, suggesting that she wasn't quite
normal; Harrison wanted to discredit her.

She shivered suddenly.

Mannering saw a woollen bed-jacket on the bed, and
handed it to her. She put it round her shoulders, every
movement easy and graceful.

'Why have you come?'

'We couldn't talk downstairs.'

'What—do you want?'

'Why did you warn me, and what's happening here?'

'I—I told you not to come.'

'We haven't much time and we may not get another chance
to talk. Don't waste it. Why didn't you want me to come?'

She hesitated for what seemed a long time. Then:

'They are going to keep you here.'

'Why?'

'I—I don't know.'

She wasn't being evasive; he felt sure that she didn't know.
Disappointment came, sharp and dismaying.

'What do you know?'

'They said they wanted you to come and they wouldn't let you get away. That happened—once before. A man was killed. They said it was an accident—said he fell out of a window and broke his neck. It wasn't true; they pushed him out; I'm sure they pushed him out.'

'*Can* you be sure?'

'Of course, I——'

'Hush!' urged Mannering. Her voice had risen in her indignation, but she stopped at his warning, and looked past him towards the door, moistening her lips again.

'Yes,' she whispered, 'I'm quite sure. Rundle saw them.'

'Who is Rundle?'

'An old—servant.'

'Did he escape today?'

'Yes,' she said, and caught her breath. 'He saw what they did, and they locked him in a room and wouldn't let him leave. It made him ill. Later, they let him move—move about the house. He managed to get a key to the back door and slipped out this afternoon; he was going to warn you—although he was too sick to go out. I followed him. They didn't know I was going, didn't know I knew that you were coming. I went on Glim.'

'Glim?'

'Harrison's horse,' she explained, and caught her breath again. 'You shouldn't have come; you can't escape. The doors are guarded by night, and you can be seen from the house for miles by day. You shouldn't have come!'

'I'm going to get away,' Mannering said with quiet assurance.

She shook her head, and her voice rose again.

'You can't; you're helpless now.'

'I shall get away, and I want you to come with me, Stella.'

'No,' she gasped. 'I can't!'

He knew something of the reason for her dread now. He could understand the little man by the stream. He could imagine how both man and girl had felt that fear of Bellamy and Harrison, and perhaps of others, which had robbed them of logic, making them utter their vague warnings without a word of explanation. Poor Rundle, who was so tired and ill and frightened, and was now alone on the wild, bleak moor.

'I want you to come with me,' Mannering repeated.

'Even if you could escape, I couldn't—come with you.'

'You must listen to me,' insisted Mannering. 'You're terrified of them, and you're in danger yourself, in as much danger as I am. We must get away together, and——'

'I can't leave here!'

Would any sane woman refuse to try and escape? Would anyone willingly stay in this house, subjected to such indignities, possessed by such fear? He watched her closely, her tension making him forget the hovering dangers. He had almost forgotten the guard in the hall, the possibility that Stella's room might be inspected; that Harrison might have been disturbed.

'Well, I'm going,' Mannering said.

'You'll never escape.'

What made her so sure?

She began to speak, in swift, urgent tones, contradicting what she had just said.

'Listen to me, you must listen, I can't leave here, but if you can escape, go now. Don't wait here another minute. I don't know what they want from you, but it's something—something evil. They'll kill you rather than let you go. *He* threatened to give them away, that's why they killed him. No one would ever believe it; the police came, and thought it was an accident. Both Bellamy and Harrison lied, the servants lied; the servants *know* the truth about this house, but they're cowed into submission. Do you understand me? *They're* frightened, too.'

'Yes, Holmes looked scared. Mrs. Dent didn't seem——'

'*She's a bitch!*'

'And as dangerous as your uncle and Harrison?'

'In some ways—she's worse. Oh, God! Don't stay here any longer. *I* can't leave, but if you think you can—go now. Only be careful! They'll shoot you rather than let you escape.'

Mannering sat on the edge of the bed, taking her hand.

'Listen to me, Stella. I'm not going out of the room until I know why you can't come with me. I mean that.'

Obviously she knew that he was serious.

'Well?' he whispered.

'I can't—leave—my sister,' Stella said.

Five words, ordinary words, which conjured up a vision in Mannering's mind, gave him a glimpse of the horror which possessed her. She was not the only one kept here against her will, she was not thinking only of herself. 'I can't—leave—my sister.' It would have been easy to retort: 'Then we'll take her, too,' but he sensed there was something deep and frightening here.

'I haven't seen her,' he said.

'She's in—her room. She isn't well. They never let me see her, but while she's here, I must stay. If I do anything—if I tell the police—they'll kill my Kathleen. I shouldn't have told you, but you wouldn't take my warning. If you can get away, for God's sake, go!' she cried, then caught her breath, for the words echoed loud and clear about the room.

Mannering went swiftly to the door and waited.

No sound.

He turned back to the bed, undecided what to do. As she was not frightened only for herself, she would be very stubborn. He was sure that she would not willingly leave this house without her sister. But she might be able to tell him more about her uncle and Harrison, and what they were doing.

'Please go,' she begged. 'If they find you here they might ——' She broke off, and closed her eyes.

Mannering said: 'Stella, believe it or not, I can get away from here whenever I choose. I shall stay tomorrow, and I'll talk to you again. You and your sister will be safe enough; I'll see to that. Don't think it's hopeless.' He found himself gripping her hand tightly, felt the vice-like tension of her fingers. 'Do you understand, it isn't——'

Footsteps came along the passage!

The girl's face blanched. Mannering switched off the flashlight and swung round, crossing to the door. The footsteps stopped, and a key was pushed into the lock.

CHAPTER V

MRS. DENT

MANNERING drew swiftly away and backed to the wall. As
the door opened, a dim light from the passage filtered in.
Whoever it was came hurrying in, and crossed to the bed.
It was a woman; Mrs. Dent. He could just see the wardrobe,
and, heart in his mouth, he edged towards it. He could have
slipped out of the room, but—he might learn much by
staying. He reached the wardrobe and squeezed himself in
the angle which it made with the wall.

'Stella, are you awake?' called Mrs. Dent. '*Stella!*'

There was a sound, rustling, rattling; the woman was
shaking the girl and making the bed creak. 'Stella!' Stella
stirred, and Mannering could imagine her opening her eyes
and blinking in the gloom.

'Who—who's that? What is it?'

'Get up, I need you.'

'But——'

'I thought you wanted to see your precious sister!'

'Kathleen!' gasped Stella. Mannering could see every
movement as she flung back the bedclothes and jumped out
of bed. She would have rushed straight to the door, but the
housekeeper pulled her back roughly, and made her put on
a dressing-gown and slippers. Stella's eyes glistened, she
looked distraught, her breathing was quick and laboured as
she ran towards the door with the housekeeper padding
after her.

She went out.

And screamed! A wild, piercing cry which brought
Mannering forward, ready for any horror.

'What the hell's all this about?' demanded Harrison harshly.

So Stella had seen him loom out of the doorway, after being disturbed by Mrs. Dent's call, and it had been too much for the girl's taut nerves. Now she sobbed, but made little sound.

'I can't do anything with the other brat,' Mrs. Dent said.

'He said——' began Harrison.

'Just this once, I can't help what he says,' snapped Mrs. Dent, 'we've got to get the brat quiet. Come on, Stella.'

Stella was quiet now.

'I'd better come with you,' Harrison grumbled.

'Please yourself.'

The housekeeper had not troubled to close the door, and Mannering crossed to the passage and peered along, in time to see Harrison going down the stairs behind the others. All three walked noisily, especially when they reached the bottom of the stairs. Mannering reached the landing as Harrison disappeared into the passage which led to the garage.

The guard stood in the middle of the hall, looking doubtfully at Harrison's back.

The temptation to go down, overpower the guard and find out more about Kathleen was almost overwhelming. But Mannering went back as far as Harrison's room. A bedside lamp showed Harrison's clothes strewn carelessly about the room. He must have slept soundly, for the bed was hardly disturbed. Mannering picked up the coat and weighed it in his hand. He wanted to find out whether Harrison kept a gun, but there was nothing heavy in the coat. He crossed to the bed—and, on the bedside table saw a small Luger automatic. He stretched out his hand towards it, then drew back. He mustn't let his need of a gun betray him. Harrison would miss it immediately he came back, and guess the truth—or else suspect Stella.

There might be other weapons.

He rummaged unsuccessfully through the wardrobe and the dressing-table, then went to a chest of drawers in the corner near the window. The top drawers were filled with clothes; the bottom one was locked.

He took out the skeleton key again.

The drawer was open a moment later.

44

Underneath some folded clothes was a wooden box. Mannering drew it out and found the companion to the Luger, with some spare clips of ammunition. He examined the automatic quickly; it was empty. He slipped a clip of cartridges into his pocket with the gun, pushed the drawer to and relocked it, then went out of the room.

He had taken enough chances for one night. And something was on his mind, worrying him; something he couldn't place, but which made him feel that the others might know he had been about.

It wasn't Stella.

He put the gun and ammunition under his pillow, and got into bed, but could not sleep. His ears were strained to catch the sound of the others returning. The waiting seemed endless, but it was only a little after four o'clock when he heard them return—Harrison and Stella, without Mrs. Dent.

Harrison growled:

'Now go to sleep; she'll be all right.'

He locked the door on Stella again.

Ah! That was it. Had the housekeeper noticed that her door had not been locked?

So much depended on the answer. The woman had been in a hurry, and alarmed by an emergency downstairs. She had pushed her key into the lock without thinking; turned the handle without thinking. If she had noticed anything amiss, surely she would have spoken of it to Stella immediately.

He couldn't be sure.

He was awakened by a touch on the shoulder, and blinked at Holmes, who stood impassively by the side of the bed. Sun was streaming in at the window. Holmes touched a tray which stood on the bedside table, and said softly:

'Your tea, sir, and the bath will be ready in a quarter of an hour.'

'Oh, thanks,' said Mannering, sitting up. 'The morning looks brighter.'

'It often does after a storm, sir. Is there anything else you require?'

'No, thanks.'

Holmes went out, silent as always; almost furtive. Mannering poured out the tea and drank it, then lit a cigarette.

As he smoked and drank a second cup, he went over the events of the previous night. If he had slept right through, had his suspicions not been aroused, he would have regarded this as the most normal household. Holmes's manner was perfect; but why did the butler bring morning tea to the guest? There must be plenty of maids.

Weren't they trustworthy?

Come to think, the only women he'd seen were Stella and Mrs. Dent.

He got up, took the automatic and clip from beneath the pillow and dropped them into his dressing-gown pocket before going into the bathroom. The huge, old-fashioned bath was half-filled with hot water; soap, face cloth, and a large bath-towel were there. He splashed cheerfully, then shaved and went back to his room to dress. Ready, he loaded the gun, slipped it into his pocket, hid the rest of the ammunition with his tools, and went downstairs. The ticking of the clock was hardly audible because of the sounds about the house. By day, the place lost something of the sense of vastness, and the sinister touch it had possessed by night. Everything looked a little smaller and less imposing. The banisters were beautifully carved and polished; several oil paintings on the walls of the great hall were by a master.

Every piece of furniture was old; some pieces were extremely valuable.

No one was in the room where they had first met on the previous night, but a refectory table was set for breakfast for three. Would Bellamy be down? Or was the third place for Stella?

The window faced west, and although there was no cloud in the sky, and the sun was warm, the moor looked bleak and desolate. Dotted here and there were great pools of water, a reminder of yesterday's downpour. But there was a cheering freshness over the grounds and the house.

He went into the hall and opened the front door. A man was hoeing a flower-bed which lay along the side of the house. By the wall was a rifle. He was a short, thick-set fellow, whose rhythmic movements suggested that he was used to gardening.

'Good morning,' said Mannering brightly. 'Much better, isn't it?'

'Oh, it'll be a fine day,' said the gardener, stopping at

once and leaning on his hoe. He was a round-faced fellow with a bovine expression, and Mannering wondered what he would do if the guest left the porch. 'Do with it, sir, can't we?'

'We can!' Mannering strolled towards him, lighting a cigarette. He affected surprise when he caught sight of the rifle. 'Good Lord, that looks like business!'

'Have some trouble with foxes hereabouts,' explained the gardener, glancing at the gun. 'Very bold they get at times. And the gun comes in useful to frighten some folk away. Very valuable things in this house, sir; some queer people come near. Don't do no harm to let them see we're pre- pared for trouble.'

Again that undertone and menace and threats.

'Like that, is it?' asked Mannering.

'Just like that, sir,' said the gardener, with faint emphasis. 'That frightens people off if they're not wanted.'

'I'll bet it does!'

Harrison came round the corner of the house, scowling. Mannering was seized with a sudden impulse to scare the man, to find out how he would behave in a crisis—to blast a way through his indifference. Before the gardener realised what he was doing, he picked up the rifle.

'Here, sir!'

'Nicely balanced, isn't it?' remarked Mannering, and put it to his shoulder and trained it on Harrison. ' 'Morning, Harrison!'

Harrison stood stockstill, except for his right hand. He dropped that to his pocket; doubtless the Luger was there.

'Don't do that, sir, it's loaded!' gasped the gardener.

'Is it, by George!' exclaimed Mannering, while Harrison, who had gone deathly pale, slowly pushed his hand into his pocket.

A pigeon flew out of the cedar tree.

'Ah!' exclaimed Mannering. He slewed the gun round and fired, and the bird dropped like a stone.

'What a gun! Absolutely true—that was a lucky shot though, wasn't it?'

He grounded the rifle.

'Lucky!' gasped the gardner.

'What the devil do you think you're doing?' roared Harrison, rushing forward with his right hand clenched inside his pocket. The colour flooded back to his cheeks, his eyes were bright with rage. 'If you do that again, I'll——'

Mannering changed his mood, and snapped: 'You're forgetting yourself!'

'Forgetting——' Harrison was almost speechless.

'You're too damned insolent. Why have you got armed men in the garden?'

It was good to attack; good, if dangerous.

'Mind your own damned business!'

'Talk like that just once more, and I'll break your neck!' Mannering's anger was assumed, he felt calm and exultant, for this was proof of Harrison's taut nerves—and he'd an excuse for goading him.

'You——' Harrison's voice was strangled.

'Jim!' That was Bellamy's voice. 'Jim!'

All three looked towards the front door. Bellamy was perilously near the edge of the top step. The sun shone on his grey hair; he looked very bluff and handsome. 'Jim, didn't I hear a shot?'

'Mannering was playing the fool,' growled Harrison thickly. His face was scarlet.

'Mannering——'

'I borrowed a rifle and shot a pigeon,' said Mannering in an angry voice. 'Harrison's behaviour is——'

'Now, now, gentlemen, you don't want to quarrel over a thing like that. Jim's a bit on edge, Mr. Mannering; we don't often hear a gun fired; they're kept as a precautionary measure, that's all. It must have startled him. Jim, how's your headache? Any easier?'

He was quick; and clever to blame a headache.

Harrison growled: 'Not much.'

'You really ought to rest this morning, my boy. I did advise you to earlier. Nasty thing, a bad headache, isn't it?' Bellamy asked suavely. 'One's naturally a bit sharp-tempered with a nagging pain all the time. I should certainly rest, Jim—have breakfast later. Mr. Mannering won't mind having only my company, I'm sure.'

Mannering put the gun against the wall.

'Of course not.'

He still sounded ruffled, but Bellamy nodded cheerfully, and Mannering went towards him. Harrison walked ahead, stalked up the steps, pushed past Bellamy and into the hall.

Mannering followed more slowly as Bellamy wheeled his chair back.

They went into the breakfast-room without exchanging a word. Holmes was at the sideboard.

'We're ready, Holmes.' Bellamy pointed to a chair. 'Do sit down, Mannering.'

Homes hovered about them.

'Tea or coffee, sir?'

'Tea, please,' said Mannering shortly.

There was grapefruit, followed by eggs and bacon; beautifully fried eggs with a covering of pale white, and three thick rashers of bacon, crisp and appetising. There were fresh rolls and toast, and butter—plenty to put a man in a good temper. He relaxed slowly, and looked into Bellamy's smiling eyes.

'Harrison annoyed me.'

'Between you and me, I'm not surprised,' said Bellamy, glancing round as if to make sure that Holmes had left the room. 'He's a sharp-tempered fellow, and when he gets a headache—a migraine—there's no holding him. If it weren't for his exceptional qualifications, I shouldn't employ him. I do hope you won't let it spoil your visit, Mannering.'

Beautifully said; so suave.

'I hope there's an improvement in his manner,' said Mannering.

'I think you can rely on it,' said Bellamy. 'Did you sleep well?'

'Like a log. I was tired out.'

'People *do* get tired when they come here, but I don't find it enervating myself.'

The vision of a man being thrown out of one of the top windows sprang into Mannering's mind.

'Do you have many visitors?'

'Comparatively few, we don't encourage them—as you've seen from the men outside. With so much valuable property here—real as well as of antiquarian value, you understand —I believe in taking extreme precautions.' Bellamy speared egg and bacon, and ate with relish. 'Yes, sir, *extreme* precautions. We are five miles from the nearest village, fourteen from a police station, and in desolate country like this, we should be fools if we didn't take care.'

'I suppose so,' agreed Mannering. 'Did the previous owner have a guard like yours?'

'He was an old fool,' said Bellamy contemptuously. 'I am told there were several robberies in the last year of his residence. I bought the house when he died—from his heir—a nephew called Morton Galliard. The Galliards are a bad family.' He broke off, and looked out of the window.

Into his eyes there sprang a gleam which drove all thought of personal danger out of Mannering's mind; it was a gleam of unadulterated hatred, and changed Bellamy's countenance completely. Mannering could understand this man inciting others to murder; watching with callous indifference as a man fell screaming to his death. The mask of genial *bonhomie* was torn away.

Mannering was calmly spreading butter on a little square of toast when Bellamy turned towards him; the man's expression was normal again.

'Galliard,' Mannering mused. 'It's an unusual name. I seem to have heard it before. Galliard——'

'You probably heard it during the war. Very brave young man, Victor Galliard. He quarrelled with his father, so this place was left to a nephew. Like all people who don't know what physical fear is, he has little sense. I was perhaps harsh on him, but I do not like men who have no intelligence, only a certain limited human understanding allied to a rude courage which makes them akin to the animals. Galliard won the V.C. during the war.'

'Oh, I remember. R.A.F. type.'

'Squadron-Leader Victor Galliard.' Bellamy made sure Mannering knew all there was to know. 'But I don't think he will give us any trouble; he's not interested in the house.' He did not enlarge on that, but pressed more butter and marmalade on Mannering. 'And more tea. I'm not looking after you at all well! Now, Mannering, I hope you will stay another night. It is impossible to look at everything here in a few hours.'

Mannering hesitated. Bellamy's gaze was impudent and challenging—as if he were telling Mannering he really had no choice. The familiar indifference, the implication that whatever Mannering said really didn't matter, was there again.

Better to avoid a crisis; just to take precautions.

'I'd like to,' Mannering said, 'but there's a snag. My wife expects me back tonight, and I've an appointment for tomorrow morning.'

'The appointment can surely wait,' said Bellamy, 'and I'll send a message to your wife.'

'If I can telephone——'

'There is no telephone here. Your thanks to Mr. Galliard for that. Since I took up residence, the Post Office has not had the facilities to install one. But I will send a man into the village with a telegram. Just a simple message, I suppose —to set your wife's mind at rest?'

And everything he said was calculated to cause Mannering disquiet.

'Thanks,' said Mannering.

No telephone; a message to be sent by one of Bellamy's men; no chance at all of communicating freely with the outside world. Harrison in a bitter, surly mood, and Bellamy caught out in that revealing flash of vicious hatred. Stella, upstairs, perhaps still locked in her room; and Kathleen—and, somewhere out on the moor, Rundle.

Rundle could prove his salvation; the old man might get through to a village, and, knowing Mannering was at the house, give another warning.

'I suggest that we look at the jewels first,' said Bellamy. 'You'll find them of absorbing interest, I'm sure. Have you finished? Good, then we'll go there right away, I always like the jewel-room in the morning sun. Man can't touch God when it comes to lighting!' Bellamy chuckled and swung his chair round skilfully. 'If you will just open the door.'

As Mannering went to do so, he heard someone crossing the hall. The door was thrust open and Harrison strode in.

Bellamy snapped: 'I thought——'

'They've found Rundle,' Harrison said in a gloating voice. 'He's been dead all night from the look of him—stiff as a poker.'

CHAPTER VI

MANNERING COMPOSES A MESSAGE

BELLAMY raised his hands

'My dear fellow! Rundle dead. Oh, I am sorry!'

Harrison took the cue in a flash; the smirk faded, he scowled and looked down at his feet.

'We told him not to go out.'

'Yes, yes. Rundle was an old servant of mine, a most faithful servant,' Bellamy explained to Mannering. 'If we had always lived here, I should have called him a retainer. Although he's had an illness lately, he wanted to go to the village yesterday; we warned him the storm was coming, but—poor, poor fellow. He must have died of exposure— pneumonia, perhaps, his chest wasn't strong. Where is the body, Jim?'

'Outside. Shall we bring him in?'

Bellamy considered.

'No,' he said at last, 'no, I don't think so. We can do nothing here, the poor fellow would have liked to be buried in hallowed ground, I'm sure. We had better send him into the village. The doctor can certify the cause of death there, too. Arrange it, Jim, there's a good fellow.'

Harrison went out.

Bellamy said quietly, and with hypocritical solemnity: 'You will forgive me if I don't come with you straight away, Mannering. This—this is a great shock.' He took a ring of keys from his coat pocket. 'Here are the keys to the cases. Open whichever you like; behave as if they were yours, my friend.'

Mannering took the keys. 'Thanks. Where is the jewel-room?'

'The door opposite this,' said Bellamy, and handed him a door-key.

Mannering said slowly: 'I'm so sorry about——'

Bellamy held up his hand, and wheeled himself rapidly away, as if too overcome to speak. Mannering stood alone in the hall, watching him. For sheer, hypocritical callousness, that display would take a lot of beating.

He crossed to the jewel-room, turned the key and pushed open the door, expecting to enter a sunlit room.

The room was dark.

He drew back, sharply.

'Excuse me, sir,' said Holmes, from behind him, 'but the shutters have to be opened.'

He switched on an electric light; and at the sides of the room jewels winked and glowed. But for once they left Mannering cold. He watched the butler, who went to the window and, taking another key from his pocket, unlocked steel shutters which fitted from top to bottom. Next Holmes turned a small handle which jutted out from the wall, and the shutters moved back until the sunlight shone into the room and the curtains concealed the cold, forbidding steel.

'Please ring if there is anything you require, sir.'

Holmes bowed and went out.

Mannering stood in the window, then slowly turned and looked about the room. The sun shone brightly on glass cabinets which stood against the walls; cabinets filled with jewels which sprang to life and gilded the light of the sun. Seldom had he seen such beauty, such a mass of brilliant lights, colours of such splendour. Here the green of emeralds, there the soft blue of sapphires, the glowing red of rubies, the gleam of gold, the creamy lustre of pearls and the pristine whiteness of diamonds. They flashed and scintillated and held him spellbound.

The sun was warm on the back of his neck. The reflection of the jewels in his eyes seemed to dazzle him.

Mechanically, he dropped his hand to his pocket and took out his cigarette-case. His fingers touched the cold steel of the Luger. He touched it again, for reassurance. Slowly, he lit a cigarette, and moved forward. Each step, each glance, revealed greater splendour.

He pressed the cigarette into an ash-tray.

He mustn't be blinded by this beauty, mustn't let his senses be dulled. Rundle was dead; his one hope of outside help was gone.

A Louis Quinze writing-table stood in one corner, and he went towards it, pulled up a chair and sat down. He had to shut out the vision of the jewels; he must contrive to send an SOS concealed in the message to Lorna. London seemed a thousand miles away; and Bellamy would scrutinise the message carefully.

He took out his fountain-pen and held it poised.

Something hit the ceiling with a thump. He started, and stared up. For a frightening moment he fancied he heard a scream, thought a body fell past the window. Nonsense! The sun was shining on a flagged terrace with a stone wall beyond it. A pale-green creeper grew on the walls, and rock plants in the cracks of the path. Beyond was the moor.

He took a sheet of paper from the rack on the table.

How could he both reassure Bellamy and warn Lorna?

He had told Bellamy of an imaginary appointment, he must turn that to advantage. He wrote: 'Been persuaded to stay extra day.' No, that wouldn't do, there was too much emphasis on 'persuaded.' He started again. 'Staying extra day amazing collection please postpone——'

Whom should he name?

Bristow, of Scotland Yard, perhaps; Lorna would jump to that, but Bellamy might recognise Bristow's name; it would have to be more subtle; or, at least, less obvious. One of Bristow's *aides?* Such as Inspector Gordon. Gordon wouldn't spring to Lorna's mind immediately, but they knew no one else of that name; she would puzzle over it until she discerned the true meaning.

Yes, that would do.

He finished: '. . . *let Gordon know; will see him as soon as possible. John.*'

Was it good enough?

He would like to hand it to Bellamy himself, to study his reaction as he read it. Instead, he rang the bell and Holmes appeared, a barrel-like figure in black coat and striped trousers, his face pale, his pale eyes protuberant.

'Yes, sir?'

'Mr. Bellamy promised to send this telegram off for me. Will you see to it?'

54

'Yes, sir, I have had instructions.'

Five minutes later, a man left Hallen House on a motorcycle, and Mannering, looking out of the window towards the cedar tree and the drive, saw him disappear.

He turned back to the jewels—almost afraid to fall under their spell. At first he was on edge for any unusual sound, and kept glancing out of the window, but gradually the jewels lured him.

There were greater collections, but all of them were famous; this was unknown. 'Bellamy's Collection'—no, the man was known to have a few stones and a few antiques, no one dreamed that he owned such a wealth of beauty.

Harrison had said that Bellamy must be one of the richest men in the country.

How much *was* this collection worth?

There were some pieces for which collectors would have paid a hundred thousand pounds. Others of comparatively little value, except as part of the collection. He recognised a few of the gems—famous pieces which had changed hands a dozen times. Absorbed now, he opened a cabinet which contained a dozen solitaire diamonds, and examined each one closely. The Big Rose Diamond was here; it had been sold in America only a year before for a fantastic sum. *Was* this really it? He took it to the window, weighing it in his hand, the flashes of coloured light dazzling him. He did not need a glass to know that this was genuine; it had a faint rose tint at one end, and was cut in the shape of a pear, with a thousand tiny glittering facets.

He did not hear the door open.

'*Mr. Mannering!*'

He swung round. 'Stella!' he exclaimed.

'*You must go!*'

She stood in the doorway, her hair looking like burnished metal, falling to her shoulders. She wore a simple green dress, and a diamond ring sparkled in her right hand.

'You said you could get away—then go!'

'I'll go when I'm ready, Stella. We have to talk first, but not here.'

'Don't be a fool! I——'

Bellamy appeared, softly, wheeling himself into the room.

'Why, Stella, my dear, I didn't know you were up. You look very well this morning—no ill effects from your drenching, I guess. That's fine—fine. And you can't keep away from

55

the jewel-room, can you? I don't blame you. It would be a strange woman who wasn't fascinated, Mannering, wouldn't it?'

'I don't believe one exists,' said Mannering.

Stella said stonily: 'I was looking for you, uncle.'

'Were you, my dear? Why?'

'Kathleen——'

'She'll be all right, and I'll talk to you about her later. Now Mr. Mannering and I have business to discuss.' He waved her away, and she went submissively; he treated her as if she were a child. 'Well, my friend, what do you think of my little collection?' he asked, rubbing his hands together. 'Not bad, I guess.'

'Do you have to ask me what I think?' Mannering gave a shrug and a rueful smile. 'It's indescribable! I didn't know such a collection existed outside the big ones.'

'I guess you didn't,' said Bellamy complacently. 'Now you see why I have armed guards about the house. If a thief were to get in here—but none will, I'm convinced of that! But I really came to tell you that I shan't be able to spend much time with you this morning. The post is very heavy and I must attend to it. Will you be able to look after yourself in here?'

'I will!'

'Don't try to run away with the Big Rose Diamond!' Bellamy said roguishly.

'Don't try to run away.' He was playing on the familiar theme.

As the chair swung out of the room, Bellamy stretched out his hand and slammed the door after him.

Mannering stood with the big diamond between his fingers, but was no longer looking at it. The spell was broken, danger grew closer and more oppressive. There was no way to escape by day, but by night—tonight—he would have to take the chance. It was useless to rely on Lorna getting the message in time to send help; useless to try to take Stella. He would have to get away by himself, and bring help. He must spend every moment he could on planning. Forget the jewels!

He knew where some of the guards were. He knew they were armed; he knew it would be useless to *walk* away. That meant he had to be able to get into the garage. But to get a car out——

There was no need for a car; the motor-cycle would serve; he could wheel it quietly out of the garage. That was the solution. He would climb out of his window—any window —and get to the garage; he'd pick that lock easily. He need only wheel the motor-cycle a hundred yards from the house; there would be a good chance of getting that far without being seen by the guards.

What then?

He could not prove that anything illegal was going on at the house. Stella had risked a great deal for him; but would she tell the same story to the police and, if she did, would she be able to prove it? He could imagine Bellamy's bland denial and plausible explanations—and the suggestion that Stella was not quite sane.

Harrison's behaviour, the look on Bellamy's face, the story of the murdered man—how could anyone make them sound alarming? There was no evidence in a look.

So he had another task before he left, he must find evidence of evil strong enough to bring the police.

The jewels—— *Were* all of them legally Bellamy's? Would Bellamy let him loose in a room where there were stolen jewels, some of which any dealer would recognise?

If Bellamy never intended him to leave, the answer was yes; it would appeal to the man's sense of humour.

But why bring him at all?

That wasn't the immediate problem.

How many of these gems had been brought here by Lark?

He lost himself again, classifying jewels and pearls, setting aside several which were world-famous, and others which bore a resemblance to jewels whose owners he knew, or which had been stolen. At Quinn's he had a file of photographs of stolen jewels; the police had circulated copies to all dealers to whom the stolen goods might be offered. Sitting at his own desk, he could have judged in a minute or so. He could picture the file and some of the photographs in his mind's eye.

The little heap of jewels which he thought were suspect increased.

When he had finished, there were three diamonds, two large rows of pearls, a pair of emerald ear-rings and a perfect set of sapphires in front of him. He took a magnifying glass from his pocket, a small one with a folding handle. He pored over each stone.

He did not know the precise moment at which he realised that he was being watched.

The realisation began with a slight uneasiness which broke through his concentration and made him look round. Then he glanced at the window and towards the orchard. No one was in sight, but the disquiet increased. He became restless, shied away from giving the gems such close attention. That warred with an increasing excitement. He held up a single diamond, the size of a hazel-nut, and peered at the faint red tinge at one side—the rose-tint which helped identification. It was smaller than the Big Rose, and he had seen a picture exactly like it. But where?

Ah!

Photographs seemed to lie in front of him, one of a diamond of this size next to an enlargement of the same stone; he could remember the caption: The Wild Rose Diamond, stolen from the collection of Mr. Rupert Hoys of Chicago. Of Chicago—that explained why he had been so slow in identifying it, why he was doubtful about some of the others. If these gems had been stolen overseas—and Bellamy had travelled extensively—it would explain much.

The new thought drove disquiet back, but not away.

He recalled large-scale robberies which had been reported in obscure connoisseurs' journals. The emerald ear-rings, pendant-shaped, were the Green Tears, stolen in Berlin before the war. One of the ropes of pearls could only be the Gironde necklace, stolen in an impudent burglary in Paris. He classified them one after the other, quite sure of his facts.

He sat back, hands in his pockets, looking unseeingly into the garden; and then the disquiet returned. It was as if someone was staring at the back of his head. He turned sharply, but could see no one. He studied the walls, where portraits hung.

The eyes of a woman in one of the pictures moved!

He picked up the Green Tears and took them to their case, nearest the picture of the woman. As he restored them to their stand, he glanced covertly at the picture. The eyes *were* painted—dull and lacking the clearness which he could have sworn he had noticed before. He went closer to the picture; yes, they were painted. Was this place getting on his nerves, giving him illusions?

He rubbed his finger over the forehead and eyes, very softly. There was a slight ridge near the top of the nose. He peered closer, and distinguished the main canvas from pieces which had been cut out and replaced—the eyes were movable!

At least he had been right.

What of the other pictures?

He touched them all; only the one had been tampered with.

His neck and forehead were damp with sweat as he lit a cigarette, strolled to the window and looked out for some time, before replacing the other jewels. Now he had ample reason to send the police here, so only one problem remained: escape.

Into the tenseness of the moment there came a tap at the door.

He called 'come in,' and Holmes entered, and put a tray on a table.

'Mr. Bellamy thought you would like some coffee, sir. Is there anything else I can get you?'

'No thanks. You're looking after me very well.'

'Thank you, sir.' Holmes's hand lingered on the coffee-pot, a beautiful piece of Georgian silver. He fiddled with the knob at the top of the lid, and looked at Mannering with his protruding eyes. 'Shall I pour out, sir?' He kept rubbing his finger over the knob.

'No thanks,' said Mannering again.

Holmes stared intently at him, then glanced at the knob, and back again. 'You will ring if there is *anything* you require, sir, won't you?'

'Yes.' Why was the butler so insistent? Why had he looked so hard at the coffee-pot?

'And if you would like anything to read, sir, you will find plenty of books in the library—the next room,' said Holmes. He bowed, and turned away, but as he reached the door he swung round again and looked not at Mannering but at the coffee-pot.

The door closed on him.

Mannering thought of the false eyes in the picture; he might be watched now. But Holmes had wanted him to look at the pot. He poured out coffee, sipped it, turned his back on the suspect picture, and held the coffee-pot firmly with one hand. With the other he gripped the knob and pulled; it did not move. But there was a joint; it might be screwed on.

His fingers were tingling with the heat as he steadied the coffee-pot and twisted the knob.

It moved.

CHAPTER VII

FRIEND IN NEED

FOOTSTEPS sounded on the flagstones outside the window. Mannering put the coffee-pot down, and picked up his cup. Harrison and one of the gardeners appeared. The gardener stared in with undisguised curiosity, Harrison gave Mannering a perfunctory nod—that might be construed into an olive branch. They were quickly past, but Mannering waited until all sound had faded before he turned to the lid again. The loosened knob unscrewed easily now.

It was hollow inside.

He held it to the light, and saw a tiny screw of paper.

Holmes's voice seemed to echo in his ears.

'And if you would like anything to read, sir . . .'

He tried to shake the paper out, but it was lodged too firmly. He took out his knife, opened it and picked at the paper until it was far enough out of the knob for him to grip between his fingers. He pulled; the paper tore. He mustn't damage it, must be steady. Gingerly he skewered the paper out, slipped it into his waistcoat pocket, screwed the knob back, and poured out another cup of coffee.

Was this a trap?

What need was there to trap him? He was already a prisoner. Better to assume the obvious, that Holmes wanted to help him.

What of the other dangers?

If he could be watched in this room, perhaps he was never free from surveillance. In his bedroom, for instance; the fresco work, high up on the walls, or the ornate plaster pattern on the ceiling might conceal a spy-hole. Although he was sure it hadn't been used the night before, the danger was real—but if he were to become afraid to move for fear of being seen, it would wear his nerves to rags. He would have to take reasonable precautions, that was all.

He fingered the screw of paper in his pocket, but this wasn't the place to look at it.

He had been here for nearly two hours; no one would be surprised if he went out, and——

'*Look out!*' a man shouted.

The cry came out of the blue, and Mannering jumped up, paper forgotten. '*Look out!*' The shouting came from the hall, followed by a flurry of footsteps; someone was running across the hall. '*Stop her!*' Mannering reached the door in time to hear Harrison say in a savage undertone: 'Be quiet, you fool!'

Mannering heard a sound nearer at hand, a sharp click. Then a cry, in a woman's voice, and the slamming of a door. He turned the handle and pulled.

He was locked in.

Two or three men were running across the hall now.

There was no time to pick the lock.

He crossed to the window, slipped back the catch and tried to push the window up. It wouldn't budge. He drew back, tight-lipped, breathing hard. There was no further sound, yet the echo of that cry seemed to ring in his ears: he had to get out.

The windows were electrically controlled; that was the only explanation of the jamming. He drew back, picked up the chair beside the table, and banged it against the glass.

Ordinary glass would have broken, but this resisted the blow. He struck again, more heavily; the toughened glass gave out a hollow, booming note, but did not break. It wasn't surprising; anyone would take such precautions in the jewel-room, but—he must get out. That cry—the quick flurry of footsteps—the alarm. Stella, perhaps—or her sister—had rushed out of the house and was trying to get away; and Harrison meant to stop him from interfering.

He examined the window closely, seeing the rubber-covered flex which carried the current. The frame was of painted metal, not of wood.

A knife would cut through ordinary electric cable, but if the wire were alive he would get a nasty shock. And of course the current was on. What was the voltage? Probably low, because they manufactured their own current.

Would he be wiser to pretend that he hadn't been disturbed?

Then he saw the girl.

She was tearing across the orchard, her dark hair streaming behind her, her flimsy white dress—dress?—pressed tightly against her figure. A man appeared, fifty yards behind her; Harrison, with one of the gardeners following him.

That settled it; he would get out somehow.

He opened his knife, pushed it between the electric cable and the wall, and tugged. The cable sagged. A staple which fastened it to the wall came out, giving plenty of loose cable to grip. He dropped the knife and tugged savagely.

There was a tiny blue flash as it broke.

He thrust the window up.

The girl and the men were out of sight as Mannering jumped over the stone wall and plunged across the garden towards the orchard. As he reached it, Harrison and the gardener, with the girl held between them, came walking towards the house. The girl was trying to pull herself free, and her breath was coming in great gasps. She was smaller than Stella, a tiny, dark creature; the dress was a night-dress, she was bare-footed and wild-eyed.

Harrison missed a step when he saw Mannering approaching.

'What the devil's happening here?' Mannering snapped.

'Let me go,' cried the girl. 'Make them let me go!' She looked at him beseechingly, her eyes two shining pools of fear. 'Oh, make them let me go!'

'You're hurting the girl,' Mannering said. 'Let her go.'

'Now listen, Mannering,' rasped Harrison in an ugly voice, 'while you're here, you mind your own ruddy business. The girl's ill—delirious. She's got to be taken back to her room.'

'Oh, make them let me go,' gasped Kathleen. 'I can't stay here! I can't stay here!'

Mannering said softly, angrily: 'Let her go.'

'Clear out,' growled Harrison, and tightened his grip on Kathleen's bare arm. His fingers bit deeply into her thin, pale flesh. The gardener was holding her firmly, but more gently.

'Now, Miss,' he said in a soft voice, 'don't make it difficult for us, Miss, please. And sir!'

Mannering came forward.

Harrison tried to push him away, but Mannering dodged his fist, gripped his wrist, and twisted savagely. Pain made Harrison relax his grip and Kathleen tried to pull herself away from the gardener. Before she could get free, Mannering put his arm round her shoulders, holding her tight. She was quaking and icy cold.

'Oh, *make* them let me go!' she pleaded.

Harrison, a yard away, stood with his fist clenched, his lips drawn back over his teeth.

Mannering ignored him and said to the gardener: 'Take your hand away, she'll be all right,' and as the man reluctantly obeyed, he lifted her bodily. 'We must get you back in the warm. You'll have to get better and get dressed before you leave, you know.'

'They won't let me leave!'

'They will, in good time,' said Mannering soothingly. Two or three other men approached, and one of them carried a rifle. They followed as Mannering hurried with the girl towards the house. She was pitifully light—skin and bones. The white skin had a transparent look.

She *was* ill; and she was trembling with cold as well as from fear.

She made no attempt to get free from him.

He crossed the drive, passed beneath the cedar, and carried her indoors as Bellamy appeared, swinging his chair out of the room where they had breakfasted.

'Mannering!'

'I'll talk to you about this later,' Mannering rasped. 'Where is her room?' he held Bellamy's gaze, and caught sight of Stella and Mrs. Dent out of the corner of his eyes. 'Someone lead the way.'

The housekeeper spoke.

'This way, sir, please.' She glanced at Bellamy, and presumably he gave consent, for she walked towards the long passage. Mannering followed and Stella brought up the rear.

The housekeeper turned from the first doorway into a small bedroom, with modern furniture, clean and tidy, making an unexpectedly good impression. A single bed was turned down, and Mannering carried the shivering girl to it. Stella and the housekeeper pulled the clothes over Kathleen, who looked at Mannering and ignored even her sister. Her eyes were enormous and unnaturally bright; feverish.

'You—*will*—help me, won't you?'

'Yes, I will.'

'You'll be all right, Kathie.' There was a sob in Stella's voice. 'You'll be all right, but you mustn't run off again, you'll—you'll make yourself worse.'

'Would you mind getting a hot-water bottle?' asked Mrs. Dent in her composed, authoritative manner, 'and ask Holmes to prepare a hot drink?'

She did not speak to Mannering, but the words were tantamount to a dismissal. There was no point in his staying, but he tried to reassure Kathleen by pressing his hands on her shoulders firmly and saying; 'You'll be all right.' Then he followed Stella out of the room.

From the door, he looked round. Mrs. Dent was bending over the sick girl, now hidden from him.

A fierce, uncontrollable rage gripped him as he walked slowly towards the hall—and dismay was with it. This would create the crisis he was so anxious to delay. Worse than that, he had told both girls that he could help.

Could he?

Holmes entered the passage, looked at him searchingly, hopefully. Mannering nodded, and the butler passed. Stella began to speak hurriedly, telling the butler what Mrs. Dent wanted, as Mannering went slowly into the hall.

'Mr. Mannering!' Bellamy called from the small room.

Mannering went in, taking out his cigarette-case, to find Bellamy sitting by the fire. Harrison was standing by the window, his hands deep in his pockets, his face pale and his eyes angry.

'Mr. Mannering,' said Bellamy in his mellow voice, 'we owe you a very sincere apology, but——'

No point in mincing words now.

'You owe me much more than that. You owe me an explanation.'

'My dear sir, believe me when I say——'

'I'm in no mood to believe anything you say,' said Mannering. 'Has that girl been seen by a doctor?'

'Why, of course she has,' said Bellamy smoothly, 'she is receiving treatment under medical guidance. She——'

'Then I think the doctor should be called at once, and then I think you should begin to explain to me. Harrison was behaving like a vicious brute. His handling of that girl was damnable, and if I see him touching her or anyone else like that again, I'll smash his face in. What the devil do you think you're doing here? Are your gardeners armed to stop thieves, or to prevent that girl from leaving? And what's the matter with your niece? She's so terrified of something here that she's absolutely cowed.'

Bellamy raised a hand. 'Please——'

'You'll hear me out. What would have happened to that girl if I hadn't forced my way out of the jewel-room? Why was I locked in? Why did you bring me here? Come on, out with it—*why?*'

Harrison took a step forward, menacingly, itching to strike him. But Bellamy remained calm.

'Jim, we aren't being very hospitable, let's have a drink. Sit down, Mannering.' He paused, but Mannering remained standing. 'I can understand you feeling a little put out, and the incident of the locked door *is* annoying. The door is always kept locked, you see, and one of the servants, noticing the key was in the lock, turned it without knowing you were there, and I do apologise.'

So he wanted to defer the crisis, too.

'Or Harrison turned the key to keep me away from the girl,' countered Mannering abruptly.

'I can see that it looks like that; it's a most unfortunate coincidence, but I assure you that you're quite wrong. Ah.' Bellamy stretched out a hand for a whisky and soda, and offered it to Mannering. 'I asked you to come here because I very much wanted to meet you, it isn't often I have the pleasure of comparing notes with a connoisseur, and I am really regretful that I have had so much else on my mind since you arrived. I'll be frank, Mr. Mannering. Both my nieces are a great anxiety.'

'Both?' Better not to let them know that he knew who Kathleen was.

'They are sisters, and some time ago they underwent a considerable nervous strain and shock. They have been ordered to rest; they aren't—quite normal, Mr. Mannering. You can see that yourself. It's only a temporary phase, I trust and believe. The younger girl, the one who ran away just now, is confined to her room on doctor's orders, but she is restive and resentful. And both have one particular illusion; they have passed it on to each other, I guess.

They *think*——' He paused, and sipped the drink Harrison had given him. 'They *think* they saw a man fall to his death from a window of the house. And, as a result, they have developed—what d'you call it, Jim?—a persecution complex. They are always restive when I have a guest. It's a sad business, you'll be the first to agree.'

'It won't improve if Harrison——'

Harrison licked his lips.

'She clawed me across the face; I wasn't in a very sweet temper, but I wouldn't have hurt the girl. If she hadn't been such a termagant, there wouldn't have been any fuss.'

Slowly, Mannering allowed himself to be mollified, Bellamy exerted himself to be reassuring, Harrison gradually thawed. The atmosphere was much clearer when they went into the dining-room for luncheon, but a new question arose in Mannering's mind.

Why was Bellamy determined to be friendly?

Not until they were having coffee did he remember the screw of paper in his waistcoat pocket.

The great clock downstairs was striking two when Mannering went into his room. Bellamy was soon to show him over some of the other rooms—including the Great Hall, which Mannering had not yet seen and where, according to both men, there were some remarkable art treasures.

Mannering closed the door, turned the key, and glanced round the room. Yes, there were plenty of places from which a spy might watch. He went to the window, turned his back on the room, and took out the paper.

It was a thin tissue, and as he smoothed it out he saw that someone had written with a hard pencil; the words would be difficult to read. The writing was small and even.

He read slowly:

The young ladies are in great danger. So are you. B. will ask you to value his jewels. Don't tell him you know some are stolen. If you can get away, send help at once. I am not allowed to leave the house. Be especially careful of H. I will try to help.

Mannering read it twice, with an odd mingling of satisfaction and disappointment, then burnt it.

If Bellamy had brought him here to value his jewels, it would explain his conciliatory manner. But Holmes and the girls were all frightened of Bellamy; what help could they give?

He had to handle this himself.

Escape . . . .

For the first time, Mannering was able to appreciate the architecture. The rooms on the ground and first floors were off passages which surrounded the entrance hall, and a huge arched door led to the Great Hall; it was locked and padlocked. Bellamy wheeled his chair forward and unlocked it. Harrison was not with them, but Holmes was at hand.

'Lights, please, Holmes,' said Bellamy.

Lights blazed from three chandeliers which hung from the high, carved ceiling. As Bellamy wheeled himself forward, Mannering shot Holmes an understanding glance.

Holmes smiled and turned away.

'*Now*, Mannering!' called Bellamy, rubbing his hands together, 'come and feast your eyes on these!'

Great tapestries of beautiful design, some of battle-scenes, one remarkably reminiscent of a Bayeux tapestry, draped the panelled walls. There were no windows, and the ceiling seemed lost in a gloom broken only near and beneath the chandeliers. Bellamy began to talk freely, giving the history and the origin of each piece there—relics from old battle-fields, swords of beaten gold, rare pieces from many epochs, a galaxy of antiques and fine art—with a studied carelessness as to century or value. Chased Norman goblets stood next to lustrous Ming vases and vessels taken from the tombs of Egyptian kings; relics of Greek, Roman, and early British statuary were ranged side by side on a massive carved sideboard. And Bellamy talked as if he knew and loved each piece; gradually all sense of danger faded and Mannering was lost in silent admiration for everything he saw.

'Yes, I am proud of that collection,' Bellamy said, 'it is a lifetime's work, Mannering. And I guess I'm just as proud of my jewels, although I know less about them. I wonder if you would care to value them for me? Or maybe tell me which are rare and which aren't worthy of the room they take up. Will you?'

'If you like,' said Mannering slowly.

Holmes appeared in the doorway. 'Did you ring, sir?'

'We'll have some tea,' said Bellamy, and took out the key of the Great Hall to lock the door again.

Mannering worked until late among the jewels, confirming his earlier opinion about which were stolen pieces. It was late when Bellamy came in, professed to be shocked that Mannering was still working, insisted that he should have a nightcap and then go to bed.

The moment for escape drew near.

Mannering read into the early hours. Silence descended upon the great house except for the creaking noises of the night, strange rustlings and murmurings, unaccountable but trying to the nerves. Between one and two o'clock would be the best time to leave, and the window at the end of his passage would be the best to use. His own would be watched.

At half-past one he threw back the bedclothes and began to dress.

By two o'clock he stood at a window overlooking the front of the house. It would be easy to open.

The tingling of excitement made his pulse beat fast. Sheets and blankets tied together to make a rope, a quick descent, a rush for the garage, and then freedom. Once he escaped, the girls would be out of imminent danger. Bellamy would not dare to harm them knowing the police might come; and he would realise that.

The moor beckoned Mannering as he opened the window.

Then events moved swiftly. A car swung round the side of the house, its headlights blazing, and the low beat of the engine purred through the night, away from Hallen House. He stood still listening—until footsteps sounded in the hall and then, less clearly, up the stairs.

He slipped back into his room and got into bed, fully clad.

No sooner had he pulled the clothes over him than the door was opened, stealthily.

CHAPTER VIII

ESCAPE

'*Mr. Mannering!*'

A man spoke hoarsely, his words only just carrying to Mannering's ears. A stocky figure showed against the faint light in the passage.

'*Mr. Mannering!*'

It was Holmes, who tiptoed towards the bed. His breathing was laboured; when he kicked against a chair, he gasped and stood stock-still.

'All right, Holmes,' said Mannering softly. 'What is it?'

Holmes stared towards the door before he came forward and answered. Little sounds filled the house—sounds of men walking about, of doors opening and closing. The hum of the car engine had faded.

'They've—they've been taken away.'

'Who have?' He didn't really need to ask.

'Miss—Miss Stella and her sister. Oh, God, what are we going to do? I didn't know anything about it until last thing, then I heard Mrs. Dent say she'd made sure they would sleep all night, she—she drugged them, sir. I couldn't rest. I didn't get undressed. I tried to come to see you before, but I couldn't get past the guards till now. Now the young ladies have gone, we may never see them again!'

Mannering got out of bed, and gripped the butler's arm.

'Do you know where they've been taken?'

'I—I haven't the slightest idea, sir.'

'Who's gone with them?'

'Harrison. But—you're dressed!'

'What are my chances of getting to the garage?'

'You can't get in there, sir.' Holmes began to tremble. 'There are two men on guard, I think they're afraid you might—you might try. They'll shoot you. They won't hesitate; they're devils!'

'Yes, I know, but we've got to help, Holmes. Where is the nearest telephone?'

'You'll never get away from the garage!'

'I must try,' said Mannering. 'Now pull yourself together, we'll have some of the men up here if you don't. Where's the nearest telephone?'

'At—at a house a few miles along the Corwellin Road, sir, the—the opposite way to which you came. It's a small house, near the road. You—you can't miss it, it's just past the bridge. But——'

'I'll get there. Tie two sheets together for me, and make a good job of it.'

As Holmes pulled off the bedclothes, Mannering went to the wardrobe and opened the tool-case. He took out half a dozen tools—a screwdriver, file, the knife, and skeleton key, a small hammer, and a diamond glass-cutter; he might need any one, or all of them. He stuffed them into his pocket, added a coil of stout cord, tapped the gun in his pocket, then rejoined Holmes. He didn't want to think, only to act.

'I—I think this will do now, sir.'

'Hold one end, and pull hard,' said Mannering.

They gripped the sheets near the knots, and pulled as if in a tug-o'-war. The knot tightened and did not give.

'That's all right,' whispered Mannering. 'Now go to the landing, and whistle softly if you see anyone coming upstairs.'

'You—you'll *never* get away, sir!'

'And when I've gone, get back to your own room and undress. You don't want to be caught.'

Holmes made no further comment. He went to the door, stopped on the threshold, muttered: 'Good luck, sir,' and disappeared. Mannering gave him time to reach the landing before going to the open window.

Harrison gone; the girls gone; and the guards were watching for him.

He tied one end of the sheet to a bracket in the wall, tucked the other end into his trousers, and, with the sheets making a big loop which touched the floor, climbed up to the window. He crouched, peering into the grounds. He could hear nothing. This window looked on to a group of thick holly trees which stood between it and the path; even if one of the guards passed along, Mannering wouldn't be seen.

He dropped the end of the sheet, turned and faced the house and then, gripping the sheet tightly with both hands, began to lower himself. The drop at the bottom was less than a yard. He bent his knees to take the impact, and landed softly.

The white sheets hung down, a clear streak against the dark wall.

He should have told Holmes to pull them up; Holmes wouldn't think of it, in his present frantic state.

He walked round the house, keeping to the muffling grass. It was a clear, still night, and stars were shimmering and giving a welcome, pale light. The huge pile of the house towered above him. As he reached the corner, he heard a man speak, but couldn't catch the words. On again. The garage, a long, low building, showed up clearly against the sky. As he drew nearer, he saw two men standing near the doors. A pale red tip glowed in the darkness; one was smoking.

He preferred to tackle one at a time.

The cigarette curved in a red arc, and sparks flew when it hit the ground.

'It's damned cold,' one of the men muttered. 'Let's get a move on.'

They walked from the doors towards the corner of the garage nearest Mannering. Would his face show up against the wall? They moved slowly, one of them beating his arms across his chest.

Mannering held his breath as they reached the corner and turned back.

No chance of overpowering them one at a time.

Mannering stepped from his hiding-place and went forward on his toes. He made a faint sound on the smooth asphalt, but the footsteps of the men drowned it. He passed the doors when the men were only ten yards ahead. They would turn when they reached the far corner, and a single shout would put an end to his hopes.

He took the revolver from his pocket.

At the corner they paused.

'Wonder how long Harrison will be,' one man remarked.

'Asking for trouble, I reckon.'

Mannering held the gun by the barrel as he crept closer. One man was hatless, the other wore a cloth cap. Both were big, powerful fellows.

'The old man——' began the one with the cap.

Mannering brought the butt of the gun down on his head; he gasped and slumped down. The other swung round, mouth wide open to shout, and Mannering's fist smashed into his face, Mannering followed with a punch to the stomach and, as the chin jutted forward, shot home an uppercut; the man's teeth snapped together as he went down.

Mannering snatched a handkerchief from his pocket, and stuffed it into one man's mouth. He gagged the other with his own handkerchief. He could count on a few minutes' grace.

He grabbed them by their coat collars and pulled them along the ground, their heels dragging noisily on the asphalt. At the door—one of three—he dropped them and took the torch and skeleton key out of his pocket. He shone his torch on the lock; it was a simple one, large and old-fashioned.

Metal scraped against metal; he couldn't afford the caution of silence now.

One of the men stirred, but didn't try to get up.

The door yielded, and Mannering pulled it open and switched on the garage light. Let the world see him!

The motor-cycle was near the wall, almost within arm's reach.

A man stirred again.

Should he drag them into the garage and lock them in? No, the din of the motor-cycle engine would arouse the rest, anyhow; only speed mattered.

It was years since he had been on a motor-cycle. It might be wiser to use one of the cars, but he would have to open another door to get it out.

He grabbed the handle-bars of the motor-cycle, swung it round and pushed it into the yard, within a foot of one man's head. A light glowed in a downstairs room, but the only sounds were the creaking of the machine.

He examined it quickly, found the throttle and the starter, and wheeled it towards the drive. He passed the cedar tree, and still all was quiet.

Should he push it a little further? Or——

'What's that?' a man called sharply.

Mannering straddled the machine and kicked the starter. The engine spluttered and faded. He moved the throttle and trod heavily again. He could hear someone hurrying forward; any moment he expected a shot.

The engine roared!

He eased off the brake, swayed, felt himself falling; but the machine righted itself and leapt forward; he had started off too fast.

A flash stabbed the darkness on his right, and the report rang out loudly, but the roar of the engine drowned all other noise. The drive gates loomed up in front of him. Would they be open or closed? Was there a man on guard there?

One gate was open.

Crack! The same man fired at him.

He was through the gateway! The pale, wavering line of the road stretched in front of him—the path to escape. He was already two hundred yards away from the gates, the machine went like the wind: he would be a couple of miles away before they could get a car out.

He had to go in the opposite direction to that from which he had come.

He hadn't seen the road clearly because of the rain!

He remembered a fork and a turning towards the house, but had he turned right or left? Right or left? Right or left? He had come from the south, followed Harrison, reached the fork and turned—right, yes, that was it, he had turned right; so at the fork he would have to turn left.

He reached the fork and turned slowly, taking too wide an arc. The wheels left the road and bumped over rough moorland, he was nearly thrown off; one hand was jolted off the handlebars. He clutched the grip again, steadied, and got back on to the road.

A house with a telephone was near the road, just past a bridge.

The rutted track made high speed impossible now; dark holes and shining puddles showed up in the bright beam of the headlamp. He bumped and rattled along at no more than twenty miles an hour. Once or twice he looked over his shoulder. There were other lights on at the house, but he could not see the glow of headlights.

How far away was the bridge?

Something flew into his eye, hurting him; he closed it spasmodically and nearly lost control again. His eye began to water and the pain made him grit his teeth. He couldn't see clearly, and the machine was wobbling dangerously. Must keep going.

It was no use, his eye was getting worse, he would have to stop. He took one hand away and rubbed it, trying to get relief from the sharp, stinging pain.

That eased, but both eyes were watering freely; he couldn't——

There was the bridge!

The road was wider just there, and he could see the stone parapet and make out the line of the river, shimmering beneath the stars. There was a sharp incline before the bridge. He felt the machine slacken speed, opened the throttle, and next moment struck something in the road. The motor-cycle skidded, the front wheel crashed into the parapet and he was flung violently off.

He fell on his side, and on a knee, but he saved his head. He lay gasping for breath, then slowly picked himself up and wiped his eye with his finger.

In the distance he could see the pale glow of car headlights; he would be overtaken in a few minutes if he tried to ride again.

He picked up the machine, wincing with the pain in his knee. He wheeled the machine towards the far side of the bridge. It nearly ran away with him, but he kept it back, reached the bottom of the incline and turned round. He pushed the machine down the river bank, while the distant sky was brightened by the glow from a car's headlights.

Near him was the lapping of water; in the distance, the throb of the car engine.

He let the machine fall, turned back, and approached the bridge, and crouched out of sight behind the parapet. The pain in his knee was agonising, and he pressed it gingerly; it was already swelling. But the house with a telephone couldn't be far away.

The bridge showed up vividly in the powerful beams of the car as it sped past.

'May you crash,' Mannering said fervently.

There was no point in going back for the motor-cycle; he wouldn't trust himself on it again. And Holmes wouldn't have been mistaken, the house couldn't be far away. But what did 'near the road' mean? Ten yards? Fifty? A hundred? He stood still, resting his injured leg. Not far away he thought he saw a shape blotting out the stars. He limped towards it, his knee gradually becoming less painful, but warm and glowing.

Yes, it was the house! He could pick out the fence which surrounded it.

The house was small and square, and in darkness—that was to be expected. He opened a small gate and went towards the front door.

He could make out the telephone wires above his head.

Holmes would have warned him had there been danger here. As he put out his hand to grope for the bell, he felt dizzy; he paused, leaning against the door. He must be ready to talk intelligently when he went in.

What should he say? Tell the blunt truth?

He heard movements inside the hall, although he hadn't rung the bell. Suddenly a light showed behind frosted glass, and as the door opened, fell on to his face.

'Who——' a man began.

The light hurt Mannering's eyes as he peered through his lashes at a perky, little fellow, hair on end, dressing-gown clutched round his waist.

The bottom fell out of Mannering's hopes.

'Why, it's *Mannering*!' exclaimed Mr. Lark in a squeaky voice. 'Come *in*, Mr. Mannering.'

And Lark took a gun from his pocket.

Another figure appeared at the foot of the stairs, a big, hulking lump of a man.

The hefty man pushed past Lark, took Mannering's arm, and pulled him over the threshold. Mannering winced from the pain in his knee.

Lark slammed the door.

'Now don't be 'ard on him, Jackie,' he said, 'you can see he's had a rough time.' The little thief stepped to Mannering's side and slipped a hand into his pockets, with the practised speed of an expert. He took out the Luger, and tossed it to his companion, who caught it neatly. 'I 'ope you've got a licence for that gun, mister,' Lark said virtuously. 'Arf a mo', Jackie; he's got something else.'

He took out the skeleton key.

Jackie's eyes rounded. Lark shot Mannering a quick, wary

glance. The spurious geniality faded and Lark became deadly serious. He looked closely at the skeleton key, then dropped it on a table and dived his hand into Mannering's pocket again. This time he found the small file.

'Strewth!' gasped Jackie.

'You shut up,' said Lark in a strained voice. Delving once more, he produced the knife and the screwdriver, and a moment later the glass-cutter. The tension increased with the appearance of each tool. Huge, shapeless Jackie stared goggle-eyed at the growing pile, and Lark's breath was hissing through his nostrils.

He found the cord, tossed it on to the table, then tapped Mannering about the chest. He took a wallet and the small case containing the Lake emeralds. Jackie's eyes bulged. Lark's fingers were unsteady as he picked at the case and opened it. The glowing green gems lay on the black velvet.

Lark looked at Mannering through his lashes. Jackie breathed: 'Cor blimey!' but Lark silenced him with a wave of his hand.

These tools were the stock-in-trade of the cracksman— their stock-in-trade. Mannering was one of the mugs; a man to be robbed; in his way famous; a connoisseur and collector whose reputation was irreproachable. But the tools and the emeralds gave the lie to that.

And there *was* honour among thieves.

CHAPTER IX

LARK LISTENS

LARK'S whistling breath was the only sound in the room. Jackie seemed dumbfounded, a mountainous, silent block of a man.

Mannering put all his weight on his right leg, to ease the pain in his knee.

Slowly, Lark stretched out his hand and picked up the Luger. He gripped it firmly, and jabbed it into Mannering's side.

'We're going to have a little talk, *Mister* Mannering. Go in that room there. Lights, Jackie.'

Jackie drew a gargantuan breath, lumbered across to an open door, groped for the switch and pressed it down. With the barrel of the gun poking between his ribs, Mannering limped into a small, crowded room. A round table stood in the middle; nearly every inch of floor space was taken up with hideous Victorian chairs, upholstered in a mauve plush, with small tables, an ornate sideboard, rococo bric-a-brac of every description. Here and there, gaudy striped wallpaper showed between sepia-coloured photographs, cheap prints, and oleographs. The light was reddened by a silk shade with a long fringe which hung down to shoulder-height.

'Siddown,' ordered Lark.

Mannering sat in a winged arm-chair, leaned forward and pushed a stool into position and, with a grunt, raised his left leg.

'S'matter with your leg?'

'I've twisted the knee,' said Mannering.

'S'ave a look.'

Mannering pulled up the leg of his trousers. At least he had time to think—but he would have to think fast to outwit little Lark. What was the best line to take?

He looked at his swollen, discoloured knee, with a sharp sense of dismay. The gravel had cut through the cloth, the flesh was badly grazed, and blood was oozing out. Better that than a sprain, perhaps—but never mind his knee, how should he deal with Lark?

Lark shot Jackie a quick, meaning glance.

'Get some water. Get everything. Come back—in five minutes. Got me?

'Okay,' said Jackie in a strained voice, and lurched out of the room.

Lark closed the door and turned, still covering Mannering with the Luger. He put his left hand into his pocket, drew out a packet of cigarettes, deftly extracted two, and tossed one of them to Mannering. He lit his own cigarette with a lighter, then threw the lighter on to Mannering's lap.

'Thanks,' said Mannering. He lit the cigarette and threw the lighter back. Lark caught it neatly.

'How long you been in the game?' Lark demanded abruptly.

'I've never been in the game.'

'Just picked them play-things up at a pawnshop I suppose. Quit lying, Mannering. I know a screwsman when I see him. Didn't think you——' He broke off; there was a glint in his eye; perhaps of admiration. 'You did a swell job! Not many men could get into the jewel-room—and get out. How'd you manage it?'

'I bought those emeralds,' Mannering said.

'I told you to stop lying,' Lark growled. 'Bellamy wouldn't sell any of his stuff. I know Bellamy. Rather lose his right 'and than sell the smallest sparkler he's got up there. Jackie's not here now—he won't talk anyway. But——'

'I've told you the truth.'

Lark thrust his head forward. His grip tightened on the gun, but his forefinger was not on the trigger. His eyes were narrowed to tiny slits.

'Listen, Mannering, I know what you are. Maybe you know what I am. Maybe we could do business. I said

78

maybe. I've got a lot of stuff I can lay my 'ands on. *You've* got Quinn's. Gawd, what a cover!' Yes, a glint of admiration showed through the tension and the menace in his manner. 'But don't make any mistake, Mannering, it's only maybe. I can work two ways. Keep you safe or turn you over to Bellamy. I sell a lot o' stuff to Bellamy, but I don't like the cove. Don't like 'Arrison, neither. They're mean. You and me might be able to do a lot o' business together, *if* you'll talk.'

Mannering drew on his cigarette.

'Lark,' he said.

'Make it snappy!'

'Ever been held on a murder rap?'

The little crook straightened up and let the Luger droop towards the ground. Mannering continued to draw at his cigarette. There were sounds in the house, of Jackie gathering the first-aid equipment for Mannering's knee, but the uncouth man wouldn't come in until he was called: Lark was boss here.

'Don't try any tricks on me,' Lark said. The question puzzled him, he was stalling now. 'I'm not a murderer.'

'You'll be mixed up in one if you don't keep clear of Bellamy.'

'I don't get you, and we ain't talking about murder. I asked you——'

'A man fell out of a window at Hallen House and broke his neck,' said Mannering. 'That's Bellamy's story, and he got away with it, but two people saw what happened—the man was pushed. And another, named Rundle, died on the moor last night. They said it was from exposure, but he was a prisoner at the house and escaped. He came to warn me not to go to see Bellamy; he said that there was death at Hallen House. There *is* death—for anyone who works with Bellamy. Death at the end of a rope, death after the eight o'clock walk, death——'

'Shut up!' Lark's voice was strangled.

'I'm just telling you.'

'I wasn't born yesterday.'

'Oh, you're not a fool, that's why I'm talking to you. Lark, I came up here to buy those emeralds. I didn't know that Bellamy had a collection of sparklers which had been stolen from places all over the world. I didn't realise he wanted me to value his stuff, perhaps force something else from me, and then——' He drew his finger across his throat, and Lark winced. 'But Rundle——'

'Rundle!'

'Rundle escaped and waylaid me, to try and stop me going to Hallen House. So did Stella Bellamy. I wouldn't listen. You'd better not make the same mistake, Lark. You'd better keep away from Bellamy and keep me away from him, too—especially just now. Because I sent a warning to the police.'

Lark said: 'It's a lie!'

'It isn't a lie; it——'

The gun moved and was trained on Mannering's chest.

'No one could get a message out of that house to the police. No one did, see? You sent a telegram to your wife—I know, I telephoned it for Bellamy. Don't lie to me, Mr. Bloody Mannering. And don't think you can get away with it——'

'Remember the telegram?' demanded Mannering, and when Lark did not answer, he went on swiftly: 'Remember the last few words? "Let Gordon know, will see him as soon as possible." ' He put the emphasis on 'Gordon' but Lark didn't comprehend. 'You know the Yard. You know Bristow and Inspector Gordon——'

Lark's breath hissed.

'I hadn't any appointment; I don't know another Gordon. My wife would know what I meant—go to the police. I didn't name Bristow in case Bellamy knew the name; Gordon was safe. And Lark—that telegram was delivered this afternoon. The Yard will get in touch with the local police. Before noon tomorrow they'll visit Bellamy. If I were you, I'd be a long way from here by midday tomorrow. You've said yourself that Bellamy's mean. D'you think he'll keep quiet about you? You've supplied a lot of his stuff, he'll swear he didn't know it was stolen. What you say to me doesn't matter a tinker's curse, but what he tells the police—well, just ask yourself.'

Lark licked his lips.

'Bellamy's too smart to let the dicks get him.'

'This time he won't be able to help it,' said Mannering. 'If you turn me over to him, the police will search until they find me. They'll prod and probe everywhere, and Bellamy won't have any warning—unless you warn him, and you'll be a fool if you do. Use your head—clear out of here.'

There was a long silence—in the room and outside.

Lark rubbed his thumb against the Luger, absently, and did not shift his gaze. He was worried; his quick, clear mind was grappling with a new and unpleasant situation. He would make his own decision, not let someone else make it for him.

Mannering shifted his position, to ease the pain in his knee. Time was passing too quickly. Bellamy must know that Lark was staying here and might come to the house, to find out if the motor-cycle had been heard. The house might be watched and—he sat up abruptly—Bellamy might even know that he was here!

Lark squashed his cigarette out in a saucer decorated with pictures of Queen Victoria. He had reached some sort of decision. The throbbing in Mannering's knee seemed to ease as his tension increased.

'I asked you a question,' Lark said. 'How long have you been in the game?'

'I'm not in "the game." '

'Why'd you carry those tools about?'

'I find them useful.'

Lark repeated his one-handed trick with the cigarettes and lighter, but this time did not throw Mannering a cigarette. He blew smoke over Mannering's head.

'You can't fool me, I *know*. Better let Jackie 'ave a look at that knee. I'm going to take your advice, mister, but I'm going to take you with me. You and me are going to be as close as brothers for a little while. I still reckon we can do business, and if Bellamy stops buying——'

Lark turned, and bellowed to Jackie, who lumbered in, proving that he had been waiting for the summons.

Lorna Mannering let herself into the Chelsea flat, pulled off her wide-brimmed, black straw hat, and poked her fingers into hair as dark and glossy as a raven's wing. She looked tired and disappointed; it was partly because John wasn't here to greet her. Whenever he was away for a few days, it left her subdued, lonely; in moments of quick introspection, she knew that it was partly because of the strain of waiting, in the old days, for word of his safety; she lived more in their troubled past than John.

He should be home.

But if he were, he would have called out the moment he heard her key in the lock.

She dropped her hat on to a table and went into the living-room, the largest in the flat, every corner and every piece of furniture with its association with John. She'd sent their maid off for the night, so as to be alone with him, and——

She saw the telegram, propped up on the mantelpiece. She drew back, knowing it meant he was delayed, then tore it open.

Gordon?

Who was Gordon?

Why on earth did he talk about an appointment he hadn't made? The next day they had planned to spend together.

Gordon? Gordon, Gordon, Gordon——

No, she knew no one of the name. But John hadn't dragged it into the telegram without a reason. He was trying to tell her something. What?

Disquiet grew like a shadow in her mind.

Gordon?

She found herself looking at the telegram again as she sat in front of her dressing-table mirror. When she glanced up, she looked at her reflection—knew that if John were here, he'd laugh gently and his hands would rest lightly on her shoulders and steal down, and the frown which drew her thick, black eyebrows together would clear, lights would spring into her grey eyes, now dull and slate-grey with anxiety. He'd make some absurd remark about the love-liness of her white skin, or trace the line of her short, rather broad nose and her full lips. Every word would delight her; every touch would be welcome.

But he wasn't here.

Gordon, Gordon——

Gordon!

There was a detective at Scotland Yard of that name, he worked with Bristow!

Superintendent Bristow, in shirt-sleeves and slippers, put down the *Evening News* and picked up the telephone. He could hear his wife in the kitchen, getting supper.

'Bristow here . . . who?'

'Lorna Mannering. Bill . . .'

Bristow listened; and knew she was really worried, and probably had cause to be. He didn't envy the lot of John Mannering's wife. But she was composed and brief—not a woman to waste words.

'And that's all?' he asked.

'Yes.'

'I wouldn't jump to conclusions,' Bristow said. 'But I can see why you're worried, and I'll have a word with the Cornshire police at once. You'll be at the flat all the evening, won't you?'

'Yes.'

'And tomorrow?'

'You'll get me some news by tomorrow, won't you?'

'You'll probably have some yourself,' said Bristow, 'Good-bye—and don't worry.'

But he knew that if he were in her shoes, he would worry a great deal. If Mannering were driven to appeal covertly to the police for help, things weren't so good.

Soon he was speaking to Superintendent Dando, of the Cornshire C.I.D., and Dando asked questions. No, Bristow couldn't think of any grounds for a call at Hallen House that night, except to inquire for Mannering. He didn't *know* that there was anything desperately urgent about this, and if it were difficult to get to Hallen House tonight, early morning would have to do, but—was there any reason to suspect that the man Bellamy was a crook?

No, Dando told him, none at all.

True, a man had been killed by falling out of a window at the house only a few weeks ago. Servants had given satis-factory evidence; the inquest verdict of accidental death had been unquestioned, certainly no one had suspected violence. What? Oh, the dead man was the previous owner of Hallen House, although he had only owned it for a few weeks—he had inherited it from his uncle and sold it to Bellamy. The circumstances were not suspicious in themselves, but if Mannering had stumbled upon a mystery, the thing would be worth investigating. He would send men to the house early next morning.

What about this John Mannering? Was he reliable? Jewel collectors were notoriously amoral, in Dando's opinion; seemed to imagine they were a law unto themselves.

'Oh, yes,' said Bristow thoughtlessly, 'Mannering's all right.'

He looked up from the telephone to see his wife, who knew about the Baron, grinning at him.

A request from Scotland Yard was not a thing which Superintendent Dando took lightly, so he was at his Cor-wellin office at half-past eight next morning. Partly because it was a glorious day, he decided to drive to Hallen House himself, and to take a sergeant.

The sergeant was getting a car out of the garage and Dando was looking through the morning's post, when the telephone-bell rang.

Five minutes late, he replaced the receiver, stared at a picture of his twin daughters which stood on his littered desk, then drew a writing-pad in front of him. He wrote swiftly:

Telegram to Superintendent Bristow, New Scotland Yard:

'BELLAMY OF HALLEN HOUSE HAS JUST REPORTED A ROBBERY. DANDO.'

Bellamy sat on the porch of the house, sunning himself, smoking a pipe and watching the little trail of dust on the road which led from Corwellin, the nearest town. A car was churning up a cloud of dust on the dry, sandy track between the puddles. Two gardeners were working at the front of the house, but no rifles were in sight. Now and again Bellamy smiled to himself, and once he chuckled; a gardener glanced at him with a nervous grin.

Harrison came on to the porch, shading his eyes with his hand against the brilliant sunlight.

'They coming?' he demanded abruptly.

'They'll be here in ten minutes.'

'If you ask me, it's suicide!' Harrison's eyes were red-rimmed and glassy from lack of sleep. His movements were quick and nervous; his hand was unsteady when he took the cigarette from his lips. It's——'

'But I am not asking you,' murmured Bellamy.

'If you'd taken my advice——'

'I've already told you what I think about your advice. Jim, go indoors, lie down; try to get some sleep. You're in no condition to talk to the police. I tell you that I can handle the situation *very* easily. Mannering won't bob up—and if he did, he couldn't show the receipt for £3,000, you stole that from him. We had to get our blow in first. The only alternative we had was to leave here. That would have meant a hue-and-cry. I'm not prepared to go into hiding, or to go abroad yet.'

'I'd rather be in Buenos Aires than in an English jail!'

'I would much rather stay here,' said Bellamy. 'Now go up to your room, Jim. I shan't send for you unless it's urgent. I hope it won't be. If I do have to——' his voice grew steely. 'You better control your nerves.'

'I'll be all right,' muttered Harrison, and flung himself off.

The approaching car, now near the gates, was a shiny Austin, with two men in it. The driver looked young, and Bellamy turned his attention to the passenger, a dark-haired man whose broad shoulders made the blond driver look slender.

When the car stopped outside the front door, the passenger jumped out. Although he was a heavy, thick-set man, he moved quickly and lightly. His shoulders were not only broad, but rounded—a bull of a man. He had a broad, sallow face and a bushy black moustache, and looked a typical Cornshire native.

This would be Dando, decided Bellamy. He wore a suit of homespun, brown tweed and the knees of his trousers were baggy. Beside him, the driver looked an elegant, young fop, fair-haired—probably a 'foreigner.'

'Good morning,' greeted Bellamy in his most mellow voice. 'Are you Superintendent Dando?'

'That's right, sir. Mr. Bellamy?'

'Yes. I'm sorry I can't get out of my chair.' said Bellamy, smoothing the black rug over his knees. 'I'm rather incapacitated, Superintendent. And your companion——'

'Detective-sergeant Whittaker.'

Bellamy nodded genially.

'Good of you to make it snappy—and to come in person. Thanks. But come in, won't you—just follow me.' He startled the detectives by the speed with which he swivelled his chair round and sped across the hall.

The sunlight made that cavernous chamber bright, and picked out the colours of the oil paintings on the walls.

Bellamy disappeared through an open door, and Dando and Whittaker followed, Whittaker appearing to take much more note of the house than his senior. When they entered the room, Bellamy was pressing a bell-push.

'Now come and sit down, and I'll tell you everything I can, Mr. Dando. I'm insured, of course; the loss isn't serious financially, but——' His expression altered, his brows knit together. 'I am very attached to my collection, humble though it is, and the emeralds were very fine specimens.'

Dando sat down; Whittaker remained standing.

'Was anything else taken?' asked Dando.

'Several smaller gems, but they're not really part of my little collection—just makeweights I had been forced to buy in order to get stones I really coveted. I find the obvious solution almost unbelievable, but—what other explanation *can* there be?'

'You're going a little too fast for me, sir.' Dando gave an apologetic smile. 'Will you start from the beginning.'

He had a bovine expression and rather sleepy, blue eyes, and was not a man to fill anyone with alarm. And he looked an easy man to bluff. The sergeant, who was standing with a notebook and pencil in his hand, looked a fathead.

'I'm really sorry,' said Bellamy. 'From the beginning is the right place to start, Mr. Dando.'

He had seen Mannering's advertisement for the Lake Emeralds in *Apollo*. Perhaps the Superintendent was familiar with the magazine which circulated among dealers and connoisseurs of fine art and jewellery. Being interested, Bellamy had telephoned Quinn's and spoken to Mannering, making it clear that he would not sell the emeralds but might consider an exchange for other rare gems. Mannering had surprised Bellamy by saying he would come to see them at Hallen House. He, Bellamy, had been quite prepared to go to London, but Mannering had said he had other business in the south-west, and Bellamy had raised no objection. Yet it had surprised him, of course, in the light of after events—but he was anticipating the story again.

He broke off, as the door opened.

The housekeeper came in with a coffee-tray and biscuits. Her pale, grey eyes seemed riveted on Bellamy, until he nodded dismissal. Mrs. Dent closed the door softly behind her, and Bellamy leaned forward to pour out the coffee.

Mannering had arrived in the middle of a storm, nothing had deterred him from coming, although, in such weather, most people would have stayed in Corwellin overnight—didn't the Superintendent agree? He had shown great interest in the collection, as well as in the emeralds, but had not been prepared to exchange, he wanted to buy. Obstinate fellow! Bellamy had been firm, and:

'I couldn't understand the man. I got the impression that he was worried about something—it made him abrupt and bad-tempered—why, he even threatened! Obviously he wanted the emeralds badly.'

Dando made understanding noises.

Bellamy admitted that he had been uneasy, especially when, next day, on the pretext of indisposition, Mannering had not returned to London but had invited himself for another night. Bellamy had thought that he was going to try to persuade him to part with the emeralds, but Mannering appeared to have accepted his *congé*. He had been sullen, uneasy and irritable.

'But we didn't dream what was in his mind,' Bellamy declared in a shocked voice. 'I was up and around first next morning, I sleep badly, and I came out of my bedroom and found the jewel-room door had been broken open. I—I can't tell you the shock it gave me. I thought the door was burglar-proof! Well, I wheeled myself into the room. The window was still shuttered, I just can't believe anyone could break in that way—but the door had been opened. And the lock was specially fitted a month or two ago. Only a really expert thief could have broken it open. But there it was—open. The emeralds and these other things were gone.'

'Curious he should leave some stuff behind,' remarked Dando.

'I thought that, Mr. Dando, but my housekeeper explained it. She heard sounds during the night, and came downstairs. She noticed nothing amiss, but presumably the thief was disturbed and thought he'd better get away while he could.'

Dando nodded.

Bellamy raised a pointed finger.

'I soon made another discovery. My butler had also run away.'

Dando blinked, and looked more bovine than ever.

'Then either of them could have taken the jewels.'

'I haven't told you yet that Holmes, the butler, and Mannering seemed on very good terms,' Bellamy said smoothly, 'Looking back, it sticks right out that they were conspiring together. Find one, and you'll find the other! They had to force a way out, you know. I take great precautions, as jewels represent only a trifling proportion of my valuables. The doors can only be opened with a key. They escaped by a window near Mannering's bedroom. Holmes I can understand, but Mannering, a man of such position! It's incomprehensible, except that——'

He broke off.

'Go on, please,' said Dando.

'Well, I guess all the time he was here, he gave me the

impression that some danger, some threat, was hanging over his head. He was so desperate to get those emeralds. Of course, you'll say I'm pre-judging the man, there *may* be another explanation, yet——' Bellamy broke off, and shrugged. 'Now the investigation is in your capable hands, Superintendent!'

'Thank you,' said Dando heavily. 'I'd like to see the jewel-room.'

'Of course. Finished your coffee? Then follow me.'

Bellamy wheeled himself vigorously out of the room.

A cursory glance was enough to convince both detectives that a brilliant cracksman had forced the lock of the door. Dando knew of no one in the south-west capable of it; it was the work of a London specialist. He did not spend much time examining the lock, but followed Bellamy into the room.

Five of the cabinets were filled with china, porcelain, and rare glass; only one contained jewels, a fraction of the collection which Mannering had seen. The jewel-cabinet had three doors; one had been forced, and a few trinkets were strewn about the shelves; the other partitions were undisturbed, diamonds winked and rubies glowed in the sunlit room.

'You see, it's a small collection, but there are some lovely pieces,' murmured Bellamy. 'What would you like to do first, Superintendent?'

'Look round here,' said Dando. 'Sergeant, fetch my case from my car, will you?'

Soon they were brushing grey powder over the cabinet and the door, blowing it away, welcoming the sight of the finger-prints which showed up. There were several at the door, also, but none at the window, where the broken cable had been mended.

Dando felt an unwilling admiration for whoever had forced the lock. But he couldn't waste much time; there was a lot to do; get finger-prints of all the servants and of Bellamy, for instance, without letting them know what he was doing, so that he could compare them with the sets. Then he must search Mannering's room; and the butler's. He must send an urgent message to Scotland Yard, too.

He did that first, and it was sent off by one of the gardeners, who drove to the nearest village; the gardener also had instructions to summon more men from Corwellin Police Station.

Dando also sent out a general call for John Mannering and Holmes.

CHAPTER X

SHOCK FOR BRISTOW

BRISTOW walked briskly along the passage of Scotland Yard, whistling cheerfully. He thrived on warm weather, and this morning's burst of Indian summer could stay as long as it liked, there would be no complaint from him. Moreover, he was enjoying a welcome lull in the crime wave. The long dark nights of winter were an ally of thieves, an enemy of the police, but this autumn the new outbreak was later than usual in starting.

As he passed the Assistant Commissioner's door it opened and a sergeant came out. Bristow saw Colonel Anderson-Kerr who raised a hand.

'Oh, come in a moment, Bristow, will you?'

Bristow went in and closed the door.

'Good morning—grand, isn't it?' he asked.

'For those who like it,' said Anderson-Kerr. He was a lean whippet of a man, but his dislike of London heat was a by-word. 'Sit down, and don't look so disgustingly pleased with yourself.'

Bristow chuckled as he took a cigarette from a box the A.C. pushed towards him.

His neat, close-clipped moustache was stained yellow with nicotine. His iron-grey hair was parted in the middle, and brushed down very flat, his fresh complexion reflected glowing health, and his eyes were sparkling. This was one of the days when Bristow was good-looking. His even features were nothing much to boast about, but they had a pleasing effect. He looked kindly, and he was, although under strain when dealing with hardened criminals the kindliness disappeared and took good looks away.

'What's this about a message from Mannering?' Anderson-Kerr tapped a file of reports on his desk.

'I don't know whether it really amounts to much, although Mannering wouldn't send mysterious telegrams for the sake of it,' said Bristow. 'I haven't heard from Corwellin yet.'

'Why did Mannering go down there?'

Bristow told him what Lorna had already explained over the telephone, and added:

'It is just possible the name "Gordon" was an error in transmission, and nothing at all may come of it. Mannering isn't on the look out for trouble.'

'I hope not.' Something in the tone of the A.C.'s voice startled Bristow. 'I suppose there isn't any doubt that Mannering *was* the Baron?'

'Short of legal proof, no doubt at all,' said Bristow. 'Why?'

'I didn't know him—or you—in the Baron days, and I only know him as a clever dealer and a trustworthy expert to consult,' said Anderson-Kerr. 'And he's made himself useful in other ways——'

'If Mannering had been a policeman, he'd have been our star performer.'

'So I've gathered. Ever feel uneasy about what he's up to these days?'

There was silence; long and thoughtful. Then:

'Just what are you driving at?' asked Bristow.

Anderson-Kerr took a buff-coloured memo from his desk and handed it over; and Bristow's eyes narrowed as he read. '*Bellamy of Hallen House has just reported a robbery.*'

Another silence, short and tense this time, before Bristow asked:

'When did this arrive?'

'Two hours ago. As you were at Marlborough Street, I held on to it. First a mysterious message from Mannering then this. I'm wondering if——'

The telephone-bell rang.

'For you,' said Anderson-Kerr.

'Hello?' Bristow barked.

The brightness, already dimmed, faded completely and his good looks were scattered.

'All right, that'll do. Send confirmation to my office immediately, with a copy to the Assistant Commissioner.'

He banged down the receiver.

'That's another telegram from Corwellin. Dando wants to know if we can telegraph Mannering's finger-prints.'

Anderson-Kerr did not speak.

Bristow's voice was as hard as his expression.

'According to Bellamy, Mannering got up in the middle of the night, broke into a locked room, and cleared off with some jewels—including the emeralds he went down to buy. The butler left with him. There's no trace of forced entry into the house, only an open window. Knotted sheets hanging down. Motor-cycle stolen from the garage. Dando's put out a call for Mannering throughout the Western Counties, and wants us to broadcast it.'

He pressed a new cigarette against a glowing stub.

'Well?' said Anderson-Kerr. 'A leopard and his spots?'

Bristow said: 'A leopard can't change his spots any more than the Baron would leave finger-prints behind, or do a job when he is the only possible suspect. And he would never use an accomplice. According to that telegram, Dando thinks he worked with the butler. I don't believe it. But——'

'Worried?' asked Anderson-Kerr.

'Badly. Can't understand why I wasn't before. Always known one thing which might start the Baron off again.'

'Is he hard up?'

Bristow laughed mirthlessly.

'He's very rich. But he's got that past and if anyone else knows about it, he might be blackmailed. Why did he travel to that god-forsaken place to get some trumpery emeralds?'

'You may be right,' said Anderson-Kerr.

'I'd better get busy,' said Bristow.

Half an hour later, the finger-prints had been telegraphed to Corwellin, and the general call was out for Mannering. If the call were picked up by the newspapers, it might be construed into a request for Mannering's help. Bristow did all this efficiently but with a cold weight of oppression on his mind. Now and again the thought of Lorna Mannering intruded, and he expected a call from her.

It didn't come.

Bristow did not leave his desk that lunch-time, but sent for sandwiches and coffee from the canteen. He might as well have had a square meal, however, for there was no further news until half-past two. This time a telegram was brought in, written on a memo form.

'PRINTS ON DOOR AND CABINET MANNERING'S. YOUR HELP WELCOMED. DANDO.'

Bristow telephoned the A.C.'s office, but there was no answer. Next, and very thoughtfully, he put in a call to Mannering's flat. There was no answer from there, either. A curious glint appeared in Bristow's eyes as he put in a call to Quinn's.

A soft-voiced man answered him.

'This is Quinn's, sir. Can I help you?'

'Is that Carmichael?'

'Yes, sir. Is that Mr. Bristow?'

'Yes. Do you know where Mrs. Mannering is?'

Carmichael didn't reply at once.

'Do you?' snapped Bristow.

Carmichael murmured: 'Well, sir, she did ask me to treat the matter as confidential, but I am a little worried by events. I understand that she had gone to Cornshire.'

So she'd heard from Mannering; or had news.

'When did she leave?' Bristow asked flatly.

'By the ten o'clock train from Paddington.'

'Alone?'

'I think so, sir.'

'Did she have a message from Mr. Mannering?'

'I was not told of any such message,' said Carmichael. 'Mrs. Mannering telephoned from the station and informed me where she was going. I gathered——' he broke off.

'Go on,' ordered Bristow sharply.

'I gathered that she was worried by the telegram which she received yesterday, and wasn't satisfied that the police were taking the matter seriously enough.' There was gentle reproof in Carmichael's voice. 'She felt that she could not stay in London. Of course——'

'That'll do for now,' said Bristow. 'I'm coming to see you in half an hour.'

Hart Row, London, W.1, slumbered in the sluggish warmth of the afternoon. Traffic crawled along New Bond Street, which was at one end of the Row; pedestrians hurried or dawdled past the exclusive, expensive shops. New Bond Street was thronged, but Hart Row was deserted except for two or three people looking in a gown-shop window.

The sun caught the facia board of the antique shop, and the gilt Old English lettering of the name stood out clearly. The narrow window was dressed in wine-red velvet, and a Genoese silver cabinet stood exactly in the middle. A single light glowed inside the shop, shining softly on priceless things.

Carmichael stood near the door. Tall, thin, white-haired, he looked as if he should be clad in robes and surplice, not in a cutaway morning-suit. His bushy, white eyebrows curled up to his high, pale forehead.

A green Morris stopped outside and Bristow jumped out, a sergeant following him.

Carmichael stepped forward.

'Good afternoon, Mr. Bristow. Shall we go into the office?'

Years of habit had made Carmichael weigh his words; he talked slowly and rather prosily.

'Yes.' Bristow was curt.

Soon Bristow sat at Mannering's desk, the sergeant by the door, Carmichael in front of the detective.

Bristow studied the old man's face as he announced abruptly: 'Mr. Mannering is missing.'

'*Missing*, sir?'

'I want to know everything you can tell me about his trip to Cornshire—and about the Lake Emeralds. You knew that he had advertised for them in the *Apollo*, didn't you?'

'Yes, sir.'

'Did you insert the advertisement?'

'No.'

'Does Mr. Mannering usually insert his own?'

'He has been known to, sir.'

'But usually he leaves it to you?'

'Frequently.'

'Do you know the customer for whom he wanted to buy these jewels?'

Carmichael hesitated.

'Carmichael, I'm in a hurry,' said Bristow in an ominous voice.

'I am thinking, sir.' said Carmichael in a tone of gentle reproof. 'I cannot recall the name of the client who wishes to obtain the Lake Emeralds, but Mr. Mannering had many friends who ask for his help to complete valuable collections of jewellery, and it is quite customary for such buyers to desire their interest to be kept secret. Mr. Mannering would respect a confidence in every way, and——'

'How long has he been looking for the emeralds?' Bristow switched the subject abruptly, and took Carmichael off his guard. 'Well? How long?'

'My first intimation of it was when I saw the advertisement,' said Carmichael. 'Yet had he wished to conceal *his* interest, he would have advertised under a box number.'

Bristow thought: 'Yes, that's a point,' but did not relax his brusque manner. 'Has Mr. Mannering been restless lately?'

'Restless, sir?'

'Worried. Nervous. Irritable.'

'On the contrary, sir, I have never known him in better health or spirits. He has never been one to allow business to harass him and of late it has been most flourishing. No, sir, Mr. Mannering was not at all restless, I assure you.'

'And Mrs. Mannering?'

'On the few occasions that I have seen her, she has been her usual self, sir, if I may say so.'

Bristow switched again.

'When you saw the advertisement, did you ask him what it was all about?'

'Most certainly I did not. He mentioned it to me himself, asking me to tell him immediately if we had a—a bite, sir.'

'I see. And the only bite came from Mr. Bellamy in Cornshire?'

'To the best of my knowledge that is correct.'

'Have you got any correspondence about it?'

'Mr. Mannering took it with him,' said Carmichael, 'although there was not a great deal. Mr. Bellamy's secretary telephoned about the matter in the first place, and there were several subsequent telephone calls. I have *no* idea what was said,' added Carmichael.

Bristow said: 'All right, Carmichael. If you think of anything else, let me know.'

'I will indeed, sir,' said Carmichael. 'Your visit has greatly disturbed me, because you are so obviously worried about Mr. Mannering. Are there any reasons for——'

'He's disappeared from Hallen House,' said Bristow. 'And understand this. I want to hear the moment you have any news about him.'

'You will, I assure you,' promised Carmichael.

94

Bristow went on to the Chelsea flat, and had an unsatisfactory interview with the maid. She only knew that during breakfast that morning her mistress had announced that she was going away for a few days. The maid was a new employee; Mrs. Mannering had not told her where she was going; but had given her instructions to refer any callers to Quinn's.

Bristow moodily summed up what little he had learned. There might be some mystery about the man who wanted the Lake Emeralds; it was at least possible that someone was exerting pressure upon Mannering in order to get them. But Mannering would never have acted like a Borstal boy cracking his first crib.

As Bristow got out of his car at the Yard, a lanky, sallow-faced man approached and grinned at him.

'What do you want?' growled Bristow.

'Lowdown on Mannering. How about it?'

'I've nothing that you can't get from the Back Room Inspector.'

'Don't give me that,' said the reporter, 'I don't want handouts. Mannering have a brainstorm and run off with the jools?'

'If you're fool enough to think so, go ahead and print it,' said Bristow.

It wouldn't be printed, of course; the reporter's suggestion showed how black the situation looked against Mannering.

Bristow didn't like it.

And it forced him, not for the first time, to probe deeply into his attitude towards Mannering. That was the one thing which continually pricked Bristow's conscience. Mannering as the Baron had been his natural enemy; Mannering as a jewel expert and dealer was a consultant to the authorities— a situation which Bristow had once fought against and now accepted; and Mannering as a man, he liked.

Policemen had no right to let personal liking creep into their attitude towards thieves. But there was nothing wrong in liking—if necessary, helping—an old lag who was running straight; and Bristow was no cynic, for he knew many cases of crooks who had genuinely reformed. Mannering fell into that category—until something like this cropped up, and all the old, nagging doubts were revived: fear, almost, that something would drive Mannering back to the Baron.

This wasn't a Baron job; it was far too clumsy.

But if Mannering came under suspicion, Bristow would have to go for him, couldn't just rely on his feeling that the Baron was really a thing of the past. If this were a case of blackmail, that past might come out——

Bristow took a grip on himself.

Mannering must have a square deal, but that was all; no favouritism. But it could become a delicate matter, since Dando was involved, and the Press had started guessing.

First task; find Mannering.

CHAPTER XI

DANDO FINDS THE BUTLER

SUPERINTENDENT Dando was in his element. This case had all the appearances of a major mystery. The life of a provincial detective was seldom brightened by such excitement. Routine became monotonous; the ways of small crooks never left the common rut; one went along at a steady jog-trot and envied the pundits at Scotland Yard.

Dando reserved his opinion of Bellamy and Harrison, but studied both men closely. He did not like the housekeeper; her curiously blank eyes worried him. Two or three of the servants seemed a little nervous when he was about, but others were affable and normal.

Broken routine was not the only good thing, for Dando had a hobby; a love of old buildings. And here he was, in a house with some parts as old as any in Cornshire, at liberty to go where he pleased. Bellamy had been insistent about that.

It was the hobby which led him to inspect the fireplace of the jewel-room. The wall there was much older than the outside wall or those on the other two sides. The design was different; larger pieces of grey stone had been used; the plaster had been replaced in some crevices, but in others centuries-old plaster remained intact. He could imagine men of Norman days working here. There would have been a stone-flagged floor, then, not this polished parquet with the skin rugs. The stone floor would have been covered with rushes; a bit smelly of course. The fireplace had been built on Norman lines, although anyone with half an eye could see that it was of modern workmanship. His gaze travelled up the wall, and he caught his breath. Surely—

surely there were some narrow slits in the original wall, slits which had been bricked in. He stood back to see them more clearly. Yes, there they were! Long, narrow apertures, used for firings arrows as well as for ventilation—by Jerusalem, this had been an outside wall!

The Great Hall—Bellamy had taken him inside—must have been the original building. Now in there he could feast his eyes for hours. Days!

Steady, now; he was on a job.

Not a bad piece of reconstruction, this fireplace. There was some rough plaster work, a series of rather primitive figures. Interesting although faked. It might have been done twenty years ago, or a couple of hundred. He examined it more closely. It *was* old work, and . . .

'By Jericho!'

There was a door in the wall, he could see the outline of it, concealed by the decorative plaster. A door which probably led into the Great Hall. It might be part of the original Norman wall. He wanted an excuse for going to the Great Hall again, and this might be it. Were there any secret passages or hidden cupboards? Over the centuries, concealed cavities had been popular; priests' holes had been two a penny in Cornshire.

He was running his fingers over the plaster when he felt something give. He pressed harder; yes, there was a knob here; this was a secret panel.

Nothing happened.

He put his mind to the task. This 'button' hadn't been installed for no purpose. It was too much to expect a sliding door, but—if he pressed the 'button' in the right way, a door *might* open.

He pushed and pulled.

The door *did* open!

Dando became so excited that he pulled harder than he intended, and the door flew wide, hitting his knee sharply. But in spite of that, he stood absolutely still, lips parted, eyes rounded in growing stupefaction.

The body of a man slowly toppled out of the doorway and fell at his feet.

The barrel-shaped corpse, knees and arms twisted oddly, was stiff with *rigor mortis*. But it was not long since this man had died.

He was dressed in a black coat and striped trousers, and

wore no collar and tie. His eyes were half-open, his lips were parted. He had been strangled; the scarf was twisted round his neck.

'It—it's the butler,' Dando muttered. 'I've found the butler.

Dan Chittering of the *Daily Gazette* was a meek-looking little man with a lock of fair hair dangling into his eyes, a slight stammer, a timid manner. He was in Bristol on a drab murder case when he heard that Mannering was missing, and that Corwellin had been mentioned as the trouble centre. Chittering, who looked too young and incapable to drive a powerful car, sent it hurtling along the West Country roads, became a menace to man and beast until, entering Corwellin, he slowed down, edged the car into a narrow parking space between two others, and went as if diffidently to the police station. There was some excitement at that unattractive stone building, so much so that he thought that knowledgeable people in the town might be able to tell him what the fuss was about. He sought out the local newspaper office, a stuffy, smelly place. He learned that a body had been found at Hallen House. He telephoned London before wandering back to the police station, and was there when the ambulance arrived with the body.

He went to the morgue at the back of the station. There was a great deal of coming and going, and several other newspaper men were hanging about. Chittering, however, was the first to discover where the morgue-keeper lived.

He was waiting near the man's house later that evening, and discovered a mutual liking for beer.

Nor did the morgue-keeper object to mixing his drinks.

The *Daily Gazette* came out next morning with a story sensational in every detail, with Mannering's name splashed across four columns.

Mannering put his foot to the ground, and gingerly tested his knee. It was not so painful as it had been on the previous day, and the swelling had gone down. He limped across the floor of the small bedroom, a dingy, gloomy place, although in the garden at the back a dense mass of trees was already beginning to change colour.

How long would Lark want to keep him here, in this little country-town pub?

There had been no question of escape the previous day; he could not have gone a hundred yards. If he were wise, he wouldn't try his leg too much today, either; by tomorrow, it should be able to stand up to most strains.

Probably it would have to.

Lark and Jackie seemed confident that he wouldn't try to get away. In their way, they were blackmailing him. No, that wasn't fair to Jackie. The uncouth Cockney did exactly what Lark told him; he was completely under Lark's domination. A queer relationship, but not important just now, he need only take Lark into account. And Lark, believing he had discovered Mannering to be a cracksman, thought he had a strong hand.

Mannering had encouraged the belief.

Without acknowledging or admitting 'the truth' he shied away from the subject. Lark never visited the room without referring to it, sometimes directly, sometimes obliquely. The little crook was outwardly friendly, but told him nothing of what he had learned, passed on no news of Hallen House or Bellamy. That was part of a deliberate policy, tightening Lark's grip on the whip.

The burglar and Jackie shared the next room.

A dray pulled up almost immediately outside Mannering's window, and two dark-haired, sallow-skinned Cornshiremen began to unload the beer. There were inexhaustible supplies of beer. Six bottles, one empty, five full, were standing along the wall near the door. Jackie had brought them up, dumped them, said 'From the Boss,' and gone out again.

Standing behind a dirty net curtain, Mannering watched the men at work. Was this town Corwellin? There was no lettering on the dray, nothing to indicate its owner or where it came from. This window overlooked small, grey stone houses, many of them in long terraces, rather reminiscent of a mining village. In the distance were two slag heaps, and what looked like a derelict shaft-head; and Corwellin was a tin-mining district. By craning his neck, he could just see the twin spires of a church or minster; but he did not know what the mother church of Corwellin was like, so that didn't help him.

He knew that he was about fifteen miles from the house on the moor, because the journey from Lark's place had taken half an hour. In the darkness of early morning, he had been hustled into this place after a hurried, whispered consultation in the doorway. He knew that Lark and Jackie were among friends; beyond that, he could be sure of nothing.

His meals had been sent up to him. That morning he had breakfasted in bed, on eggs and bacon, toast and marmalade, as generous in quantity as that as Hallen House. The breakfast tray was on a bamboo table by the side of the bed.

It was now nearly ten o'clock, and he had just finished dressing.

The room was poorly furnished—a huge, brass-railed feather bed, a marble-topped washstand with a cracked jug and bowl, and a narrow, old-fashioned wardrobe. These were the only large pieces. Two cane-seated chairs, a dilapidated fireside chair which sagged on one side whenever he sat in it, and the table, made up the rest. A huge black-and-white print, *The Last Supper*, hung over the bed, and two or three religious texts on the other walls. By the empty fireplace hung a yellowed pre-war calendar, without a single sheet torn off it, and a small mirror was fastened to the wall. The linoleum was old and cracked; a strip of threadbare carpet was beside the bed.

Everything was clean; Jackie himself had 'done' the room the previous day; he hadn't been talkative.

The unloading finished, the dray moved off.

Mannering turned away from the window.

The stairs creaked as someone came up—he had learned to recognise that sound quickly. Jackie? No—these footsteps were lighter and quicker; Lark was coming to see him.

He took out his cigarette case and lit one of three remaining cigarettes. He heard the key turn in the lock—a mere formality, for he could open it whenever he wanted—and Lark slipped into the room.

A cloth cap pushed his ears out further than nature had intended, and she had pushed them far enough. His bony nose was red, and his eyes were wary. Ugly and painfully thin, there was an air of repressed energy about him.

He had several newspapers under his arm.

There was no love in the way he looked at Mannering.

'Siddown.'

Mannering sat on the bed.

'So you didn't bust that jewel-room.' He was angry; Mannering felt his own pulse racing.

'No, I didn't.'

'You didn't, eh? And you reckon that I'll get mixed up in a murder rap if I have anything to do with Bellamy?'

'You will.'

Lark drew in his breath and thrust his head forward menacing and dangerous—yes, dangerous; all friendliness was gone. He had his right hand in his pocket, poking something against the cloth; undoubtedly a gun. There was now an expression of intense dislike on his face; dislike, contempt, hatred, anger.

He growled:

'I'd like to cut your ruddy throat.'

Mannering did not answer.

'You talked to *me* about the eight o'clock walk. To *me*!' Lark paused, let the newspapers slip, picked one up and folded it across and across; he could do most things with one hand. He folded it into a tight roll, stepped forward and slapped Mannering across the face. Mannering thrust out a hand and wrested the paper away. His face stung, but that wasn't important. What had come over Lark?

'Don't you try no tricks on *me*,' growled Lark. 'Take a look!'

He pulled the gun out of his pocket, and backed away a few paces.

Mannering turned away and went to the window, unfolding the newspaper. It was a *Daily Gazette*. At the half-fold, he saw a photograph—his own. There was Chittering's four-column headline: POLICE SEEK MANNERING IN MURDER HUNT. As he stared down, the black letters seemed to swim in front of his eyes. POLICE SEEK MANNERING IN MURDER HUNT.

The light from the window shone straight on the paper. Gradually the wavering lines straightened, and he could see more clearly; he read the caption beneath the photograph.

'John Mannering, jewel-expert and connoisseur, famous for investigations into sensational crimes, whom the police want to interview in connection with the Corwellin Moor murder.'

There was a sub-heading: SUPT. DANDO'S GRIM DISCOVERY.

'Superintendent Dando, believing the theft of valuable emeralds from Hallen House, until lately the home of Sir

Mervaise Galliard, now owned by Mr. Silas Bellamy, to be important, took over investigations personally. Two men were missing from the house, John Mannering, a guest, and Edward Holmes, the butler. Supt. Dando shrewdly suspected that one of these had not left the house. He searched every corner, and eventually found a secret cupboard. Opening the door, Supt. Dando was horrified to see the body of a man topple out. The missing butler had been strangled, and had been dead some hours. A scarf round his neck was tied fiendishly tight. Although the house was subsequently searched by a squad of police and detectives, no trace of John Mannering was discovered.

'Corwellin Police immediately asked for Scotland Yard's help. Yard officers are expected at Hallen House today. Meanwhile, a general call has been sent out for John Mannering. (*Photo, side.*) Mannering is famous for his collection of jewels and knowledge of all works of art and antiques. Owner of Quinn's, a two-hundred-year-old shop in Hart Row, W.1., Mannering has been known to assist the police in the past; now he is being hunted by them himself! One time dilettante, man-about-town, and London's wealthiest eligible bachelor, he married Lorna, daughter of Lord Fauntley, some years ago. Mrs. Mannering is a well-known painter whose pictures are frequently exhibited at the Royal Academy.

'*Gazette* reporter called at Quinn's and at the Mannerings' Chelsea flat-cum-studio. Mrs. Mannering "had gone away." It is believed that the police are anxious to interview her, also. Superintendent Bristow is the Yard's representative in these inquiries.'

Mannering lowered the paper.
The little thief was still standing with his chin thrust forward and his eyes narrowed; and the gun was pointing straight at Mannering.
'Well?' Lark grunted.
Mannering pulled one of the upright chairs towards him and sat down. His voice was very quiet.
'I'm in a spot, Lark, aren't I?'
'I'll say you are. Flicking murderer!'
'I told you——'

'You told me plenty, and I didn't believe you. I don't believe anything you say. You can go to hell. I'm quitting. You'll be handed over to the dicks as soon's I'm clear. Got that? I'll look arter myself, but——'

'I told you that Bellamy was a murderer——'

Lark said hoarsely:

'Now you do some listening, cock. I've got ears. An' I've got pals. They've been picking up a lot of dope about this job. Your prints are all over the door of that jewel-house, over the cabinet. You busted that lock and took the greeners. Holmes caught you at it and you croaked him. I don't help flicking *murderers*, Mannering.'

'You're falling for what the police think and what someone's guessed, but it isn't true. I *bought* those diamonds from Bellamy and he stole the receipt from me.'

Disbelief showed clearly in Lark's reddish-brown eyes; how could he convince the man? If he failed, Lark would carry out his threat; Mannering knew the repulsion that some crooks felt towards crimes of violence.

Disbelief, hostility, condemnation, all showed in the crook's eyes.

'You can't fool *me*,' Lark rapped, backing towards the door. 'Jackie's outside in the garden. I've got a pal on the stairs. Don't try to get out.' He went backwards slowly, without moving his gun.

How *could* the man be convinced?

Mannering spoke sharply: 'Lark!'

'Keep yer trap shut!'

'Lark, you took my wallet. You've still got it. There's a cheque-book in it.'

'So what?'

'Have a look at the cheque-book. You'll see the last stub was for £3,000 drawn in favour of Bellamy, dated the day before yesterday. I made out that cheque just before you came that night. Have a look, that can't hurt you.'

Lark hesitated; then his left hand moved to his inside coat pocket. He took out the wallet, opened it, felt inside and extracted the chegue-book. Only three or four of the original dozen cheques were left. He felt for the stubs, reached the last one, rubbed it between his fingers and then, for the first time since he had entered, took his gaze away from Mannering.

'Well?' Mannering's voice was dry.

'That don't prove anything!'

So it was there.

'Keep that cheque-book safely, Lark, because I'm going to need it if I ever stand trial. Bellamy won't cash the cheque, but I handed it to him. Harrison was with him. I came to buy the emeralds; he let me have them for several thousand pounds less than their value. I told you before, he wanted me to value all his jewels and didn't intend me to leave alive. He would have taken the emeralds back. The deal was just to keep me quiet.'

'*I* ain't keeping quiet!'

'I can't make you, but don't forget the other things I told you about. Don't forget Stella Bellamy. And Rundle. And the man who fell from the window. Don't forget any of them.'

'This won't help *you*,' muttered Lark, but there was doubt in his eyes now.

'I'm in a spot, and if I can't get out of it, Stella and the other girl certainly can't,' Mannering said. 'They were taken away—they're locked up somewhere. They——'

A creak on the stairs made him pause. Lark glanced round, as if surprised, and there was a tap at the door. Jackie always thumped as if his fist was a battering ram.

'Whossat?' snapped Lark.

'Me, Larky,' said a man nasally. 'It's only me.'

'Okay, open up,' said Lark.

A tall, thin man with beady eyes and a long, wriggly nose slid inside the room. His short sleeves were rolled up showing thin, sinewy brown arms, and a green beige apron stretched down to his knees.

In his hand was a letter.

'Bloke come,' he said, in that nasal Cockney voice. 'Said he'd got a message—for 'im.'

'For Mannering!'

Mannering felt a swift spasm of alarm. Who knew that he was here?'

'S'what he said,' declared the lanky man.

'Gimme!' Lark snatched the letter and tore it open. Mannering stood quite still, taut nerves stretched to their limit.

Who knew that he was here?

Lark read once, twice. Then he handed Mannering the letter and at the same time, lowered his gun.

CHAPTER XII

GREASE-PAINT

THE note was written in pencilled block capitals.

'*Who's it to be, Mannering? You or the girls?*'

There was nothing else on the sheet of poor quality paper. No address, no signature, nothing but the succinct questions. '*You or the girls?*'

And Lark read the truth into it.

'W'ass come over you?' whined the lanky man.

Lark glanced up. 'It's okay, Perce, it's okay. You don't have to worry. Scram.'

The other man turned round and shuffled out, closing the door behind him.

Mannering was thinking: Bellamy knows he's finished if I talk; thinks that I might put my head in a noose because of the girls; thinks I might keep quiet to save them. But he's not sure; he's worried—I'll say he's worried!

No, it wasn't so simple.

The evidence was so black against Mannering that anything he said about Bellamy would probably be disbelieved. Bellamy was banking on that, but was uneasy and wanted to keep him on the run. The longer he kept away from the police the blacker things would look. Bellamy knew that.

And yet . . .

The owner of Hallen House had planned everything down to the last detail. The moment Lark had told Mannering of the finger-prints, he had realised that his *were* on the door and on the case. He had left them on his first day at the house, Bellamy had probably made sure that the door and furniture weren't polished afterwards. The evidence

106

was damning; Bellamy must know that; yet he had sent this note, which might frighten Mannering but *might* also serve to strengthen his position when he saw the police.

The police might even think he had sent the note to himself.

Did it really help him?

Why *had* Bellamy sent it?

But supposing Bellamy hadn't?

'Perce!' he shouted.

'What's up?' snapped Lark.

'Want me?' Perce called.

'Get him back,' ordered Mannering.

'Perce!' shrilled Lark, then added sharply: 'Why?'

'We want to know who brought this.'

Perce opened the door, this time without knocking, and Lark put the question.

'Never saw him meself,' sniffed Perce, 'but Lucy says he was a long streak. Quite a toff.' He sniffed.

'Tall and fair-haired?' Mannering demanded.

'Yeh.'

'Harrison!' exclaimed Lark.

Yes, that was it: Harrison, not Bellamy, had sent the note, there was a ring of his overbearing manner in the phrasing.

'Come in a car?' asked Lark.

'Nope,' said Perce. 'Just walked up. Lucy was cleaning the steps. "Give this to your new lodger," he said to 'er.' Perce looked at Mannering covertly. 'Dunno what you think, Larky, but it won't be so good if Lucy twigs. She reads the pipers. Never meant 'er to know we'd got 'im.'

'Okay, Perce,' said Lark, 'I'll look after it.' He nodded dismissal, waited until the door closed on the lanky inn-keeper, then rubbed his bony jaw. His attitude had turned full circle. He didn't say another word about it, but he believed Mannering's story. And he was worried on other accounts; the fact that anyone *knew* where Mannering was staying meant danger for them all.

'This,' he announced suddenly, 'is a rum do.'

Mannering said: 'The police may have been following Harrison. In any case, he might talk. I can't stay here, I don't want to see the police just yet.'

'Fancy that,' said Lark, with half-hearted facetiousness. 'Any ideas about this?'

'Harrison took Stella and her sister away, so probably

they're somewhere in the neighbourhood. I doubt it he'd take them far. Do you know when he arrived back at Hallen House?'

'The next morning,' said Lark; 'it's in the piper.'

'So he couldn't have gone far. And he knows where I am and where you are.' Mannering allowed time for that to sink in. 'What about finding out where the girls are? You've friends about here, haven't you?

'Plenty. I dunno that I want trouble with Bellamy or Harrison, though. I don't want any trouble at all, cock. But those girls——'

'You can put the question round. Perce must know a lot of people. Just make inquiries, and tell me what you find out. I'll do the rest.'

'You're in easy street, you are,' said Lark heavily. 'The minnit the cops——'

'Get me a box of grease-paint, Lark, and give me a couple of hours. I'll be ready to leave after that.' When Lark did not answer, he went on: 'Grease-paint and a suit of old clothes and some peroxide. Bellamy's put me in this spot, but I can get out.'

Lark rubbed his chin. Would he take the risk?

'Okay,' Lark said. 'I dunno how long it'll take me to fix it, though. The sooner you're out've 'ere the better I'll like it.' He turned towards the door, then swung on his heel. 'But if you croaked Holmes——'

'I didn't croak Holmes,' said Mannering.

Every creak on the stairs, every footstep outside, wore at Mannering's nerves in the next three hours. Once he saw two policemen walking past the back of the pub, and while they were approaching he stood watching them nervously. They did not linger; but they made the ensuing waiting even more intolerable. He went over everything he had read and been told. He knew the *Gazette* story off by heart. He felt sure that Lark wouldn't have talked of finger-prints if he weren't sure the police had them. The danger in which he stood seemed to increase with each reflection. Periods of uncertainty and vacillation followed each other quickly. Was he wise to stay away from the police? Wouldn't it be best if he gave himself up, told the whole story, and set the police searching for the missing girls?

Would that help the girls?

Bellamy would lie easily and be suave, plausible, convincing. He would deny Mannering's story categorically and might even frighten Stella into saying she had never talked to Mannering, or gone out on the moor.

No, he couldn't go to the police; he would have to find his own way out; for himself and for the girls.

What about Lorna?

He could imagine her set face; the drawn lines of worry, the way her eyebrows would meet, how her lips would tighten and the glow would fade from her eyes.

And so the hours passed.

Just after two o'clock, when he had toyed with a heavy steak-pudding and apple-tart, Lark came briskly up the stairs, followed by the lumbering Jackie.

The door was unlocked, a measure of Lark's *volte-face*.

Lark carried a black case, about the size of Mannering's tool-kit. Jackie had a brown tweed suit over his arm, and a bottle of peroxide in his knuckly left hand. He dumped the clothes and bottle on the bed and went out, while Lark handed the case to Mannering.

'That do?'

Mannering looked inside.

'That's wonderful,' he said fervently.

'Mirror good enough?'

'I'll manage.'

'Get you another,' said Lark.

'Before you go, there's another thing,' Mannering said. 'Yeh?'

'Can you get me a commercial traveller's order book and some stationery? Almost anything would do. I need a plausible reason for being in Corwellin.'

'How do you know where you are?' demanded Lark. 'I'll see what I can do.'

He was soon back with a larger mirror, but said nothing about the other things.

Mannering stripped to the waist when he was alone, mixed the peroxide, and bleached his hair; then he touched up his eyebrows and lashes, a delicate operation for which he used one of two small brushes.

His hair finished and drying, he sat down again in front of the new mirror. The fair-haired man at whom he looked already seemed unfamiliar. He became absorbed in the work with the grease-paint, watching the transformation feature by feature. Shading at his nose made it look broader at the base, and thicker at the bridge. More at the eyes gave them a slanting look. There was a bottle of spirit gum; he touched the corners of his eyes gingerly, narrowed them and kept them narrowed while the gum hardened. Lines at his chin and on his cheeks made him look older.

He forgot time . . .

His hair, nearly dry, looked naturally blond.

He changed into the brown tweed, and was knotting a frayed tie when the door opened and Lark came in. He saw Mannering's back at first, but when Mannering turned round, the cracksman stepped back a pace, gaping.

'It's a ruddy miracle, that's wot it is!'

'If it caught you, it'll catch anyone who's only judging from a photograph,' said Mannering.

'It—it ain't natural!'

Mannering chuckled. 'You're dead right, Larky! What news?'

Lark had been busy.

Mannering was not to come back here. If he called at the *Red Lion*, at the other end of Corwellin in River Street, and asked for Lark, he'd get help. Lark and Jackie were going to be ready to move from here at a moment's notice; they didn't trust Harrison. Mannering could stay at any one of three pubs; the *Red Lion*, the *Corwellin Arms* which was at the northern end of the High Street, or the *Norman's Head*, a river-side 'hotel.' Perce was a 'retired' screwsman, and when he said retired, he meant retired; there were several old lags about there. There was some local smuggling from Spain and Portugal, too; that was to be the story for the crooks—Mannering was bringing silks and wines over. But he wasn't to talk to anyone except to Lark or Perce—not even about Bellamy.

He'd fixed the order book, too. A few days ago a man travelling in cheap cigars and tobaccos had left a book and some letter-heading at the inn. Mannering could use that. There were carbon copies of some orders, and the name in the book was Browning.

'Got all that?' Lark asked.

Mannering repeated the gist of it.

'You're good,' admitted Lark almost reluctantly, 'I hope you'll live to do business with me! Ready?'

'All set.'

''Ow you fixed for dough?'

'All right, when I've got my wallet back!'

Lark grinned. 'It's a pleasure. Any chance of your notes being checked up?'

'I doubt it,' said Mannering. 'I took them from the cashbox at Quinn's. It's customers' money. I'll take the wallet but leave most of the papers and everything with my name on. Parcel them up and send them care of Chelsea Post Office, will you? And look after the emeralds.'

Lark nodded.

'Anything else?'

'A pair of cotton gloves, if you can find them. Is there any chance?'

'Nice, useful thing for a burglar, a pair o' cotton gloves,' remarked the screwsman knowingly. 'I'll see Perce.'

He went out, to return in a quarter of an hour, empty-handed. There were no gloves that would suit Mannering. If there were any message Perce would leave it at the *Red Lion* that night—for a Mr. Browning. Was that okay?

'Fine.'

Lark gave him the order book, forty Players, a box of matches and his wallet, also a battered attache case. 'Look better to have some luggage,' he said.

'And I could do with one or two of those tools that you took from me,' Mannering remarked.

Lark grinned. 'They're in the case!'

Mannering put his head on one side, and gave a long, thoughtful smile.

'Lark, I won't forget this in a hurry.'

'I won't ruddy-well let you, don't you worry! Going out by the side door?'

'Why not use the front? I'm a business man.'

It was strange to walk down the stairs—free.

Perce and Jackie were talking in the hall, and Jackie caught sight of the 'stranger' first. His eyes nearly popped out of his head. Perce made a curious little gasping sound.

Lark grinned broadly.

'Good, ain't it?'

'Good!' gasped Jackie.

'It——' began Perce.

And then the front door of the inn opened, and two men stood on the threshold.

One of them was Superintendent Dando.

CHAPTER XIII

DANDO MAKES AN ARREST

MANNERING stared blankly at the detective and at the elegant younger man just behind him. The Superintendent ignored Mannering, and looked hard at Lark, whose hands were twitching as he fingered his chin.

Behind Dando's plain-clothes companion stood a policeman in uniform.

Perce found his voice first.

'S'matter, Super? W'assall this about?'

'Don't you know, Grey?' asked Dando, his deep voice rumbling about the narrow passage. He did not look at the innkeeper, only at Lark. 'I want a word with your guests. They won't mind, I hope.'

'Dunno why they should,' muttered Perce.

Mannering said in an undertone: 'Well, Mr. Grey, I'll see you get delivery as soon as I can, but you know how difficult supplies are. Good afternoon.' He moved towards Dando and the door.

'Where do you think you're going?' asked Dando.

Mannering looked astonished.

'You don't want *me*, do you? I've only just called on Mr. Grey——'

'Who'd you travel for?'

'The Regency Tobacco Company. If you would like to see——'

'Have a look at his papers, Whittaker,' ordered Dando, and turned to Lark. 'You're Edward James Lark.'

'That's me.' Lark had recovered his poise, and truculence crept into his voice.

Mannering handed the order book to Whittaker, who glanced at it quickly. The police could not have been watching the inn for long, or they would have known that he hadn't 'just called.' The sergeant turned over the pages, closed the book and handed it back.

'All right.'

Mannering walked out.

The policeman moved aside.

'Now, Lark,' began Dando.

Mannering sat in a window seat in a café opposite the Corwellin Police Station. Toasted buns and a pot of tea were in front of him, and the attaché case between his feet. He could see into the street, which was almost deserted that afternoon, when most shops closed. A few cars were parked along the curb; a policeman stood on the steps of the police station. The hands of a clock on a small stone tower in the middle of the road pointed to half-past five.

Mannering had come straight to the High Street and had been at the table for nearly a quarter of an hour.

He poured out some tea.

A car drew up outside the police station, and he recognised the 'Super.' He had not yet fully recovered from the shock of the encounter, and its possible consequences. If Lark were detained, it might go ill with the little man.

It did not occur to Mannering that Lark would betray him; but Jackie might; Jackie's loyalty was only for Lark. Perce Grey might also talk.

Lark and Jackie got out of the police car, and Whittaker followed them. Dando said something to the policeman on duty before he went into the police station.

Mannering lit a cigarette, although a half-finished bun was on his plate. A little waitress with untidy hair smiled, and Mannering went on with his tea. If Dando had any reason to believe that he, Mannering, had been at the inn, this disguise would lose most of its value. Dando may only have glanced at him, but policemen took a lot in at a glance. It wasn't easy to concentrate on the three main problems: Stella's; Lark's; his own. Stella's and his were connected, but Lark's was another matter. Even if he discovered the truth about Bellamy, would it help the screwsman?

Another car pulled up outside the police station. There was something familiar about the passenger who jumped out and hurried towards the steps. He was partly hidden by the car, but once on the steps came into full view.

Bristow was here!

So he already had the Yard to fight; as if the local police were not enough.

He finished his tea, picked up his case, and went out. Only one shop was open near the police station; a newsstand. He bought a local evening paper, the *Cornshire Echo*, and was not surprised to find that most of the front page was devoted to the crimes at Hallen House. Much of it was a rehash of the *Gazette* story, and there was nothing new to help Mannering, except a paragraph: 'The *Echo* believes that the police are of the opinion'—what journalism! —'that Mr. Mannering would not stay in the district a minute longer than necessary.'

That might well be the police theory; if so, it would help.

There was nothing about Lorna. If she had come down here, she would come openly, and stay at one of the larger hotels.

There were two in the High Street. *The George*, a comparatively modern building, only a few doors away from the *Corwellin Arms*, and an old coaching inn, the *King's Head*. He crossed the road opposite *The George* and went into an airy entrance hall. The furniture was modern; there was nothing picturesque or quaint. No one was at the reception desk, but a porter at the end of a wide passage was talking to a page. Mannering went to the desk, where the register stood open.

Lorna had not registered here.

The porter hurried up.

'Good afternoon, sir.'

'Good afternoon,' said Mannering, speaking in a low pitched, hard voice, unlike his normal one. 'Have you a Mr. Kinnard staying here?'

'I don't *think* so, sir——'

Soon Mannering returned to the sunlit street.

The High Street widened opposite *The George*, and here the brown-grey stone buildings had dignity. Even a cinema, a little way along, was built in keeping with the older buildings.

He passed the *Corwellin Arms*, a double-fronted shop,

114

with two bottle-glass windows and a side entrance over which was a sign: 'Hotel.' He sauntered along, sunning himself, until he reached the *King's Head*. Here the entrance hall was gloomy, the ceiling low. It was old-fashioned, and comfortable chairs and sofas were dotted about. Brass gleamed in the poor light. A single electric lamp burned over the reception desk, where a grey-haired man sat poring over his books.

The receptionist looked up.

The register was upside down to Mannering, who smiled as he asked:

'Have you a Mr. Kinnard staying here?'

'Kinnard, sir? I feel sure we have not. I'll just check for you, sir.' He ran his finger down the list of guests, while Mannering scanned it. He could recognise Lorna's signature from any angle, and—yes, there it was! 'Lorna Mannering,' in her heavy, clear writing.

'No, sir Mr. Kinnard hasn't registered.'

'Then he's probably not arrived,' said Mannering. 'Unless that signature——'

He turned the book round, and saw that Lorna's room was Number 27. He scrutinised an almost illegible signature beneath hers.

'That is Mrs. Kennedy, sir,' said the clerk. 'I assure you Mr. Kinnard hasn't registered, but if you would care to wait in the lounge——'

'Thanks,' smiled Mannering. 'I'll wait here, I think.'

He sat in a gloomy corner, and a porter came up to ask if he would like the light on? No, thanks! Mannering sat back, crossing his legs.

Should he register here as Browning? It would probably be as safe as anywhere, and he would have an excuse for going to Lorna's room. But would it really be safe? Bristow and other detectives might come in to see Lorna.

His knee was throbbing rather painfully, and he pulled a pouf towards him and put his leg up.

He smoked cigarette after cigarette, out of a paper packet. Only his wallet, which contained no clue to his identity, and the tools in the borrowed attache case, remained of the things he had brought from Hallen House.

Was Lorna in or out?

He looked up every time he heard the sound of woman's footsteps, but Lorna did not appear.

A fussy couple came in and registered.

A young, affectionate couple made a great palaver over their baggage and held hands as they went up a flight of narrow, twisting stairs.

A tall, boyish-looking man, not unlike Harrison in build, came in briskly and waited at the desk; the clerk had left only a minute or two before. The young man was dressed in a well-cut grey flannel suit, was bare-headed, and had a broken nose which spoiled an otherwise excellent profile. He glanced about him almost furtively, failed to notice Mannering, and pulled the register towards him. He ran his forefinger down the names.

'Ah!' he exclaimed.

The clerk came hurrying back.

'Good evening, sir; I'm sorry you've been left unattended.'

'That's all right,' said the young man. His smile was attractive, his voice pleasant. 'You have a Mrs. Mannering staying here, I believe.'

Mannering raised his hand sharply.

'Yes, sir, we have.' Was there a quickening interest in the clerk's voice?

'Is she in?'

'I believe so, sir.'

'Ask her if she can see me for a few minutes, will you?'

'Very well, sir, I will send a page,' said the clerk. 'What name, please?'

'My name is Galliard—Victor Galliard. And I'm most anxious to have a word with her, although she won't know me.'

'Very good, sir.'

The clerk rang for a page.

Victor Galliard stood waiting by the desk.

Mannering seemed to hear Bellamy's voice and see the invalid's expression of livid hatred when he had talked of this man and his cousin.

Lorna came down the stairs.

Mannering felt his heart beating faster.

She was so lovely; a vision in dark green, carrying herself with an easy grace and fine distinction. She smiled at Galliard, but Mannering saw the strain beneath the smile and knew that she was praying that this meant news of him.

'I'm Mrs. Mannering,' she said.

Galliard thrust out his hand.

'I must apologise for intruding, Mrs. Mannering, but—I should very much like a word with you. I wonder if there is somewhere quiet where we could go?'

Lorna eyed him evenly.

'Just what do you want to see me about?'

'It's confidential, but I assure you I—I won't waste your time.'

'I think one of the small lounges is free,' said Lorna; how like her not to hesitate.

'Thank you,' said Galliard.

As she turned and led the way along the passage, Lorna's gaze swept Mannering and went past him. A tribute to the disguise. But Mannering hardly thought of that. What did Galliard want? The man whom Bellamy hated, the man whom Bellamy had said would 'give no more trouble.'

The clerk, brooding over his books, glanced round as Mannering stood up, then looked back at his desk. Mannering was torn between curiosity about the clerk and desire to know what Galliard had to say. He sauntered towards the passage, but paused on the far side of the stairs.

Only the clerk remained in the entrance hall, and he spoke in a soft voice. He was giving a number.

A pause.

'Hallo? Is that the police station——'

Another pause.

'Yes, Mr. Whittaker, please.'

A clock ticked, loudly.

'Mr. Whittaker . . . the *King's Head Hotel* here. A Mr. Galliard has just called to see Mrs. Mannering . . . I heard him say that his business was confidential . . . Yes, they have gone to one of the small lounges . . . I'm happy to be of service, sir.'

A bell went ting!

So the clerk was acting as stooge for the police, who would soon be here.

Mannering walked along the wide passage, passing a large lounge where half a dozen people were sitting, and a spacious dining-room, where two waiters were laying tables, and, beyond that, three small lounges, labelled *Writing Room*, *Smoking Room*, and *Coffee Room* all with glass-panelled doors.

Lorna and Galliard were in the middle room.

Mannering did not appear to take any notice of them, but entered the coffee room. It was empty and there was a solid door, communicating with the smoking room. A thick carpet deadened the sound of his footsteps, and the door was closed. He could hear the murmur of Lorna's voice, then Galliard's, louder and more eager, but none of the words was distinguishable. He turned the handle of the communicating door softly, and the door opened an inch.

'My story may help,' Galliard was saying, 'and I certainly hope it does, Mrs. Mannering. It must be worrying for you.'

'I would hardly say that,' said Lorna lightly.

Galliard sounded startled. 'Surely——'

'There must be a simple explanation, very different from the present silly guesses.'

Anyone who heard Lorna must have been convinced by the carefree voice—but Mannering knew how the shadow of the Baron pressed down upon her, like a great weight.

Galliard said: 'But you don't know Bellamy, Mrs. Mannering.'

'Do you?'

'Well enough to be sure that he's a thorough-going rogue.' Galliard was in deadly earnest. 'It is a long story, Mrs. Mannering, but I think it might help your husband.'

'Just what do you know of Bellamy?'

Galliard gave a hard little laugh.

'I've only met him twice. You see, my father owned Hallen House before Bellamy. My father and I didn't get on too well, and I knew that the house would be left to my cousin, Charles. I—I'm compressing this rather, but want to make it clear.'

Mannering could imagine Lorna's quick nod, telling him to go on.

'It was left to my cousin, and he sold the house almost immediately to Bellamy. He and Bellamy were friends—of short acquaintance, I believe. My cousin went to stay at the house and met with a fatal accident. *Accident*,' repeated Galliard, in a harsher voice.

'So you don't believe it was an accident.'

'I'm damned sure it wasn't! And the whole atmosphere of the house had changed. I met——' Galliard paused, then gave an explosive little laugh, rather like Harrison's. 'I met a niece of Bellamy's. A charming girl. She—she was scared out of her wits. She tried to speak to me in confidence, but a shrew of a housekeeper prevented her. I came away from the house feeling that I had to do something to help her, or bust.'

'Yes,' encouraged Lorna.

'And then a queer thing happened. Look here, don't misunderstand what I'm going to say. I'm not worried about the personal angle. Money, I mean. But my cousin had left everything to me in his will. And as he'd just sold the house and everything in it, the estate should have been pretty big. It wasn't—it amounted to just a few thousand pounds. The sum which Bellamy had paid him was purely nominal. I went to see Bellamy again. He——'

Galliard broke off, and this time Lorna did not prompt him; the silence lengthened.

Would the story be finished before the police arrived?

'He told me rather crudely to mind my own business,' Galliard continued at last. 'Said that my cousin had owed him a large sum of money and he had accepted the house in settlement. There were papers, purporting to prove it. I wasn't satisfied, and by then I was really worried about that girl. We—er—had a bit of a row.'

'You and the girl?' Lorna was deliberately obtuse.

'No, Bellamy and I. I was shown the door pretty fast. Bellamy had bodyguards there—a proper gang of pluguglies. He didn't threaten in so many words, but—well, I knew what he meant, that I'd run into trouble if ever I went back. But I couldn't get that girl out of my mind. She looked—haunted. I'm—I'm quite serious, Mrs. Mannering, and this isn't just a yarn.'

'I'm sure it isn't,' said Lorna, who knew when to respect the earnestness of youth. 'What did you do?'

'I wrote to the girl, but Bellamy answered my letter. He wasn't polite.'

'But surely, Mr. Galliard, if you told the police about this, they'd investigate your cousin's death.'

Galliard said grimly: 'Bellamy spiked my guns. Damned hard to realise that it really happened. He spoke to me on the telephone; he wouldn't commit himself by writing anything. It was from here, funnily enough—he was staying here for a day or two, there isn't a telephone at Hallen House. He as good as told me that if I took any action the girl would suffer. And—he absolutely dominates that girl. She's terrified of him. I couldn't screw myself up to do

119

anything because I thought he might take it out of her. It's a week since we had that showdown. It's been preying on my mind every minute since. I went to Bristol, and turned the thing over in my mind, determined to do *something*. I stayed up at Clifton, near the Suspension Bridge. Strolling across it just after dark three nights ago, I was nearly thrown over.'

'*What!*'

'This is the sober truth. A man lit a cigarette as he drew near me, and I'm pretty sure it was one of Bellamy's so-called gardeners. Next moment, he came at me. I managed to bump him pretty hard on the nose, but another thug came from behind me. I was nearly over that damned bridge when a car came along, and I managed to get free. I keep seeing that drop into the gorge, though.'

'You *must* go to the police.'

'Look here, if they'll try to murder me, what will they do to the girl?' asked Galliard. 'I can't think clearly, I'm so worried about it. I was on the point of going to the police when this business got in the papers. I saw you were out of London, and wondered if you'd come down here. I tried three hotels before I found you. The thing is—your husband has a pretty good reputation for this kind of thing, hasn't he? Knowing Bellamy's a rogue, I don't need telling that things aren't what they appear to be. You—you *are* here to meet your husband, aren't you?'

CHAPTER XIV

NEWS FROM 'PERCE'

'I FEEL sure you are,' Galliard went on. 'And he ought to know what I can tell him. I might be able to help, I'll gladly try. If I could only be sure that Stella's all right, I'd tell the police the whole story. And your husband stayed at Hallen House, so he might have seen her, might have got something from Bellamy. I—I know I'm a bit confused,' Galliard confessed naively, 'but you see what I'm driving at? If your husband discovered something at Hallen House, caught Bellamy out, perhaps, he—he might know where the girl is.'

Lorna still did not answer.

'Mightn't he?' insisted Galliard.

'I suppose he might,' said Lorna at last. Her voice was colder, fainter. 'Yes, I suppose he might.'

'Look here, I haven't scared you, have I? A chair creaked. 'Your husband got away from Hallen House, you know.'

'But—*did* he?'

Her dread sounded in her voice: if murder had been committed twice at Hallen House, why should Mannering have escaped with his life?

Galliard spoke quietly.

'Well, I wondered about that, Mrs. Mannering, but I think he did get away, you know. Otherwise—why should Bellamy worry about making it look as if he killed Holmes? Holmes was—well, rather friendly to me. We tried to have a word on the side once or twice, but never got the chance. I meant to try to see him outside, but he never left Hallen

House—didn't come to Corwellin, anyhow.' He paused, but Lorna didn't speak. 'Bellamy must be worried, Mrs. Mannering, that's why he's tried to make your husband look guilty.'

'You may be right,' said Lorna quietly, and she had recovered. 'You seem fond of this girl Stella, Mr. Galliard.'

'Oh, no! I hardly know her. Nothing—I mean, I hardly know her,' Galliard repeated. 'The point is, she was terrified of Bellamy, and as he threatened to injure her—I've thought about little else. One minute I feel like rushing to the police, the next I'm scared stiff lest Bellamy make her pay for it. You see—I feel sure I'm followed wherever I go. I was certainly followed here. There's a man outside, a little fellow, looks like a salesman. All gent's natty suiting! I can't shake him off. Perhaps the police will scare him away!'

'But if you're not going to the police——'

'Now look here, I'm not quite a fool,' said Galliard. 'The police are almost certainly watching you, and they'll wonder why I've come to see you. But I promise not to tell them anything you care to tell me.' He paused hopefully but in vain. 'Er—well, if you communicate with Mr. Mannering, will you tell him I'm ready to put all I've got into lending a hand?'

'I've no more idea where he is than you have,' said Lorna quietly.

'You—but that can't be true!'

'It's true,' said Lorna.

She sounded nearer to Mannering—and suddenly the door by which Mannering stood moved slightly. Had she noticed that it was open?

Time to go.

He went out into the passage, saw Lorna and Galliard look at him through the glass door, and stared blankly at them.

In the next room were Whittaker and another man. Both were standing by the door, and Whittaker's back was towards him.

The police had also listened. He'd no idea how much they'd heard, and didn't greatly care. The one sure thing that emerged from Galliard's story was confirmation of Stella's danger.

No argument was possible now; he had to find the girl.

122

And he needed a car; a fast car.

At the reception desk, he booked a room in the name of Browning, took his key and went upstairs to leave the attache case.

He transferred his tools and flashlight to his pockets, then went to the hall and out into the street.

It was not yet half-past six, and still broad daylight.

A green Bentley stood outside the *King's Head* and behind it a small rakish-looking sports car. At the wheel of the second, reading a newspaper, sat a little man wearing a Homburg hat, and so smartly dressed that Galliard's 'gent's natty suitings' described him to a T.

The Bentley was probably Galliard's.

Yes, he needed a car, to follow the man.

He reached the end of the High Street, where a tiny Methodist church stood back from the road, its doors and windows freshly painted. A few white tomb-stones rose out of the trim grass of the churchyard, and beyond the church lay the first drab stretches of the moor. Straight ahead, the country was green and broken, rising to a range of low hills.

The chase wouldn't start just yet. Galliard would probably be questioned by the police, for Whittaker must have over-heard enough to make him take Galliard to the station.

Whittaker was coming out of the *King's Head*. Was Galliard with him?

Yes, and the other detective was following Galliard. Mannering saw Galliard in a new light now. A man who'd won the Victoria Cross would be no coward, but Bellamy had him scared, and he was probably in love with Stella.

Whatever his thoughts, Galliard looked composed. He had a long, easy stride, his clothes hung well, and but for his broken nose, he would have been as handsome as a young Greek God.

The man in the sports car looked at Galliard furtively, his head buried in his newspaper.

Lorna didn't come out.

Lorna might be able to help Mannering to get a car.

Near the hotel, Perce Grey came cycling along the road towards him. Perce was not at ease on the machine. For one thing, it was too small, and his boney knees were bent outwards, his toes turned inwards on the pedals. For another, he lurched from side to side, his thin shoulders drooping.

His mouth was open and the breath whistled in and out as he passed Mannering. Whether he recognised the fair-haired 'stranger' Mannering did not know. Perce laboured on, and Mannering strolled past the *King's Head*, no longer doubtful about his next move.

When he turned round, Perce was getting off the little machine; he went into the *Corwellin Arms*. Mannering approached the pub casually and hesitated outside before going inside. He went into the bar, where Perce was leaning against the counter. A little old man with a big, bald head was drawing beer.

Perce took his glass to a table in the window. He selected one by the bottle-glass panels, through which he could not be seen. Mannering ordered a beer, sauntered over, and murmured:

'Nice day it's been.'

'Not ser bad,' agreed Perce. He tapped a chair, and Mannering sat down.

'Want me?' asked Mannering.

'Dunno that I do. They took Larkie. Dunno wot charge. Come in to find aht.' Perce drank deeply, and wiped his lips with the back of his hand. 'Anyfing *you* want?'

'A car.'

'What kind've a car?'

'Anything fast. I need it in a hurry.'

'See what I can do. Go to Andrews' Garage in 'arf a n'hour.'

'Twenty minutes,' said Mannering.

'What do yer think I am?' demanded Perce, 'a ruddy streak a'lightnin'? See what I can do.'

He got up, drained his glass, nodded to the bald-headed man and went out. Mannering waited for five minutes before following him. There was no sign of Perce or the bicycle.

A large sign, hanging at right-angles from the wall of the garage opposite the little Methodist church was easy to read even from that distance: ANDREWS.

Was there time to see Lorna?

No, he mustn't risk it yet.

She came out of the hotel!

She wore a long tweed coat and was pulling on a pair of gauntlet gloves. She hesitated, as if not sure which way to go, then turned and went away from Mannering. But she walked slowly, and stopped at a small dress-shop which had two models in the window. Mannering quickened his pace and, as he drew near, spoke quietly, in his natural voice.

'The bar of *The George*.'

She started and half-turned her head, recovered herself quickly and looked back into the windows.

Mannering strolled on, and entered the big hotel, going straight to the bar where a dozen people were drinking; a young girl was already very merry. Two or three men looked up when Lorna appeared, glanced round, and took a stool next to Mannering.

One man grinned.

A waiter came up.

'A gin and orange, please,' said Lorna, and the man turned away for the drink. When he came back:

'Allow *me*,' said Mannering, in his assumed voice.

He slipped silver across the counter. 'Thanks,' said the waiter.

Lorna looked at Mannering with a restrained smile.

'Thank you,' she said.

'Pleasure,' said Mannering, and grinned at her blandly. God, it was good to see her! Two men, who had noticed the exchange, whispered together. 'Let's get more comfortable seats,' suggested Mannering. 'Never could stand these stools.'

They were soon sitting in easy chairs in a corner away from the others.

Mannering leaned back and smiled easily—and spoke very softly.

'Why did they take Galliard?'

'For questioning.'

'Did he tell them anything?'

'He told me he wouldn't. You heard about the girl?'

'Girls. There are two of them! As far as you know, Galliard won't tell the police about them?'

'No.'

'Then it depends how much Sergeant Whittaker heard.'

'How much did *you* hear?'

'Pratically everything. Darling, I can't stay long, because I want to keep an eye on Galliard. I may look in at the hotel tonight. Be in your room by ten o'clock.'

Lorna said: 'John——' and stopped. 'John, they think it's you. *Bristow* thinks it's you.'

'He might pretend he does, but he knows I wouldn't touch this job.'

'John, listen to me. I've seen Chittering of the *Gazette*.' There was no better crime reporter on the Street. 'He's got a lot out of one of the local police, and says the case against you looks cast-iron. They were your prints; your scarf was used. Even if Bellamy's not all he seems, Chittering doesn't see how you're going to get out of it.'

'He'll find out. Darling. I love you.'

'John, don't risk too much for that girl. Don't take too many chances.'

'Stella and Kathleen can tell the whole truth; no one else can. Save them, and I'm out of trouble. Must do.'

Lorna said: 'I'll never let you out of my sight again.'

Mannering touched her hand.

'I must go,' he said. 'Don't forget, ten o'clock tonight.'

The sergeant who had been with Dando was outside the hotel, as he had followed Lorna. Mannering stared at him blankly, and Whittaker showed no interest in him.

Next thing to find out: was Perce reliable? Had Lark arranged for the car, Mannering wouldn't have worried. Now he was on edge. If Perce betrayed him——

A plump, red-faced man in overalls came out of a small office at Andrews Garage; a greasy-looking boy stood at a distance.

'I want to hire a car,' Mannering said without preamble. 'I believe a friend of mine——'

'You Mr. Browning?'

'That's right.'

'I've got a beauty—a real beauty,' said the plump man brightly.

Good old Perce!

'Only been in a few days. Took it out myself for a trial. Touched ninety. Wouldn't think so to look at it, but it's a fact. Can't tell a filly by her looks, always, can you? Ha-ha-ha!'

He went on talking while he led Mannering to the back of the large garage. In a corner near an open door leading to a back street, was a rakish-looking but dilapidated Lancia. 'She's all tuned up for anything *you* might want out of her,' said the young man. 'She do?'

'She's just right.'

'Twenty quid deposit—you can't grumble at that. And twelve gallons of juice thrown in.'

'Wonderful.' Mannering produced the notes, and drove out through the back door of the garage, turned right, then right again, and was soon in the High Street. 'Gent's natty' was still reading the newspaper.

Mannering turned into a side-street and parked where he could see the man and the *King's Head*. Lorna returned, and went inside. Whittaker and the man in the sports car looked at her with unveiled curiosity.

Then Galliard appeared, unescorted, and not looking unduly worried. He hesitated by the side of the sports car, and, to Mannering's surprise, said something, grinned, waved his hand and disappeared into the hotel. The little man reading the newspaper muttered under his breath. Then 'gent's natty' got out of his car and went to a telephone booth outside the nearby post office. When he returned, he immediately started the engine of his car.

Mannering pulled his self-starter.

The sports car hummed past the end of the street, and, as Mannering nosed into the High Street, took a right-hand fork at the far end—the Bristol road. So the fellow was not going straight to Hallen House.

The Lancia was in good shape, and responded well.

At the crest of a hill outside Corwellin, Mannering saw the other car in the valley beyond, travelling very fast. Ahead the road stretched over a series of hills; it should be possible to keep the man in sight without being noticed.

Both cars roared on, Mannering with a sense of freedom and exhilaration he had not known for days.

CHAPTER XV

RIVER COTTAGE

DUSK was falling over the green country-side. In the distance, the hills grew dark in a purple haze, and to the west the sky was golden where the rays of the setting sun caught furry trailers of light cloud. Yet Mannering could still see the small, neat fields, the isolated farm-buildings and cottages and, a golden ribbon twisting and turning along the valleys; a river which was flowing gently towards the west. A road ran alongside the river, and Mannering could just discern the dark shape of the car he was following.

He could see a bridge, on a by-road.

As the other car took the by-road, its headlamps flashed on. The river and the bridge were lit up; so was a small white house which stood close to the river bank. Its white walls showed vividly beneath the beams of the headlamps.

The lights went out.

Mannering slowed down. He was still driving along the main road, half a mile from the turning towards the bridge.

There was a little copse in which he could hide, beyond the house, but he did not want to go too near yet. He turned a bend in the road, and came upon an old quarry, with a pool of water glistening beneath the fading sky. He pulled into the side of the quarry. From the car he could not see the house by the river, but when he climbed to the top of the quarry he saw a light shining from one of the windows. It struck the side of the sports car, which was parked in front of the house.

Gradually the light at the window grew brighter, until at last Mannering felt that he could safely go nearer. He started the engine of the car, turned right at the road to

128

the bridge, and found that it went downhill. He switched off his engine, and coasted down until he was within a few yards of the bridge. He pulled up within a few yards of the river, just off the road and hidden by a row of trees.

He walked over the bridge.

He reached the sports car and made a complete circuit of the house which was only a cottage. At the back was a single-storey out-building, with long windows; a faint light shone from them. There were no other lights except in the room which he had already seen. In front of the cottage was a small landing; he had noticed it from the quarry; now he went nearer and saw a motor-boat. A faint smell of petrol suggested that it had recently been used.

How long should he stay outside?

What were the chances of breaking in and frightening the man into betraying Bellamy? If only one man were inside, they would be good.

If there were more than one, or others came——

A car changed gear behind him. Swinging round, he saw the headlights turned towards the bridge.

He hurried from the cottage and stood in the shadow of the hedge. The car purred on a low, powerful note; he thought it was a Bentley.

Galliard's?

The car drew up with a scream of brakes. The white walls showed up vividly until the lights were switched off. A man jumped out. Was it Galliard? Had the younger man been lying? Was he——'

The front door opened, and the light shone on Harrison.

Of course, there had been a Bentley at Hallen House.

The 'gent's natty' was at the door, and Harrison's voice sounded clearly across the quiet of the night.

'Why the hell aren't you ready, Foss?'

'Can't work miracles,' retorted Foss sharply.

Harrison growled a rejoinder and stepped across the threshold; the door slammed; footsteps echoed and then died away.

Mannering rounded a corner of the house and approached the lighted window.

Harrison was lolling in an easy chair, his back to the window, and Foss was sitting at a writing-desk in a corner, looking round at Harrison; the little man was smoking a cigar. The window was tightly closed, and the men were

129

talking, mouths opening and closing like puppets in dumb-show.

If there were any servants here, would Foss have opened the door?

He felt the quivering of excitement, just as he had at Hallen House, the old, familiar keynote which had been born with the Baron.

But soon he was cool and ready.

He went to the front door; the lock was a Mortis. That couldn't be opened quickly.

He was examining a window at the far side of the house, when he heard a door open and saw a pale light shine out on to the road. A shadow appeared, tall, thin, and was joined by a much shorter one. The door slammed. Both men were leaving.

They came towards him!

He would be seen against the white wall if they glanced his way.

'Plenty of petrol on board?' asked Harrison gruffly.

'What do you take me for?'

They rounded the corner, and Mannering pressed tightly against the wall. Harrison was hurrying; a tall, vague figure, he passed within a yard of Mannering but did not look towards him. Foss was a couple of yards behind; evidently the men were on bad terms.

The little man passed, too preoccupied to notice Mannering, who kept absolutely still, watching their shadowy figures. 'Plenty of petrol on board' probably referred to the motor-boat. Yes, they reached the landing, their footsteps echoing clearly. Mannering crept forward now, still uncomfortably conscious of the white background of the wall.

'I'll untie her,' said Foss.

'Just a minute,' said Harrison. There was a thump, as if he had jumped into the boat. Water lapped noisily against the bank and the wooden sides, while Foss crouched over the stanchion to which the boat was moored. The lapping of the water was suddenly lost in the spluttering note of the engine. By the time Foss had jumped down into the boat, the engine was ticking over smoothly. A faint smell of exhaust fumes crept up the bank towards Mannering.

The men had left a light on in the house—deliberately, it seemed.

The boat swung out into the river, and two lights showed

—a green and a red. Mannering kept concealed, until the boat began to move swiftly down-river.

The lights disappeared when it went under a bridge, but broke the darkness again as Mannering moved. He ran towards the bridge; by the time he reached the Lancia, the boat was half a mile away.

Better be bold about the chase.

He switched on the headlights and let the Lancia go all out. He could see the tiny light in the stern, reflected on the water. The motor-boat was travelling fast. He passed it, seeing the men just visible in the headlights. Harrison stood in front of the engine; Foss sat beside him.

Mannering drove ahead, looking again for a vantage point from which to watch. But while the river and the road ran almost parallel, he had to keep on the move, or they would wonder what he was doing.

He rounded a bend, and just in front of him were several buildings, and the light picked out the words: *Guest House*. This was as good a spot as any. He switched off the headlights and slowed down. Faint radio music was coming from one of the buildings. Soon he could hear the chug-chug of the boat's engine, which drew nearer. Were the two men coming to this place? Was it possible that the girls were in the guest house?

No. The boat went past.

Mannering waited for five minutes, then went off again in pursuit. Harrison and Foss would probably think it was a different car.

He picked out the boat in the headlights, and, just beyond it, something large and white in the river; soon he saw that it was a house-boat. Two or three dim lights showed at curtained windows.

Further along, the road left the river in a sharp bend. Mannering felt a pull on the engine; he was going up-hill. He changed gear, breasted a hill and, once he was starting down, switched off his lights again.

He pulled into the side of the road, jumped out and hurried to the top of the hill.

The boat was still moving—but more slowly! He could tell that only from the lights, for he could see nothing of the two men. Soon the lights went out.

After a long pause, a brighter light from an opening door shone from the house-boat.

The house-boat was moored on the other side of the river, and Mannering had not passed another bridge. He walked quickly down to the river bank. A cold wind, blowing along the river, made him shiver. No night for a swim; he wanted a boat.

He climbed down the river bank, wishing that he dared bring the car down and switch on the headlights; he might grope for hours in the darkness. He had passed no houses on this side of the river; and boats were not likely to be moored to the banks away from buildings.

Swim?

No—there was a boat!

He came on it suddenly, not far down-stream. Near by was a small boat house and a landing, and the dinghy made a dark blotch against the river. He stepped on to the landing, and groped for the rope with which the boat was tied to a post. His hand brushed it. He untied it, wound it round his arm, and felt the boat pulling at him on the tide. He bent down, stretched out and caught the side, pulled the boat close, and crawled into it.

The boat rocked perilously.

He crouched in the bottom, waiting until it steadied, coiled the rope and dropped it on to the floorboards. Then, carried slowly into midstream, he groped for the oars. He found them neatly placed, one along each side. He took them out, making a lot of noise as he slid them into the rowlocks; the blade of one splashed into the water.

He decided to row straight across the river and walk along the bank to the house-boat.

The keel grated on stones, and he stood up cautiously, swaying from side to side, and pushed one oar into the river bed, in order to get the boat closer to the bank. The swaying eased as the boat grounded. He shipped the oars carefully, peered over the side, then pushed his hand downwards. There were several inches of water.

He took off his shoes and socks and stepped ankle deep into icy water; two strides took him onto slate which hurt his feet, a third to a grassy patch. He sat down, dried his feet on a handkerchief, and rubbed them to get them warm, then put on his shoes and socks.

Twenty minutes must have passed since he had found the boat.

A steep bank rose above him. When he stretched up his

hand, he could feel the grass at the top. He hauled himself up and walked quickly towards the house-boat.

There were more lights this side.

There was a gap of several yards between the bank and the house-boat. On the bank were several boards, obviously used for a make-shift gangway; if he tried to put them into position, he'd drop one and rouse everyone within earshot. Should he jump? He'd land too heavily, even if he made it safely.

He wanted a length of rope. There should be some about.

Without switching on his flashlight, he scanned the path and the ground near the boards. Just to one side was a coil of rope, long enough for his purpose. He made a loop at one end, and, standing close to the edge, tossed it towards one of the rail-posts on the house-boat. The rope dropped gently back against the bank. He kept trying and mis-judging the distance by inches. No one appeared; he could hear nothing except the sound of the water and his own breathing.

Ah!

The loop fell over a post, and pulled taut. He leaned back with all his weight, to test it.

He tied the other end high up to a tree, then went down on his knees, gripped the rope, and let himself go gently over the side. His feet dangled just above the water. Hand over hand, he moved along the rope; the gap was much wider than he'd thought; yards wide. Would the rope hold?

He gripped a rail!

He'd be on deck in a trice now.

The boards creaked under his weight, but the boat was moving gently, there were other creaks, and now and again a sharp crack as a wave hit the side. He passed a lighted window. Net curtains prevented him from seeing clearly inside until he pressed close to the glass.

Harrison and Foss were in there—and Mrs. Dent!

How secure they felt!

He left the window, and crept along the deck towards another lighted window.

Stella was sitting in a small easy chair by the side of a bunk, on which her sister lay!

CHAPTER XVI

ALARM

STELLA was reading. Kathleen appeared to be asleep. She was lying on her side, facing the window, with her eyes closed. Stella's face was sideways to Mannering, and she seemed immersed in her book. At that quick, first glance, there seemed nothing wrong; it was a pleasant, peaceful scene.

Stella looked up, but did not glance towards the window. Could he get them away?

Kathleen's pallor was unhealthy, it would be risky to take her on a wild and dangerous journey—on which they might be followed. There was no real chance of taking them off now, but he could arrange with one of Lark's friends to watch the house-boat; or even send an anonymous warning to the police. No, not the police, until he could be quite sure the girls were free from Bellamy's influence.

Standing on the deserted deck, he grew aware of a faint glow of light further along the river. A car on the road before it turned away from the river? No, the light was nearer than that turning. He could hear a chugging sound— a low, monotonous beat of an engine. A launch was coming up-river, with its searchlight on.

A bell rang, so sharply and unexpectedly that it made him jump. *Brrr-brrr; brrr-brrr*. That was the unmistakable ring of a telephone bell. Stella looked up at the door, but Kathleen did not open her eyes. A man's footsteps sounded inside, then Mannering heard Harrison say clearly:

'Hallo?'

The short pause seemed long; Mannering felt on edge, as if some tension inside the cabin was passing itself on to him.

Yes, there was tension.

'Are you *sure*?' Harrison's voice was harsh.

Stella rose slowly from her chair.

Harrison snapped: 'All right. Tell the old man.'

He banged the receiver down.

Next moment, the door of the girls' cabin opened and Harrison appeared inside the room.

Harrison said in a harsh, grating voice:

'The police are coming here. You're staying of your own free will. Understand?'

Stella gasped.

Harrison gripped her arm; twisted.

Mannering turned away; and in that moment he knew that Stella would lie to the police, she would obey orders.

The light from the approaching launch was much nearer. He slipped to that part of the deck where his rope was tied—and saw a car coming between trees, towards the river!

He swung himself across the gap to the bank, took out his knife and slashed at the rope. It was tarred and thick; the small blade had little effect as he cut furiously. The head-lights of the approaching car drew rapidly nearer, and the river near the house-boat was clearly visible in the light from the launch.

The rope parted! He heard it flop against the side.

He did not wait to unfasten the piece round the tree. It might not be noticed in the general commotion. He coiled the rope swiftly and hooped it over a branch, then made off along the path. The trees which grew close to the river's edge were showing clearly in the beams from the approaching car. He was soon out of their reach, and only a few yards from the small boat in which he had crossed the river. He stood by a big tree, watching.

Yes, more policemen had come in the car. Two or three jumped out and approached the house-boat, but made no attempt to get on board. The motor-launch was very near now, and someone was hailing from it. A door nearby opened and a bright light shone out. Mannering thought he could hear Harrison's voice.

The wind was freshening, and it was getting very cold.

Mannering began to move about, stamping his feet, beating his arms across his chest. There was too much noise near the house-boat for that to be noticed. The minutes dragged past. Muttered voices floated along the river.

Ten minutes passed; twenty.

Half an hour.

A man appeared on the deck opposite the policemen on the bank, and, in the light from the police car, Mannering saw Bristow. Dando stood beside him.

'It's all right,' Dando called: 'you can go back.'

'Any luck?' That was Whittaker.

'I'll see you later,' said Dando.

He could not have said more clearly that he had not found what he had sought. So Stella had obeyed Harrison. Why?

Both she and her sister would have been safe with the police.

Had Bellamy some other hold on her? Or had Harrison?

Mannering had to find the reason for that fear of Bellamy before he could get either girl to tell the police the truth—before he could be free from danger and from probings into the past.

Just after nine o'clock that night, Mannering went to the *Corwellin Arms*, asked for the use of a private room, and gave his name as Browning. He was soon visited by a short, breezy man, who declared himself to be a friend of Perce Grey.

Mannering told him what he wanted, and the man's eyes rounded in astonishment.

Lorna sat on her bed, her knees tucked beneath her, a newspaper open by her side; but she wasn't reading: she was listening.

A clock struck ten.

She got off the bed, glanced into the mirror, tucked a strand of hair into position—and then a swift gleam shone in her eyes and she turned to the door.

A man was approaching.

He stopped; and knocked.

Her heart was beating so fast that she could hardly speak, but she called:

'Come in.'

Victor Galliard entered.

Lorna backed against her chair, tripped, and saved herself from falling by putting a hand on a table. The table rocked, an ash-tray fell to the floor. Shock, disappointment, and relief, all mingled as Galliard closed the door behind him and approached her.

He looked concerned. 'Are you all right?'

'I tripped over the mat,' said Lorna. 'Yes, of course I'm all right. What do you want?'

The light shone on Galliard's wavy, auburn hair, and into his clear grey eyes, showing the anger and frustration in them.

'Well, I hardly know! It doesn't make sense.'

'What doesn't?'

'I've just seen the police.'

'Will—you—tell—me—why—you've—come—here!'

This affected John; it must affect him; and Galliard was standing as if he were tongue-tied, afraid to break bad news.

He threw up his hands.

'They say that she—she told them she's staying with Bellamy of her own free will. But it's damned silly! They found her on a house-boat down river. Dando *says* he spoke to her himself, and she told him that I'd been talking a lot of drivel. And yet—I could have sworn——'

He went on talking, explaining.

Lorna was seeing Mannering's face in her mind's eye; and seeing the situation starkly; as he had seen it.

Everything—*everything* depended on the evidence of the girl Stella; she had lied.

Galliard kept talking, bewildered and hurt. He gave her a cigarette and lit his own, forgetting hers. On and on he talked, about how incomprehensible it was, how certain he was that Bellamy was frightening the girl.

Lorna looked past him towards the door.

It was opening.

She dropped the cigarette and took a quick step forward. She must send John away, he mustn't be seen by Galliard.

Galliard swung round towards the door.

An untidy man with a lock of fair hair dropping into his eyes, an old raincoat hanging open, a white shirt, a hideous tie and a pair of baggy flannel trousers, stood before them. He carried a battered trilby hat in his hand.

'I hope I'm not butting in,' said Chittering of the *Gazette*.

137

Galliard snapped: 'Who the devil are you?'

'You wouldn't know, but Mrs. Mannering does. I'm from the *Gazette*.' When Galliard looked blank, he went on in a careless, easy voice: 'You know—a reporter. On a newspaper. Specialist in crime. I think I should like a little chat with Galliard, V.C.'

'You can go to hell!' roared Galliard.

'Unkind chap. Nasty place to be consigned to.' Chittering closed the door. 'Hope I'm not unwelcome, Mrs. Mannering. I heard odds and ends of what Galliard said.'

'Mrs. Mannering——' Galliard's voice was thick with unreasoning anger.

'It's all right, we're old friends. Come in and sit down, Mr. Chittering.' Lorna pressed a bell. 'I'll send for some drinks. And sit down, Mr. Galliard. You still believe that Stella Bellamy *is* in trouble, don't you?'

'Of course I do. But I don't see how publicity——'

'Wonderful thing, in regulated doses,' said Chittering. 'You'd be surprised. Cure for many ailments. Shyness goes in a flash! Policemen get more careful when the newspapers say the public's not satisfied. The beneficial effect of one censorious leading article is astonishing. Especially in a matter of a miscarriage of justice. Also when the police are duped. I——'

Someone tapped on the door; a floor waiter.

'Now if there could be a *bottle*.' Chittering perched himself on the arm of a chair. 'My poison's whisky.'

In the next hour, Galliard was won completely round.

Chittering knew as much as Lorna; as the police; as the young man. They all came to the same conclusion; pressure had been brought to bear on Stella. And they asked the same question: how could they remove it?

They couldn't.

But at least talking with Chittering and being sure of his understanding, helped Lorna, and she felt better when they left; but on edge, because John was an hour late. She didn't want him to come, the risk was too great, and yet if only she could be sure that he was safe.

Outside, a cold wind blew down the High Street.

'Where are you staying?' Chittering asked Galliard.

'With some friends, in Church Street. Can I give you a lift?'

'I'm only a step along,' said Chittering. 'Good night.'

He stood and watched the Bentley move off, and waited until it had turned the corner. Then he returned to the hotel and hurried up to Lorna's room, tapped lightly, and went straight in. Lorna was standing by the window, and obviously not surprised to see him back. She looked sombre; austere; afraid.

Chittering picked up a half-empty bottle.

'We've been too sober,' he remarked. 'Known Galliard for long?'

'I hardly know him at all.'

'Earnest young man, with a fondness for jumping to conclusions, or else for pitching a tall story. When you first heard it, I expect it sounded okey-doke. In the light of after events—some doubt, don't you think? Mr. Galliard might be at his own particular game. He is not'—Chittering paused, and went on carefully as he poured himself out another drink—'he is *not* a fool. He likes to create the impression that he is. You haven't been foolish enough to tell him where your husband is, have you?'

Lorna said: 'I don't know where John is.'

Chittering grinned and drank.

'To your discretion! You aren't going to be foolish enough to tell me either.' When he saw her wince, he crossed to her side. 'Sorry. I want to help, you know. I did not believe young Galliard, but one never knows. He may be a simple romantic. I imagine that John is always suspicious of romantics.'

'*Must* you talk like this?'

'You know me. Trying to get the old thoughts clear. Difficult on three doubles.' He finished his drink, but did not pour himself out another. 'What's your chief worry, Mrs. Mannering?'

'Isn't it obvious?'

'No help from Stella Bellamy? Was John relying on her story to corroborate part of his own?' Lorna didn't answer. 'So he was, eh? The obvious, when all's said and done. And now Stella is either scared out of her wits and won't allow herself to be rescued *or* she's been leading John up the garden path. It would have to be a long, winding path to take him as far as this, wouldn't it?'

Lorna moved to a chair and sat down.

'*Will* you be serious?'

'Yes,' promised Chittering.

'If that girl won't give evidence—is there *any* chance for John? Are you sure about the—finger-prints?'

Chittering pushed the lock of hair out of his eyes.

'Yes. Sorry. Had an interview with Bristow earlier in the evening. Most garrulous mood. I've no doubt he told me most of it so that I could pass it on to you. Crafty bloke, our William. On the other hand, he seemed to have everything at his finger-tips. He let me *see* photographs of the prints. Showed me the scarf.' Chittering paused. 'Can you take it?'

'Go on.'

'The police made an arrest this afternoon. Man named Lark. Believed to be the next best screwsman to a merchant who once operated as the Baron.' Chittering did not alter the tone of his voice as he said that, and Lorna kept her face absolutely blank. One couldn't trust—not wholly trust—even Chittering. 'The police have never been able to pin anything on Lark, but apparently they scared him. Accused *him* of busting open that jewel-room. Lark couldn't stand it. Made a statement.'

Lorna gripped the arms of her chair.

'All this, you understand, was off the record.' Chittering went on. 'And I'll keep it there, of course. Can't do the dirty on the dicks. But this story of Lark's does the dirty on John. He told a queer story, of John fetching up at his house, near Bellamy's. Breaking in. Holding them up—but Lark wasn't alone, and overpowered John. John *had* the emeralds.'

Lorna closed her eyes.

'Only hearsay, but when you take it in conjunction with the rest of the story, it makes you think,' said Chittering. 'I repeat—I think Bristow told me this so that I could pass it on to you. Thinks you will be a good girl if you know that the situation is really black. Probably expects John to get in touch with you, and wants this passed on to him. I wouldn't know. The ways of the police are weird and wonderful. The one outstanding and unalterable fact is that John is in a very bad spot indeed. I think probably Bristow was getting at this: when you see John, tell him he can't expect help from anyone, and that surrender is his only wise course. Every hour he keeps away from the police strengthens suspicion against him. Mind you, that was before Bristow knew Galliard's story was phon—no, I won't say phoney . . . that it just won't stand up.'

140

He poured a little whisky into Lorna's glass, and took it to her.

She drank it eagerly.

'Another thing. I went downstairs with Galliard just now. There's a bright young detective named Whittaker on the other side of the road. When I first came in, I saw a watcher at the back door. I think Bristow has this place so closely watched that John can't get in, even if he can out-Lark Lark, as one might say. Even if he did get in, he couldn't get out. Now, understand me—I don't want anything, Mrs. Mannering. I only say that if you can get a message to John to stay away until he's decided what to do, you'd be wise.'

'But—I *can't*!'

Chittering's eyes rounded. 'So you really can't? That's bad. I hope——'

A shout from outside cut across his words; a man bellowed: 'There's someone there!'

The man seemed to be standing immediately beneath Lorna's window.

CHAPTER XVII

MANNERING LOOKS IN

MANNERING stood in a dark corner of the *King's Head* yard. Above him, a creeper which grew across an archway dangled close to his head. He pressed tightly against the weather-worn red brick of the stables. Bright lights flashed from torches and from windows. A tall man, who had been halfway up the wall, near Lorna Mannering's window, was climbing down a rope which danced wildly near the groin. The policeman who had first seen him was struggling with another man in the shadow of the great arch which led from the High Street. Two hotel residents, standing at open windows, were shouting advice. Heavy footsteps from the front of the inn told of more policemen approaching.

The man on the rope dropped the last few yards.

He stood poised for a moment; and a vivid yellow flash against a lighted window was followed by the report of a shot.

The bullet smacked into the flagstones.

The cat-burglar raced for the darkness at the side of the hotel, then towards the garden at the back. Two policemen hurtled through the main archway, and Mannering was close enough to hear their heavy breathing. The man struggling with a policeman near the inn broke away, and raced after the first fugitive.

Lights were going on all over the inn; the yard was now brightly lit. The detective who had fired at the burglar climbed out of a first-floor window, lowered himself, and dropped to the ground.

It was Whittaker. He rushed in pursuit of the two men.

Mannering continued to stand quietly in the shadows.

A door opened, and Bristow and Dando appeared. Neither was really hurrying as they went towards the back garden.

A hotel resident shouted: 'What's up?' and Bristow called back: 'It's all right now.'

Mannering's lips curved.

But there was not much cause for amusement; the police were seldom prepared to shoot on sight, nothing else could have told him so clearly that they meant to get results, at once. Absurd thought; of course they did; but the English used guns only when a criminal was dangerous.

The Baron had never been dubbed violent.

He saw a figure appear at a second-floor window; a woman's head and shoulders were outlined against a yellow blind. The window opened, and Lorna looked out. He could not see her clearly enough to judge her expression.

Mannering slipped across the yard to the doorway through which Bristow and Dando had come, and went inside. No one was in the narrow passage which led to one of the lounges.

He reached the lounge, and heard voices. A porter and a man in pyjamas with his overcoat thrown over them, were talking excitedly. The word 'police' kept cropping up; and the word 'murderer.' They were standing near the reception desk, and the staircase lay between them and him. He went forward quickly but quietly, and up the stairs. A young woman, looking nervously out of her room, bobbed inside and shut the door sharply. Two men were talking across the first-floor landing, and one of them called out to him.

'What's the matter, d'you know?'

'They think Mannering was staying here,' said Mannering gruffly.

'The Devil was!'

No one was in sight at the next floor, and all the doors were closed. He saw a light under Lorna's door. He glanced right and left before he turned the handle and slipped inside, moving so silently that she did not hear him. He closed and locked the door, the click of the key turning attracted her attention, and she swung round.

'Jo——'

143

'*Hush!*'

She stood with her hands at her breast, staring incredulously at him.

Mannering smiled gently as he went forward, hands outstretched. Next moment she was in his arms, and he could feel the wild beating of her heart. Her face was pressed tightly against his shoulder. He knew she was clenching her teeth; trying hard not to break down. She had keyed herself up to face the worst. Now—he was standing here, in the flesh; alive *and* free.

He stood smoothing the dark gloss of her hair.

She lifted her head suddenly, and her radiance made him catch his breath. She was transformed; not merely beautiful, not merely lovely, but lit up with happiness.

'Oh, darling,' she said in a shaky voice, 'I thought they'd shot you.'

'Not yet, by a long way,' said Mannering. He put his arm round her shoulders and led her to a chair. He sat down, and she sat on the arm, leaning against him. 'I wish they hadn't started popping lead, though. My friends won't think much of it, and might refuse to help.'

'Friends?'

They were both speaking in whispers.

'Friends. I don't know just what's going on down here, but there's a little group of rascals'—he used the word deliberately, lightly—'who first wanted to hand me over to the police and then decided to help. My powers of persuasion haven't wilted entirely. One of them made a stab at your window, his pal stayed downstairs to cause a distraction, and I slipped in when they'd drawn all the police off. Even Bristow won't expect to find me here just yet.'

'How long can you stay?'

'For tonight, anyhow,' said Mannering. 'I've a room on the same floor. Number 39. Ask for Mr. Browning.'

'John, the risk!'

'Well, show me a way to avoid any, and I'll take it,' said Mannering. He took out cigarettes, and they lit up. He saw the half-empty whisky bottle and three glasses on a table near the chair. 'Which is your glass?' he asked, and Lorna touched one. Leaning forward, he poured himself out a whisky and soda. 'If I need this, what are my stooges feeling like?'

'John, please don't take this lightly!'

'Now look here, it will work out—it will be *worked* out. At a rough guess, I'd say that the situation can only get worse if Bristow puts the darbies on me, but he isn't going to do that for a bit. And, as they say, his suspicions are aroused.'

'Aroused!'

'Against the real villains, I mean.'

'I wonder if you know just how bad things *are*,' Lorna said quietly. 'I've just seen Chittering—and young Galliard. And——'

'Tell me,' said Mannering.

So he learned what Lark had 'confessed'; and what the police had told Galliard and Chittering. He smoked two cigarettes while Lorna talked; now and again he smiled; and occasionally he frowned. When she finished, he stood up, walked to the fireplace and turned to face her. Lorna continued to sit on the arm of her easy chair.

There was no pretence of light-heartedness about Mannering now.

'We ought to be grateful to Chittering,' Mannering said. 'He's right, of course—Bristow told him, hoping he would tell you; it's an invitation to me to give myself up. But the answer's No. Not yet. Bellamy hasn't just been snatching any chance which offered, you know. He's had this worked out. When I escaped, it jolted him, but he must have laid similar plans beforehand. I think I was lucky, sweetheart. I don't think he meant me to leave that house alive—*and* free. Deep-laid plot. Get me there, kill me there or make it seem that I killed someone. The problem is—*why?* Not because I was after him; until I advertised for the emeralds I'd never heard of him. He deliberately tried to get me down here. But—why?'

'Does it matter now?' asked Lorna. 'Cause isn't important, but the effect——'

'If we could find out why it was started, we'd probably know what their object is, and get at their weak spot. Still, no use spending too much time thinking about that now. What to do?' He looked at her with a gleaming smile. 'We *could* go to bed.'

'Oh, you're hopeless!'

'Just in love. Get one or two things clear, sweet. Lark told the police a little, so as to help himself, but didn't tell them all. Had he done, they'd know just what I look like, and would have arrested me hours ago. Lark's dependable. So are his friends, although the shooting will have depressed them. Still, I don't think we need worry overmuch about Lark. There are two main questions—first, Galliard? What's he doing? Is he what he seems? Second—*why* did Stella tell the police that she was on that house-boat of her own free will? I was there, you know.'

Lorna drew in her breath.

'And feeling cock-a-hoop,' Mannering confessed. 'House-boat, Harrison, the evil housekeeper and the two lovely sisters, all in one fell swoop. If Stella had been there alone, I'd have expected her to lie to the police to save her sister. But both were there, as large as life, and Stella caved in at a scowl from Harrison.'

Lorna said: 'Have the girls fooled you, John?'

'Girls having the habit! No, darling, Stella's scared.'

'But if she and her sister could have escaped and didn't——'

'She's scared of something else.'

He was sure that was true. And Lorna, doubtful at first, saw how convinced he was, and accepted it. They sat silently for a while. Suddenly:

'What will happen to Lark?' asked Lorna.

He put his head back and looked at her through his lashes.

'Who else would have thought of little Lark just now?' he murmured. 'Bless you, my sweet! And I wish I knew the answer. The police might be holding him on a technicality, and I doubt if he'd have anything at his house to put himself in bad. He's a smart little beggar.'

'And he could have damned you.'

'I know. Not to be forgotten. And before it's over, I'll see him through.' He shrugged, as if to drive away thought of what might happen before all danger was gone, and asked abruptly: 'What did Galliard have to say about himself? About his inheritance, chiefly.'

She went over the story carefully; of Galliard's death, the legacy to cousin Charles, Charles's sale of the house and contents to Bellamy for a song; and his sudden death.

'It's almost too complicated not to be true,' Mannering said thoughtfully. 'I wonder how much of this Galliard told the police? If he's also scared of something we don't

146

know about, he may have told half a story. Have you passed it all on to Bristow?'

'No.'

'You'd better, I think. Bristow will check up if there's any discrepancy between Galliard's story to you and to him. If there isn't, he'll go into the case history. The answer to the puzzle's in that history somewhere, and the deeper Bristow has to look the better my chance in the long run. Still—it isn't reassuring. Candidate for the gallows! A rope for the Baron! But we aren't seriously worried about that, are we?'

'I think I have been.'

'No need. I hope! But there's plenty to worry about. The police will have to dig very deep if they arrest and charge me, so they'll dig out the truth about this job and save my neck. In doing so they might disinter the Baron. That's why I must keep away from Bristow for a bit. No charge, no digging, no digging, no ghost.'

'The ghost is always there,' said Lorna.

'At least the damned thing doesn't always clank around like this.'

She laughed, then pushed him away.

'John, no! Darling, what are you going to do?'

'Exercise stern self-control and go to my own lonely bed. Think. And evolve a way of finding out why Stella's still so scared. I can't have hysterical young women chasing my ghost around. Darling, did I ever tell you that when you look like that, you're the most desirable woman in the world?'

Mannering lay in bed in his dark room, only vaguely aware of sounds in the yard, of voices, of a car moving off, suggesting that the police were back. If they hadn't caught their man, they might conclude that Mannering had planned the disturbance as a distraction, and search the hotel. But they would also assume that he had gone again, so he felt secure. Could that be because his mind had slowed down? Was there danger which might close in at any moment? Was this temporary safety an illusion? Was he so preoccupied with the other problems that he could not see this situation clearly?

Forget all that! Back to the major question:
Why had the girl lied?

What gave Bellamy and Harrison their hold over her?

Now facts which had to be faced.

He could never prove that he had left Hallen House before Holmes had died. No one had seen him, except Holmes himself.

Other questions; one in particular.

Why had Lark told Bristow about the emeralds but not the rest of the story? Had the little crook some ulterior motive? Did *Lark* want the police chasing him, Mannering? Had it suited Lark's own purpose to set him free? What had the little man really thought when he had pulled those cracksman's tools out of his pockets? Had he suspected the whole truth—the Baron? Did he think that there was a way of escaping from the consequences of his own crimes? Was Lark, in fact, working with Bellamy and Harrison?

And why *had* Galliard turned up at the crucial moment?

Chittering, a shrewd judge of human nature, had doubts about Galliard.

There were footsteps along the passage; tapping at a door; voices.

'I'm sorry to disturb you so late, Mrs. Mannering.'

Bristow!

Mannering sat up, groped for the light, but did not switch it on.

Bristow was in Lorna's room for a long time; questioning, probing, and yet frustrated; he'd get nowhere with Lorna, she was proof against all his tricks.

What did Bristow believe?

Did it matter?

At last he heard the Yard man's quiet: 'Good night.' The door closed and the hotel settled down to its nightly stillness.

But Mannering was a long time getting to sleep.

CHAPTER XVIII

VISITOR TO THE COTTAGE

SUPERINTENDENTS Dando and Bristow were not in the best
of moods when they met in Dando's office the next morning.
Up to a point, things had gone well; when there had been a
report of a man trying to get into the *King's Head*, Bristow
had thought: 'We've got him!' If he had mixed feelings, he
concealed that well.

But they had not caught anyone.

And Bristow couldn't make up his mind whether Mannering had fooled them, or whether someone else had caused
that alarm.

Dando was angry because of the failure of his own men.
What an example of inefficiency! Bristow had been decent
about it, but the two men at the *King's Head* ought to have
been caught. Their escape created new problems. Where-
abouts in or near Corwellin could thieves hide with im-
punity?

In fact, Dando had an uneasy conscience.

There had been rumours of extensive smuggling in the
locality, but he had never been able to put a finger on the
trouble. As the reports were only rumours, he had made
tentative inquiries, no more. Now he was worried lest
Mannering was connected with smugglers, who would
certainly have hiding places. How extensive was the organisation, if it really existed? Was it centred in Corwellin?

There was Dando's real sense of guilt; he was not sure
what was going on in his own district. But Corwellin was

149

such a quiet spot; serious crime was almost unknown; the smugglers—if they existed—he kept repeating that, as if to reassure himself, had kept very quiet. Possibly some contraband was landed on the nearby coast and taken straight to Bristol or London; it certainly wasn't distributed from Corwellin; he would have known about that.

Mannering, a dealer in jewels and antiques, might easily be one of the leaders of a smuggling organisation; so might Bellamy. The more he thought of it, the more it seemed to Dando that this was a case of thieves falling out. Perhaps Mannering and Bellamy had quarrelled over the spoils?

Should he confide in Bristow?

He decided to ease his mind; Bristow had a way of encouraging confidences, and this morning his looks were at their best, in spite of his own worries, his kindliness glowed. So Dando found it easy to talk.

He exaggerated the attempts which he had made to find out if the rumours were true, and Bristow appeared to be properly impressed.

'Of course, this may be a false trail,' Dando finished. '*Would* Mannering touch smuggled jewels, d'you think?'

Bristow looked like a wise old owl.

'You can never tell with dealers. But his reputation is so good, I shouldn't have thought he would take a chance.' He lit a cigarette from the stub of one in his hand. 'Smuggling—it *might* be part of the solution. Your men Bellamy and Harrison apparently use the river a lot, and the stuff could be brought up river. They want watching closely, but I don't see that we've any excuse for concentrating too much on Bellamy. Better have Hallen House and the house-boat watched, though.'

'I've already arranged that.'

'Good. Er——' Bristow looked grave. 'Sorry to say this, but Whittaker isn't one of the best——'

'Don't talk to me about Whittaker! Always liable to do something daft. I'm keeping him here, reliable men will do the watching. But you're right, we can't afford to concentrate too much on Bellamy and Harrison. Mannering now—don't you think he left the district?'

Dando sounded almost hopeful, Bristow casual.

'Could be. We'll pick him up sooner or later. I think we ought to keep an eye on Grey, the innkeeper of the place where Lark was staying. You might get a line on Grey's friends, too. I've a feeling that I've seen Grey in London, and men like Lark usually mix with their own kind.'

He touched Dando on a tender spot.

'I know. Er—but are we justified in holding Lark any longer?'

'We could charge him with helping Mannering to escape, but whether we should is a different matter,' Bristow said. 'Better release him and his friend, and watch them. Whether it's smuggling or not, there's something very odd going on here. The murder of Holmes is only a part of it. And if Mannering is in the district, he'll have to get in touch with someone sooner or later. It might be Lark or his friends; it might be his wife; it might be Galliard—and it might even be Chittering of the *Gazette*.'

'We can't watch them *all*,' complained Dando.

Mannering left the *King's Head* just after ten o'clock, when the two Superintendents were discussing him. He walked past a policeman who was standing opposite the hotel, and went to Andrews Garage. The same plump man greeted him genially. Yes, of course, he could have the car whenever he wanted it. The garage owner winked. Just as well to have a good fast car sometimes, wasn't it? What with taxes where they were and things in such short supply, he didn't blame anyone who managed to get some stuff into the country without visiting the Customs Shed. He wished any such people good luck!

Mannering left Corwellin at half-past ten with plenty of petrol in the tank.

He reached Bristol before one o'clock, went immediately to the G.P.O., bought a letter-card, and wrote a brief note:

'My dear Bill,
    I didn't kill him, you know. I hope you realise it. If I come into the open just yet I shall spoil as nice a little plot as I've ever come across. Be patient; be careful; and get ready to say 'thanks' when I hand you the case on a plate!
    You might tell Lorna that I'm still alive. I'm afraid she might worry in case I've shared Holmes's fate.'

He read it over; about right, he decided; sufficient to imply that he'd not been at Corwellin the previous night; to

151

say he wasn't worried about his own position. But it wanted rounding off.

He added another sentence.

'You might ask Dando if he's ever heard of smuggling in this part of the world.

John M.'

He addressed the letter-card in block lettering, so that Bristow would not immediately recognise the handwriting, marked it *Personal and Private*, and posted it just before he left Bristol, at four o'clock that afternoon. He did not return to Corwellin, although his room was still reserved at the *King's Head*. He stopped at a hotel near the river for an early dinner and, when darkness was beginning to fall, drove towards the riverside cottage. Lights from several windows were glowing. A pity, for he had hoped that the house would be deserted.

He left the Lancia near the quarry, and walked to the river.

Harrison would certainly not recognise him in this disguise. Should he go boldly to the front door, knock, force his way in and . . .

Nonsense!

But the notion amused him.

He went straight to the landing. The motor-boat was tied up securely. The strains of radio music were coming from the cottage; slow, sonorous, operatic. Wagnerian, heavy on the crisp night air; so whoever was inside was settled for the evening, one didn't take Wagner in snatches. He approached a lighted window, the one through which he had looked the previous night.

Stella and her sister were inside; no one else was in the room.

He went to the back, seeing no one in the kitchen, although the light was on.

In another ground-floor room Foss was sitting in an easy chair, near a radio-phonograph. He had taken off his coat, and loosened his collar and tie. His shoes were in the fireplace, and he wore a pair of carpet slippers. A large cigar jutted out from his lips.

Only the lights Mannering had seen were on; Foss and the girls were probably on their own.

If he acted quickly, he could get results.

He hurried back to the quarry, and drove down to the bridge, leaving the car where he had left it the night before. Indoors, the music boomed out, and the girls were still in the lounge, both reading.

He approached the window of a darkened room and examined the catch with his fingers, relying only on sense of touch. Then he took out the thin screwdriver, pushed it between the two halves of the windows, and pressed lightly against the catch. It moved. He increased his pressure slightly; the latch went back with a sharp click!

The music would drown that sound.

He pushed up the window, and the music welled out, spreading into the night.

He climbed inside.

Enough light came from beneath the door to show that this room was a dining-room. He stepped to the door, opened it, narrowing his eyes against the glare from the light in the passage.

The girls were in a room immediately opposite him; Foss was in a small room next to this.

He crossed to Foss's door, put his right hand into his pocket, and pushed the screwdriver against it so that it would look like a gun. Then he opened the door with his left hand. The music swelled out, loud and deafening, a depressing medley of strings and drum and trumpets.

Foss, sitting with his back to him, was nodding his head up and down to the rhythm of the music.

Mannering stepped closer.

He was a yard away when Foss swung round!

Foss got to his feet in a flash, backed towards the window and snatched a gun from his hip pocket; the movements were almost simultaneous, he must have had some warning. His face twisted in mingled fear and determination, and the light glinted on the grey gun.

Mannering leapt before the gun was levelled, and hit him on the side of the face. The blow pushed Foss back, he tripped over a stool and crashed down. The music boomed out to a wild climax. The gun, loose in Foss's hand, was touching the floor. Mannering saw the hand move and kicked out. He caught Foss on the wrist; the gun slithered a couple of feet, without going off, but Foss jumped up and dived for it. Mannering caught him by the arm, swung him round, and drove his fist into his face. Foss's eyes rolled, he caught his breath and slumped down.

Boom!

The music stopped after a crash of drums.

The silence seemed deadly.

Foss lay inert on the floor between the stool and a chair. Mannering looked round for a cloth to bind the man, saw nothing, took Foss's handkerchief from his pocket and rammed it into his mouth. Foss's breath whistled noisily through his nostrils.

Mannering turned off the radio, picked Foss up, slung him over his shoulder, peered along the passage to make sure no one was coming, then carried the man up the stairs. An open doorway led into a bedroom. He carried Foss in, and switched on the light with his elbow. He dropped the man on a single bed in a poorly furnished room, then turned down the clothes, took the pillow-case off the pillow and tore it into strips.

Soon Foss was trussed up, and tied to the bed; no danger there, now.

Mannering took the bulb out of the lamp, plunging the room into darkness, and then went out and closed the door, glad of Foss's gun in his pocket. But he wanted something else, and went into a larger bedroom and looked through the drawers of the dressing-table. He found a pair of thin leather gloves, the next best thing to the cotton gloves Lark hadn't been able to find. He drew them on, wriggled his fingers about, and turned to the door.

He went downstairs, reached the hall and moved towards the girls' door.

He was two yards away when the door opened and Stella appeared.

She did not see him at first, but came sideways into the hall, looking at her sister.

'I won't be long, Kath.'

She turned round, caught sight of Mannering—and screamed!

CHAPTER XIX

TALK WITH STELLA

'WHAT is it?' cried Kathleen. 'What is it?'

She appeared behind her sister, who had uttered that one piercing scream, and now stood with a hand at her mouth, gasping for breath.

Mannering said quietly, in his assumed voice:

'I've come to help. Don't worry about Foss, he's having a rest.'

'Rest!' gasped Stella.

'Go inside,' Mannering ordered; and they backed into the room. Magazines lay on the floor, and open on a table between two armchairs was a box of chocolates.

Stella put out her hand to touch her sister. Kathleen's face was chalk white.

'Who—are you?'

'A friend of Mannering.'

'A friend of——'

'I hope you remember him. He wants to see you.'

'Yes, I remember Mannering,' said Stella, in a strained voice. 'He killed Holmes, the only friend we had at Hallen House. It's no use saying he didn't!' Her voice rose almost to a scream, she was as bad as her sister. 'He's a murderer; he killed my friend!'

'He risked his life getting out of Hallen House to help you, and he didn't kill Holmes.'

'But the newspapers——' Stella was fighting to speak calmly.

'The newspapers got their information from Bellamy. If

you're going to believe your uncle, we'll never get out of this jam. Stella, why did you lie to the police when they came to see you on the house-boat? Your sister could have been rescued with you—at the house, you told Mannering that you were frightened for her, only for her.'

'How—how do you *know* all this?'

'I've seen Mannering. He can't come out of hiding, so I'm doing his job for him, and I'm going to save him from the gallows.' He saw the girl flinch. 'You didn't mean Mannering harm, or you wouldn't have warned him not to go to Hallen House. What's made you change your mind?'

'Oh, stop!' cried Kathleen. 'Stop talking like that!'

Mannering said roughly:

'Mannering tried to help you without going to the police because you were so scared about your sister. Mannering put his neck in a noose for your sake. Now you're going to tell me what your game is.'

Stella did not speak.

Kathleen dropped into a chair and closed her eyes.

Mannering went on: 'You were frightened then, and you're still frightened. Your uncle has you in his power and every time you throw away a chance of escaping, you're making your own position worse. Either you were lying to Mannering, or——'

'I wasn't lying!'

'Then what is the truth?'

Stella said slowly, desperately: 'I daren't tell you. I *daren't*!'

'You'd rather live like this—frightened of every sound, every movement, in deadly fear of Bellamy and Harrison, of the police. You'd rather see Mannering die—hanged—*murdered*. You'd rather let the real murderer of Holmes get away scot free, because—you daren't tell me the truth.'

'I—I can't help myself!'

'You're going to help yourself. If you're frightened of what Harrison or Bellamy might do to you, come away with me, I've a car outside. I can take you to a safe hiding place. And——'

'No!' gasped Stella. 'No, we can't!'

'So your uncle——'

'He's not my uncle!' cried Stella.

Bellamy wasn't her uncle.

156

What crazy business was this?

'We can't leave here,' gabbled Stella. 'Not now. Please go away. You can't help. No one can help.' She talked like someone who was beyond all hope. 'Please go away. If—if Mannering is in danger, I'm sorry. I warned him not to go to Hallen House; he wouldn't listen to me.'

'So Bellamy isn't your uncle? Then who is he? Your name *is* Bellamy. Isn't it?'

'Go away; I can't tell you anything more.'

Understanding dawned. 'So you're frightened *for* your uncle.'

She drew in a hissing breath.

'No, no! No, it isn't true, it isn't true!'

'All right,' Mannering said into a long pause. 'The best thing I can do is take you to the police. They'll probe deep; they won't be influenced by danger to you or your uncle. All they'll want is the truth, and they'll find it.'

He turned on his heel.

'Don't go!' cried Stella. She ran forward, gripped his hands, hers were hot and clammy. 'You mustn't tell the police; they'd go to see Bellamy, if they did——'

'Your uncle will be killed. Is that it?'

'*Yes!*' cried Stella. 'They'll kill him!'

So he'd won that round!

'Where *is* your uncle?'

Kathleen opened her eyes.

'Stella, don't——'

'It's no use,' said Stella in a flat voice. 'We'll have to tell him now.' She released Mannering's hand. 'He—he's at Hallen House. I don't know where. It's so big—so rambling —it's full of secret rooms, secret panels, hidden passages. He's somewhere there. I didn't know until Harrison told me. I looked everywhere. I couldn't—tell the police—the truth— until I could be sure he was all right.'

Now she talked freely; eagerly; all the barriers were down.

Their real name was Ashton.

Their uncle had brought them up from childhood; been mother and father, a man they loved; adored. That came out clearly in broken words and phrases; so did the fact that they must help him, and why. Kathleen kept bursting into tears; recalling all that had been good, and showing how the horror had come swiftly, shatteringly upon them.

Ashton was a dealer in antiques and precious stones. Mannering knew him . . .

He had first met Bellamy when in America. They made a business deal through a friend; and her uncle was commissioned to sell a big collection. Bellamy had wanted to buy, but not to pay the full price. Something—the girls didn't know what it was—had forced her uncle to accept ruinous prices for some of the jewels. From then on, her uncle had changed. Back in England, he was nervous, irritable, sick.

Stella had guessed that he was being blackmailed by Bellamy.

One morning, months ago, he had been ordered to go to Hallen House. He hadn't wanted to go, but had not dared to disobey. The sisters had stayed in their London flat, Kathleen in poor health, a constant anxiety. Soon afterwards, their uncle had written to them. They were to join him in Cornshire; all was well, there was no need to worry.

They went by train, and Harrison met them at the station.

Their uncle didn't appear.

Bellamy did.

Bellamy in his suave, cruel way had hinted at dark horrors. They must stay at Hallen House; obey orders; submit to his commands; and one day they might see Ashton.

Stella had revolted.

And Kathleen, sick, frightened, had been shut away in her room, lost to Stella.

Why was it done?

They didn't know.

Stella knew that a man had come to the house, and stayed a few days; and been hurled to his death from a window. Later, another man; Galliard, who had tried to help her, but to whom she had not dared talk. Then she had heard Bellamy and Harrison talking about Mannering's visit; he was to value the jewels, but not be set free. Murder had leapt to her mind, in panic she had fled, to warn him.

Rundle had tried, too.

Rundle and Holmes had been the only people at Hallen House with a kindly word for Stella; Holmes had brought reports of Kathleen's progress—but none about her uncle.

Yet Bellamy kept telling her that Ashton was at the house.

The two people whom she cared for were completely in Bellamy's power.

And even now, she didn't know why.

She pressed her hands against her forehead as she drew towards the end of her strange story.

'Now I've told you, what can we *do*?'

Mannering said:

'Find your uncle.'

'I lived there for six months—and couldn't find him.'

'If he's there, Mannering will.'

'It's impossible!'

'It was impossible for Mannering to get away from Hallen House; but he's free.'

Stella said slowly:

'Yes—yes, that's true.'

'And you can help. There must be something to give you some hint, some clue.'

'Nothing!'

'Think,' said Mannering.

Stella's eyes were glassy, red-rimmed; she was tormented. Kathleen got up and came to her side, gripping her arm.

'Stella, *think*.'

'Kath, please——'

'You must!'

'There was—one strange thing,' said Stella, and her voice was hushed. 'They would never—let me into—the Great Hall. They had some secret there.

'One night when I couldn't sleep, I saw them go into the Great Hall. All the lights went out—everything. Harrison had a candle. I remember how ghostly it looked. And——'

'Yes?'

'There were other nights when the lights went out.'

'Did you see them go into the Great Hall again?'

'No. After that night, they locked me in.'

She stopped.

And, stopping, she looked past Mannering and in a flash he knew that the fear which leapt to her eyes was not born out of memory; and a cold draught swept into the room.

'We ought to have cut your throat,' said Harrison.

He came in, with a Luger in his hand.

CHAPTER XX

PRESENT FOR THE POLICE?

ANOTHER man was behind him; one of the gardeners from Hallen House. Stella covered her face in her hands; all colour had gone from her sister's face.

'So you're a friend of Mannering's,' Harrison rasped.

Mannering did not speak.

'The police ought to be very interested in a friend of Mannering's. What a pretty present you would make for Dando and Bristow.' Harrison gave that odd, unfinished laugh. 'Ha! Didn't your friend Mannering warn you that you were dealing with clever men? And didn't you realise that we could see you from outside?'

The other man came into the room and stood behind Mannering. Harrison's hand flashed out, knuckles smashed into Mannering's mouth.

'Talk, damn you!'

Mannering said through the salt blood: 'I'll talk—in good time.'

'You'll talk now. Where *is* Mannering?'

No answer—and another smashing blow followed the first; a third; a fourth.

The gardener held Mannering tightly.

'Don't!' cried Stella. 'Don't!'

Harrison growled: 'You keep quiet, I'll deal with you later. Come on, smart guy, where's Mannering?'

'Yes. You need to know. You will—when he gets you.'

Harrison struck out again, and Mannering let his knees bend under him. The gardener pulled him up, Harrison's fist loomed up red with Mannering's blood.

'Don't!' screamed Kathleen.

Mannering's head jarred back under the next blow. Mists blinded him; rage shook him to the madness of steeling himself to go berserk; and then he saw Stella, a wild fury of arms and legs, kicking and striking and clawing at Harrison.

The gardener's grip relaxed.

Mannering back-heeled; his heel caught a shin, the grip fell away. Mannering swung round, and hit out; the man reeled back.

The gun dropped from Harrison's hand.

Mannering took his from his pocket.

He used the butt; once on the gardener; twice on a swearing, sweating Harrison. After they had fallen, only the heavy breathing of the two girls broke the quiet. Blood filled Mannering's mouth, trickled down his chin. He hardly noticed it.

'Get your coats on,' he said.

'Stella, Stella, Stella!' sobbed Kathleen.

Stella was standing close to Harrison. Her lips were swollen, and a tiny trickle of blood was running down her chin. She brushed hair out of her eyes, and put out her hand to her sister.

'It's all right, Kathie; it's all right.' She paused for breath. 'Go—go upstairs and get—get our things.'

'But, Stella!'

'Just pack one case, for the night.'

Kathleen still hesitated; Stella pushed her towards the door. Kathleen went out, and Stella said to Mannering:

'Your face.'

He fingered his mouth, then caught sight of himself in a mirror on the wall. His lips were pulp. Blood had spread over his chin and nose and was dripping on to his shirt.

'You must clean up.'

'Yes. Later. Go and help your sister.'

She left him.

He pressed his hands against his spinning head and knelt unsteadily by Harrison's side. The man had been badly bruised, but was breathing regularly. Slowly and laboriously, Mannering went through his pockets, took his wallet, found nothing else that might be helpful except a bunch of keys. He pocketed these, and straightened up. He felt sick. But he had to go through Foss's pockets, and ought to search the house. He went out of the lounge and into the room where Foss had been sitting. There were some books in open book-cases; Foss had a Rabelaisian taste and a liking for pornography. Mannering pulled the books out, dropped them to the floor one by one, made sure there was no secret hiding-place behind the shelves, and turned to a small, modern pedestal desk. It was locked; forcing it took him several minutes, but when he had one drawer open, the rest unlocked.

A quick glance through the papers there showed nothing of interest. He needed more time—much more; but he daren't take it.

He opened a slim account book. The entries in the first pages looked innocent enough. At the top of one page were the items:

10 bales S.	£595
12 Gross W.	£2456
21 case C—one damaged	£750
Sundries	£9125

Sundries—nearly three times as much as the rest put together!

He tucked the book into the top of his trousers.

The two girls were coming down the stairs. He went to the door, and Kathleen looked at him over the banisters.

She clapped her hand to her mouth.

'You must do something to your face!' Stella cried.

'Switch off the lights, and go out. I'll follow you.'

Both girls were wearing overcoats and small, tight-fitting hats; Stella was carrying a suitcase. She put out the hall light, pushed past her sister and opened the front door. Soon all three were hurrying towards the bridge, Mannering just behind the girls, telling them where to go. When they reached the Lancia the sisters got into the back and Mannering took the wheel.

The cold night air stung his lips, and the pain was getting worse. Forget it! What should he do with the girls? Where could he take them?

'Are you taking us to Mr. Mannering?' Stella asked.

'No, to a friend. Do you mind not talking?'

The evening yawned in front of Lorna. She could not go out, because there might be a message. She couldn't settle to a book. Every time footsteps sounded in the passage, she turned her head sharply. Despair and confidence in John clashed all the time.

Someone was approaching now.

There was a tap on the door.

She jumped up from her chair. 'Come in!'

'Evening, lady,' said Chittering, pushing the door wide and slouching in with one hand in his pocket. 'Only your little newshound.' He pushed the door to and stood looking at her with a twisted smile. 'Is it tough?'

'Yes, it's tough,' she admitted.

'Must be. Only a hard-bitten thug like me would wonder. Still, while there's life, you know.' He took his hand out of his raincoat pocket, and tossed a letter on to the table near her. 'For you.'

'Who from?' Lorna asked eagerly.

'I wouldn't know. I thought it was for me. It came to my hotel. Hope deferred. Inside the envelope addressed to me was another addressed to you. I'm slipping,' he declared. 'I can't guess who sent it. The point is, I shall be imbibing bad liquor in the bar if you want me. 'Bye, lady!'

Lorna did not see him leave.

She tore open the letter, and the familiar handwriting leapt from the page. It was a dirty piece of paper; there were brownish stains all over it.

'Bit rushed, darling. Ask Chittering to take Galliard to Crossford Arms, pub on Bristol Road, to pick up Stella B. and sister. Don't send Galliard alone. Don't go yourself. Stella is scared of police but will tell them the truth if strongly advised to when the time comes for that. I'll send word. Meanwhile if police question her again, she's to stick to original story. Forgive rush. John.'

She read it twice, and then hurried down to the bar.

Later that night, a detective watching the house where Galliard was staying, reported that Galliard had left in a hurry, to return a little more than an hour later with two girls.

'Could be the two girls from the house-boat,' Dando said to Bristow.

'I should put another man on to watch that house,' advised Bristow.

Out on the lonely moor, lights shone from the windows of Hallen House. A car raced along the winding road, and the headlights shone on a pile of rocks which concealed two hardy detectives whom Dando had detailed for that bleak job. The men recognised Harrison's Bentley, with a driver and two passengers, whom they did not recognise. As soon as the car was out of sight, one of the detectives walked across

163

to a motor-cycle and side-car equipped with a radio, and a message was flashed back to Corwellin.

That was routine; there was nothing surprising about Harrison's return. Where he had been was of far greater importance.

The front of the great building shone in the headlamps, until the car disappeared round the side of the house.

An hour later, darkness descended over the moor.

'Queer thing,' said one of the detectives; 'they seem to have switched off all the lights.' He yawned. 'Hell of a beat, this. Who the devil expects Mannering to come back here?'

The door of Hallen House was opened by Mrs. Dent, who peered blankly at Harrison and Foss. If she saw that they were pale and bruised, she made no comment, and she led the way to the room where Mannering had first been received.

Bellamy was sitting in front of the fire, a book resting on his black rug.

He saw the bruises.

'Why, Jim——' he began.

'We've got to get out of here,' Harrison burst out.

'What have you been doing wrong, Jim?'

'That's right, blame me. Well, I'm *not* to blame.'

Bellamy said: 'Foss——'

'There's no one to blame but yourself!' snapped Harrison. 'We oughtn't to have stayed here. We ought to have gone when Mannering got away. I've always said so.'

'But then, you're so often wrong. Sit down, Jim—and you, Foss. You'd better not have spirits with those bruised heads, I'll send for some coffee. Have you had dinner?'

'Coffee—dinner! We've got to get out, I tell you!' roared Harrison. 'The girls are free!'

'Are they, indeed,' murmured Bellamy. 'Well, that's too bad. I thought they were going to behave themselves, and I felt sure that Foss would be able to look after them—with your help. You and the guard were watching the cottage, Jim, weren't you?'

'What the hell does that——'

'Weren't you?'

'They went off for a drink,' Foss said.

'I *see*. Yet it wasn't your fault, Jim. You have some mighty queer ideas, boy.'

The door opened and Mrs. Dent appeared.

'Bring supper, with some strong coffee,' Bellamy said. 'Now, Jim. Where are the girls? With the police?'

Harrison growled: 'I don't know. I doubt it.'

'I think you had better tell me exactly what happened,' said Bellamy. He had not once raised his voice, but there was cold anger in his eyes.

Foss began the story, and Harrison finished it. Neither man made any further attempt to excuse himself. When it was over, Bellamy told the others to get on with the supper, and while they ate, he sat looking into the fire, as if nothing at all disturbing had happened. But his very silence held a menace, and Harrison could not stand the strain.

'What the devil are you going to *do*?'

'I'm trying to decide,' said Bellamy. 'We have a great deal to think about, but the key is—Mannering.'

'You've got Mannering on the brain. If you hadn't been scared of him, you'd never have brought him down here. You made a mistake——'

'Well, son, I'm not the only one who makes mistakes, am I?' asked Bellamy gently. 'Don't get worked up. That man called himself a friend of Mannering's. How tall was he?'

'About my height, but what does——'

'And his build?'

'Do you think I took his measurements?'

'Now, Jim! How did he compare with—well, let's say Mannering for size? About the same?' Harrison stared at him without speaking, and Bellamy nodded. 'Obviously, yes—about Mannering's size. And blond—ever heard of peroxide, Jim?'

Harrison pushed his chair back.

If you're trying to tell me that fellow was Mannering, you've got another guess coming!' He swung round on Foss. 'There wasn't a scrap of likeness, was there?'

'Disguise isn't difficult. An expert can work wonders,' Bellamy said. 'And the light isn't very good at the cottage. By all accounts, you had knocked him about pretty badly before you were able to take a good look at him. It may have been Mannering. Whether it was or not, Jim, I guess we've got to hand it to Mannering for finding a "friend" when he wanted one so badly. Yes, sir, we've got to hand it to Mannering. But—*he* won't want the girls to talk to the police. He won't want them to hear about the little games at the cottage yet. Unless the police know where the girls are——'

165

'They're bound to find out sooner or later!'

'Oh, sure. The question is—will it be sooner or later?' Bellamy shifted his position slightly. 'Jim, I'm *not* a fool. And although I trust you so far, I can't rely on you to keep a still tongue in your head. You weren't frightened enough before to be told what I'm arranging, but I think you are now. We're leaving soon. All four of us—you two, Emma Dent, and I. We're leaving the country, Jim.'

Harrison sprang up. 'And you didn't tell me!'

'Because I think you would have told the servants, and we can't take them all. The police will almost certainly raid the place soon. No one else must know what we're planning, and—we want thirty-six hours' start, Jim.'

Foss and Harrison were staring at him tensely.

'An aeroplane will arrive here from France the day after tomorrow. It is due at dawn. I couldn't arrange it any sooner. But you two and Emma will have to get busy, because we want all the jewels packed up, and we want all the stuff that we can take put into small crates. You'll have to work through tonight and tomorrow until it's finished. We've done very well, but now—we'll have to leave. I shall be sorry and yet——' He shrugged his shoulders, and smiled faintly. 'Well, haven't we done well, Jim? We've a fortune in this house. Thanks to our combined efforts.' He turned to Foss. 'Of course, you needn't come with us, son. If you'd rather stay and take charge yourself, you'll be the Boss. Foss the Boss! It's been a good sideline, and there are a lot of pickings left for a smart young man like you.'

Foss gave a twisted smile. 'I'm coming.'

'That's good,' said Bellamy. He took out a cigar-case, selected a Havana, pierced it with the end of a match and lit it carefully. 'Yes, Jim, I knew we might have to go when Mannering escaped. And let's face it, son. Things have moved very quickly since then, *very* quickly. I think I could have bluffed it out if they'd caught Mannering earlier, but now both the girls are free—well, that's an end to it. I guess if you look hard you can see the funny side. Because Lark went to Perce Grey for help, didn't he? And got it! Perce has been working very nicely with Foss, here, but didn't know that Foss was working for me. And I brought Lark down because of some of those beautiful gems he managed to get for me. You know,' he smiled faintly, 'I think I know why Lark decided to rent that furnished house. I do believe he thought he *might* be able to break into Hallen House and rob us. But murder put him off—Lark's kind are always afraid of the rope.'

Foss said thinly: 'I don't *like* it.'

'Of course you don't,' said Bellamy, 'but you needn't worry about it. It's ironical, isn't it, Jim? If Lark hadn't been here, Mannering wouldn't have got any help, and maybe this wouldn't have happened. Well, there it is. You think the police are bound to find out what you've been doing, Foss, don't you?'

'They'll break up the smuggling,' Foss said. 'And the farther away I am, the better.'

'I guess you're right. Now we've got to work, and work hard. No more running to and fro. We'll get all the small stuff crated and ready to take away, and if there *is* any trouble from the police—well, I guess we'll hide in the vaults and get out when the aeroplane's due. But we needn't anticipate it. I don't reckon the police will come again for a while.'

Harrison said sharply:

'I hope you're right. But if Stella talks about Ashton——'

'Yes, I know, that's the danger. But she'll be so frightened that we'll kill him, she probably won't talk. We'll have to hope for the best, Jim, that's all we can do—and work, mind you.' He drew on his cigar. 'We'll have a man in the tower watching, so that if anyone approaches we'll see them miles away, and have plenty of warning. You boys finished your meal? Then I guess it's time we went downstairs and got started.'

The three men gathered in front of the huge sideboard in the Great Hall. Harrison was holding a candle, and the flickering light shone eerily on their faces. Bellamy, leaning forward in his chair, ran his fingers along some of the carving, and a piece moved outwards. In the plain wood beyond was a small keyhole. He inserted a key; there was a click as the lock turned.

Bellamy wheeled his chair away.

Harrison lowered the candle and pulled at a head of one of the carved warrior figures. The end of the sideboard opened, leaving a space just wide enough for the wheel-chair to go through. But in front there appeared to be only the blank wall.

Harrison this time used a key, which Bellamy gave him. He pushed open a door in the wall and, holding the candle

167

high, led the way along a passage which sloped downwards. The door swung to behind them. Bellamy braked the wheel-chair with his hands. Twenty yards along the passage they came upon an oil wall-lamp; Harrison lit it, then lit others which were placed at intervals of ten feet. The passage was circular, and went downwards all the way. Eventually they reached what appeared to be a blank wall, but closer inspection showed a doorway. Again Harrison used a key, and pushed the door open.

'Help Jim prepare some lights,' said Bellamy.

Foss obeyed.

The flames of the oil lamps burned steadily behind glass mantles, revealing a large chamber, almost as large as the Great Hall. The walls were of dark stone, the ceiling was high and gloomy. In one corner was a door over which a single light had been burning when they entered. Several large safes stood against the far wall, and Harrison and Bellamy went to them. As the door swung open, the yellow light shone on precious stones.

Placed neatly against the wall were small, exquisite *objets d'art*, of untold value. In another corner were small packing cases of strong wood, and a bench on which were hammers, nails, strands of packing wire and tools for pulling the wire tight to secure the cases. Next to the bench was packing material.

'We ought to have started this before,' Harrison grumbled.

'It is easy to be wise after the event,' said Bellamy, 'and I hoped that I shouldn't have to move. Mannering——'

'Oh, forget Mannering!'

'I shall never do that,' said Bellamy softly. 'But for him, no move would have been necessary. I think he will live just long enough to regret it.' There was steel in his voice. 'Because, before we leave, I shall leave a "confession," Jim. I shall admit to my share in the crimes—not yours, don't worry, not yours!—and I shall give a detailed explanation of how Mannering and I worked together. How we quarrel-led. How he came here intent on robbing me, and Holmes caught him in the act. There'll be a rope for Mannering!'

Harrison stared at the pale face.

'You—devil!'

'Now don't you get soft-hearted, Jim. You know what I think about Mannering. *And* what I think about Ashton. I'll go and see Ashton, but you two must set to work.'

The two men turned to the bench, while Bellamy wheeled

himself to the door in the corner. He took out another key, opened the door, and went inside.

The light was not so good in here.

It was a small 'room'; a cell. A camp bed stood against the wall; there was a chair, primitive furnishings—and an old man lying on the bed. Glittering eyes turned fearfully to Bellamy.

The man was filthy. A long, straggly beard hid his features. Thin, claw-like hands clutched the lapels of his coat, but he seemed hardly to have the strength to move.

'Bellamy.' His voice was hoarse, croaking. 'Bellamy, when are you going to let me out . . .?'

Bellamy did not speak, but grinned at him as Ashton tried to get up. The prisoner's breathing was laboured; perspiration glistened on his forehead and cheeks; veins stood out on his throat. He managed to reach a sitting position.

'Bellamy, I've not much longer to live. I—I must . . .'

Bellamy threw back his head and laughed.

Peels of that wild laughter rang through the vaults, made Foss and Harrison shudder and stare towards the cell. Ashton cowered back.

Bellamy stopped . . .

'We're leaving,' he said, in a hard voice. 'We're leaving, Ashton. The police will come here soon, but they'll never find you. They can't find you. Understand?'

Ashton raised his trembling hands.

'If I've one regret, it's that I can't leave Mannering with you,' said Bellamy, 'but he'll be looked after. He'll hang, understand, he'll *hang*. And you—damn your guts—you'll live in eternal darkness. Darkness!' Bellamy swung his chair round, picked up the small chair and flung it at the lamp. The glass broke; darkness descended on the tiny cell gradually relieved by the light outside.

'Darkness,' hissed Bellamy, 'eternal darkness!'

He laughed again, swung the chair round and wheeled himself out.

The door slammed.

Bellamy sat outside the cell, while Ashton's cries sank to a piteous moaning. Foss looked uneasily at the door, but Harrison took no notice of the cries. He was examining an unopened safe, built into the wall. After trying a dozen keys in the lock, he turned to Bellamy, who caught his eye and wheeled the chair towards him.

'What is it, Jim?'

'The jewels from the jewel-room *are* in here, aren't they?'

'Yes. We brought them down when Mannering escaped.'

Harrison said slowly: 'The key's missing, and we only had one.' He hesitated, then blurted, 'It was the bunch Mannering took from me this evening. I forgot to leave them behind.'

'Break the safe open,' Bellamy said.

'It's not so easy. We haven't an oxy-acetylene torch here, and it needs an expert. I managed the jewel-room door, but I can't manage that.'

Foss swung round.

'You mean we can't get the sparklers?'

'Not on our own.'

After a long, tense pause, Bellamy said:

'We've got to open that safe. Get Lark——'

'But——'

'Get Lark!' roared Bellamy.

Lark and Jackie walked uneasily along the darkened street near Perce Grey's pub. They had received a message from the *Corwellin Arms*, saying that Harrison wanted to see Lark. Jackie had been going out, but Lark wasn't prepared to stay away. If Bellamy and Harrison had framed Mannering, they could frame him.

He and Jackie had managed to slip the police when leaving the pub.

Now, looking warily about them, they turned along a dark narrow alley leading to the High Street. At the corner a man was sitting at the wheel of a car.

Harrison showed in the light of a match.

'You wait here, Jackie,' Lark ordered.

'I doan like——'

'You wait here!'

Jackie grumbled under his breath and Lark approached the car.

As he reached it, a man sprang out of the darkness and struck the big man savagely over the head. Lark heard a strangled gasp, and turned—but another man appeared out of the gloom, and thrust a gun into his ribs.

'Get in,' the man growled. 'Hurry!'

Very soon, the car was humming along the road. On the sidewalk Jackie groaned as he came round.

CHAPTER XXI

A LETTER FOR BRISTOW

BRISTOW walked up the steps leading to the police station, nodded to the constable on duty and, whistling, went along to Dando's office. The local Superintendent had not yet arrived; on his desk was a pile of unopened correspondence. Bristow lit a cigarette and went to the window, looking out on to the High Street. A fair-haired man was leaving a shop opposite the police station. Bristow only caught a glimpse of his face as he got into a car, but noticed that his mouth and cheeks were swollen and discoloured. 'He's had a nasty packet,' mused Bristow, and saw the man climb into a Lancia.

For some inexplicable reason, Bristow's spirits were high that morning. It might be because he had slept well; West Country air suited the Yard man. It might be because he had thrown aside hesitation and uncertainty about Mannering. For the time being, at least, he had convinced himself that he was not interested in Mannering as an individual, only as a criminal.

And Bristow felt in his bones that this was going to be a good day.

There might be a letter for him in the post. His wife had promised to write to the police station, and someone might have sent a memo from the Yard.

He sorted the letters out. Nothing for him, apparently—pity. Only two letters left—hallo, what was this? One for him after all, but not from his wife or from the Yard. It was addressed in block lettering, and the post mark was Bristol.

He tore off the perforated strips of the letter-card, and opened it.

'Mannering, the Devil!'

The door opened.

'What's that?' asked Dando. 'Did you say Mannering?'

'I—er, yes, just for a moment I thought this was from him,' said Bristow. He caught the opening 'Dear Bill'; this was not for general consumption. He slipped the letter into his pocket. 'Anything much come in, do you know?'

'I haven't looked at the reports yet,' said Dando. 'I can't burn the candle both ends.'

'I'll leave you to your mail for ten minutes,' said Bristow. He nodded vaguely, and went off. In the cloakroom, he took out the card from Mannering.

Much of the brightness faded from that morning. '*I didn't kill Holmes, of course.*' Just a flat statement, put down almost casually. The rest of the letter was characteristic of Mannering. Cheerful, confident, saying a great deal in a comparatively few words. That Mannering was working on the 'case'; knew that he dared not give himself up; and, in the postscript, suggesting that the affair might be concerned with Dando's skeleton in the closet—smuggling.

The cloakroom door opened and Bristow glanced round, expecting to see one of the Cornshire detectives. Instead, Chittering strolled in, one hand in his pocket.

'Hallo, Bill!'

'What the devil are you doing here?'

'Come to see if there's any news,' said Chittering. 'I'm funny that way. Perhaps it's because I have to earn my living. Anything from Mannering?'

'No.'

'Police baffled. Nice headline, if not original. Too bad. Not a simple job, Bill, is it?'

'You're too familiar,' growled Bristow.

'Touchy on a nice bright morning like this. Sorry, Super! But I'm by way of being a friend of the great John. Same like you. And the last time we met, you were almost garrulous. I take it the news is bad?'

'There isn't any.'

'H'm, pity.' Chittering ogled him in disbelief. 'Personally, I don't believe you. Who's the *billet doux* from?' He looked pointedly at the letter-card.

Bristow drew a deep breath.

'Now look here——' he stopped abruptly, hesitated, and then—a sense of humour had always been Bristow's saving grace—he broke into a chuckle. 'All right, Chitty. I don't see why you shouldn't know, off the record.'

Chittering raised his eyebrows.

'Okay—let's have it.'

'I've had a note from Mannering. He doesn't say much, except to deny that he killed Holmes and expects to be able to prove it. You might care to let Mrs. Mannering know that he is all right.

'Delighted. Pity we can't publish that letter, though. Would it do any harm?'

'It might.'

'Okay, I'll be good,' said Chittering resignedly. 'But if there is a story in it later, you'll think of me, won't you?'

'You'll have it first.'

'*Mucho gracias.*' Chittering looked at Bristow through his lashes. 'Of course, I wouldn't know, and I don't know what you're doing, but I've a feeling that things won't hang fire much longer. Reaching a climax, so to speak.'

'Any reason for saying that?'

'Just an opinion. I can't say more. Er—you got the same feeling?'

Bristow shrugged his shoulders.

They went out of the cloakroom together, and outside Dando's door, Chittering touched his forehead in mock humility, and said: 'Good morning, Mr. Bristow.'

Bristow took his arm, and pressed firmly.

'Just a minute, Chitty. You aren't fool enough to keep anything back from me, are you. Mannering hasn't been in touch with you?'

'William! What an idea.'

'I know you, and I know Mannering. But you will come a cropper if you try to do any investigating yourself, and don't forget it.'

'I'm just a hack reporter. If I get a lead, I'll come running to you with it.'

'See that you do,' grunted Bristow.

Chittering grinned, and went off. Bristow went into Dando's office, and found him with the letters spread out on the desk.

'Well how does it go?'

'Nothing really fresh. A report from Galliard's place—

the two girls haven't come out. My man hasn't been able to find out their names. We might try to force an issue, if they're the Bellamy girls. That's about all. Nothing new from the house-boat—no one's there now, they've all returned to Hallen House. Arrived last night. An hour after Harrison had gone in, all the lights at the house went out, and came on again ten minutes later.'

'Fault in their generator, possibly,' said Bristow.

'It didn't happen anywhere else—my night-duty man checked up.'

'Thorough fellow,' said Bristow. 'Nothing else?'

'No.'

'What about this smuggling?'

Dando looked wary. 'Now look here. You yourself said that the first consideration was Mannering, and the smuggling secondary. We can't take the smuggling for granted, anyhow. I'm going all out to trace it if I can. That man Lark might have something to do with it. I've begun inquiries about him and the people with whom he's friendly. Perce Grey—remember him?'

'Yes.'

'He's well-known throughout the town, especially in the liquor trade and among the poorer people, and he's a London East Ender. Two or three East Enders have taken over pubs here in the last year or two. I'm going to have Grey closely watched. After he was released, Lark went back to his pub, remember. He hasn't stirred from there—nor has his friend Jackie—and they've had no callers. We've got to be patient and keep our eyes on everyone with whom Mannering might get in touch, and we might find a smuggling end.'

'Yes, that's all right.'

It wasn't such a bright day after all.

'Oh, one thing did come in,' said Dando. 'Confirmation from the Yard about the finger-prints on that lock and the cabinet. They're Mannering's.'

'He's got himself into a fine old corner,' said Bristow. 'But he doesn't seem down-hearted.'

He took out the letter-card.

Two minutes later, Dando put a call into the Bristol Police Headquarters, and Bristow, getting up, glanced out of the window and saw a Lancia being driven slowly along the High Street. He remembered the man with the battered face getting into it. Must have had quite a beating up. Dando was talking to Bristol, while the Yard man made up his mind to see Galliard and the girls.

It was a waste of time.

Kathleen was in bed, on doctor's orders. Galliard said that they were old friends, and were staying with him for a rest—because the moor got on their nerves. A pale-faced and subdued Stella, stuck to what she had said on the house-boat.

Bristow's hopes for that day had faded completely.

Lorna had one thing to cling to, during the day: Chittering's message. If John felt confident enough to write to Bristow, he must be sure of himself.

Mannering had spent the night at the *Red Lion*, a small hotel at the far end of the town. No questions were asked about his battered appearance and lack of luggage. When he woke up, his face was a discoloured mess, very stiff and painful. After cleaning his clothes, he went to a chemist opposite the police station for a healing lotion, returned to the hotel, bathed his face and dried it gingerly, then returned to the High Street. He had arranged by telephone to see Chittering outside the *King's Head* at half-past ten; but Chittering wasn't there.

He drove out of town before midday, and stopped for lunch at a country inn on the edge of the moor. The inn was in the middle of a small village, a cluster of cottages, one shop, a garage, and a church with a fine Norman tower. Hallen House, he knew from a careful study of the map, was nine miles away. This was the nearest village of any size—only a small hamlet was any nearer to the house. He had been assured by the owner of the *Corwellin Arms* that this place was 'safe,' which probably meant that it was a link in the chain of smuggling in the district.

Whether Bellamy was concerned with the smuggling didn't matter; Ashton at Hallen House was his chief concern now. An old man, prisoner for twelve months, victim of a sadist. Through the whole affair Bellamy's cruelty and love of inflicting mental torment showed like a murky red glow.

How to find Ashton?

There must be a strong-room at Hallen House, and probably vaults. He conjured up a mental picture of Harrison creeping into the Great Hall with a candle, and

175

the rest of the house in darkness. Generator failure? It might be, as there was a plant at the house. But the window of the jewel-room had been electrically locked. But supposing the current had been switched off so that electrically controlled doors could be opened.

Could he break past such defences? Was he justified in trying to? Even now—could he find out the truth in any other way?

And also free Ashton?

A meek little waitress came towards him in the lounge after lunch.

'Please, sir! the telephone.'

'For *me*?'

'Yes, sir, for Mr. Browning.'

'Thanks.' Mannering forced a smile as he rose to his feet, but he didn't like this. Who knew he was here? Had Lark talked about 'Browning' after all?

The telephone was in a secluded corner.

'Hallo.' He used the harsh voice.

'Perce Grey 'ere,' said the man at the other end of the telephone. 'I've been trying everywhere to find yer.'

They were loyal.

'Why?'

'It's Larky,' said Grey. ''E's in bad. I dunno if you can help. 'E. . .'

He talked swiftly. No one knew for certain where Lark had gone, but probably to Hallen House. If Bellamy didn't mean to put him in bad, he wouldn't have sent Harrison to do the rough stuff, would he?

No. And there was no longer any lingering doubts about what Mannering must do.

'All right, Perce,' said Mannering. 'I'll see what I can fix.'

That afternoon, a local bus took a letter addressed to Chittering at *The George*, giving him precise instructions. And Mannering booked a room at this inn for the night.

Mannering drove away at half-past eight, and after three miles turned off the Corwellin road. According to the map, he would strike the road which led from Corwellin to Hallen House near the bridge where he had fallen off the motor-cycle.

Soon, he switched off his headlights.

It was difficult going; the sidelights gave only a dim glow.

But the police were probably watching Hallen House and headlights could been seen for miles around.

Bellamy probably had a close watch kept, too.

He crossed a narrow bridge over a stream; it was not the bridge where he had fallen off the motor-cycle. He slowed down, travelling at no more than twenty miles an hour, his eyes strained to pick out the faint trail of the road. He came to a junction; this was probably the road he was looking for; he had to turn right.

He made the turn, and turned off the sidelights.

The stars gave a dim light, but he could hardly see the road, and the car lurched and rattled from side to side. Ten minutes of such driving was enough for him. He drove behind some bushes, and carefully noted the spot.

As he climbed out, a keen wind made him shiver.

He could see only the starry sky, and the dark shapes of the Lancia and the bushes.

He ran through his pockets, checking that he had all the tools which Lark had returned to him, and the Luger which he had taken from Harrison. He put that in his coat pocket, the others he stuffed into his hip-pocket. He stepped on to the road and walked towards Hallen House, which was at least two miles away.

His footsteps were loud on the rough road, and he stepped on to the moorland. Here the grass was slippery, and he kept catching his feet in heather which grew close to the ground, but he made little noise. After a while, he began to long for a cigarette; but if the police were watching, they would see the flare of a match; it might even be visible from Hallen House.

Suddenly a tiny flash broke the darkness.

Standing quite still, he peered across the moor, and made out a man's face, then another, probably two hundred yards away. The flame died down and fell to the ground. He could no longer see the faces, but two little glowing red dots told him that the watchers on the moor had given way to the temptation to light cigarettes.

He smiled to himself as he made a wide detour.

He could still see the cigarettes glowing and, now when he was on low ground, saw the rocks behind which the men were sheltering. The stars were blotted out by the ragged outline. The red glows faded behind him, but he had lost the road, and it was not easy to find his way back.

There were no lights at Hallen House, or he would be able to see them.

One could easily get lost on the moors. He remembered the picture of bleak desolation which it had by day.

Another light flashed—then another.

Hallen House appeared in a blaze of lights which came from half a dozen windows. It seemed very neat—not half a mile away. He stood silent, watching, trying to judge which rooms were lighted up. The front door and the hall were in darkness.

He peered at the dial of his luminous watch; it was half-past ten.

He walked over the rough grass, slipping and sliding now and again, until he could see the trees which lined the drive. He heard a throbbing noise which he couldn't place.

One of the ground floor lights went out; another.

They were going to bed.

But there would be men on guard. Bellamy would take precautions against a sudden swoop by the police.

Mannering reached the wall.

He stood beneath it and reached up, touching the broken glass on the top. He felt along, until he could get a grip without cutting his hands.

He hauled himself up. The old excitement made his nerves tingle.

He climbed over and dropped down into soft earth. The deep throbbing note still broke the quiet; a petrol engine, probably generating electric current for the house; but he hadn't heard it before.

Another light went out. Only one was on, now—on the first floor; Harrison's room. There might be others at the back or on the far side, but that didn't matter. He crept forward to within a few yards of the drive, and listened quietly.

He could hear a man's footsteps. There were two men. They walked past him; he could have touched them.

He waited until they were at the end of the drive, then crept closer to the house. He was on the side nearest the garage.

The throbbing noise grew louder as he neared it. Apart from that he could only hear the whistling of the wind.

He stepped on to the asphalt of the drive near the garage, as the engine's regular throb was interrupted. It stopped,

178

with a gurgling, rumbling sound, and fell silent. Now all seemed still.

Had they deliberately turned off the current? Or had the last light in the house been switched off as a man got into bed? The plant was probably operated from the switches, and did not run unless current was being used. But if it weren't in use now, the electrical devices at the windows and the strong-room could not be operating.

He entered the garage, and using his torch, he approached the engine. There was a strong smell of petrol.

Ah! There was another plant, a battery set; so they were used alternately, there was no mystery about that.

He found the main switch and pushed it up—off.

Still no sound. He approached the back door.

The lock would take five or ten minutes to force. He took out his tools, trying the skeleton key first; no use. He ran his fingers over the lock fittings and touched the heads of the countersunk screws. He took out his screwdriver.

He had three of the four screws out and in his pocket, when he heard footsteps.

He moved swiftly towards the garage, and waited there. Two men were talking this time, and their footsteps rang clearly on the asphalt. They passed him, without troubling to try the back door lock. When they were out of earshot, he went back to the door.

The fourth screw soon came out.

He pulled the facing of the lock away, and switched on his torch. The mechanism was bared; he could press the barrel back now. He used the screwdriver; there was a familiar sharp click as the lock went back.

He stepped into the darkened hallway, then into the passage which led to the front hall. Oil lamps flickered in the draught, so the battery set wasn't in use for ordinary lighting purposes.

He went along on tiptoe. The silence in the house was unnerving.

He opened the door leading to the entrance hall.

A single oil-lamp was burning on the table where once a guard had been.

Was a man here now?

If so, would he notice the door ajar?

Mannering opened the door wide and stepped boldly into the hall.

No, no one was there! Bellamy was relying on the two men outside.

Mannering went to the door of the Great Hall.

It was padlocked, just as it had been when Bellamy had wheeled his chair towards it and taken out a key, but there was light enough for Mannering to work by. He used the skeleton key, and after two minutes the padlock opened; he took it out of the hasp and let it hang.

Now for the main lock.

It was more formidable, but to force it would be only a matter of time. The simplest method was to unscrew the lock and remove it; the danger was that anyone who came would see that it had been forced.

In any case the padlock would be noticed.

He took out the screws, and they jingled in his pocket. He was alert for any warning sound, but the house seemed dead.

He slid back the lock.

Slowly, he turned the handle and pushed one of the great doors. It opened, creaking slightly. Beyond there was only darkness, a great black void.

He stepped inside and closed the door. Darkness and silence, except for the fluttering of his heart and the blood drumming in his ears. He switched on his flashlight.

The pale beam stabbed the darkness, and he began to swivel it round.

Next moment, another light came on!

CHAPTER XXII

THE VAULTS

FOR a wild moment Mannering thought that he had been fooled, that someone was waiting here for him. He took in the great room at a single glance, and saw no one. No one spoke. Yet the light *was* on, over the sideboard.

Had a switch been pressed on in the hall?

He stepped swiftly across the room, and hid behind a suit of Dutch armour.

This was uncanny; the single electric light, but no movement, no voice, no challenge.

He heard a creak—as if someone were tiptoeing towards him. He glanced round; no, the room *was* empty. Yet the creaking continued and . . .

The end of the sideboard was moving!

Someone was approaching from inside the walls, coming from the secret hiding place that Stella was sure existed.

The gap by the sideboard was wide, now.

Harrison stepped into the room, in his shirt-sleeves, wiping his forehead. He did not close the secret door, but walked quickly towards the exit doors.

If he once reached them, he would know the lock had been forced.

Mannering stole out from his hiding-place, the thick carpet muffling his footsteps. Harrison was still unsuspecting, but dangerously close to the door. Mannering got within two yards of him, and he whispered:

'*Put your hands up!*'

Harrison turned round, into a punch which rocked him

back on his feet. Another, carrying all Mannering's weight and all he owed this man for the ordeal in the cottage. A third—and Harrison crumpled up, with a little groaning sound.

Mannering rubbed his knuckles slowly and looked round the Great Hall; he saw a coffer in one corner—Bellamy had pointed out that it was a William and Mary relic. He dragged Harrison by the arms towards the coffer, which was not locked. He eased back the lid.

Grunting with the strain, he lifted Harrison into the box. It was not quite long enough for the man to lie full-length. He bent his knees, turned round and picked up a rug, rolled it and pushed it beneath Harrison's neck. Then he stuffed the man's own handkerchief into his mouth.

He examined the coffer more closely.

There were cracks at the sides, which were unlined, and others in the lid; there would be plenty of air. He closed the lid and sat on the top to recover his breath. He would have to put something on the lid, or else tie Harrison's hands and feet.

Better do that——

Ten minutes after Harrison had come into the Great Hall, he was bound hand and foot, and the lid of the coffer was closed.

Mannering went towards the sideboard.

He examined the mechanism closely.

It *was* electrically controlled and, the current being off, had opened without any difficulty. The light which had come on was worked off a dry cell, fastened to the wall. Harrison had pressed the usual switches, not knowing that the current was off.

Mannering worked at the lock with the screwdriver, took it off, and pushed it out of sight, beneath a chair.

Now he could not be locked in from behind.

He entered the sloping, circular passage, lit by the little oil lamps, and heard a sound of hammering mingled with a curious high-pitched wailing. There was something uncanny about that wail—its banshee note was like the cry of a tormented soul, a cry that would delight Bellamy.

He reached the open door leading to the vault. In the mellow light, he saw a man working at a bench—hammering a box or crate. It was Foss, his dark head bent over his work.

Mannering drew nearer.

Bellamy was in the wheel-chair in front of a safe, and was taking out jewels. He glanced up now and again, at someone Mannering could not see. Mannering drew a shade nearer.

Lark, chained to the wall, was packing jewels into another case.

Mannering saw the wide steel band round his waist, and the chain which led to a stake in the wall. Lark had been badly knocked about, his face was still sore and bleeding. He worked slowly and sullenly, glancing malevolently at Bellamy from time to time.

Bellamy said suddenly:

'Lark, if you don't hurry, you'll get another beating-up. Harrison won't mind doing it, and he'll soon be back. Maybe he would even like it! You ought to be grateful that nothing worse will happen to you. Something like—that.'

He nodded towards the corner.

The wailing, which had faded, suddenly grew louder. Mannering stared towards the corner with sharp alarm. Could *Ashton* be making that noise?

Lark said harshly:

'Listen, Bellamy. If the police find me 'ere, I'll go down for a stretch. I've opened your ruddy tin-can; lemme go!'

'But you helped Mannering,' Bellamy said softly, 'and you have to suffer for that. Seven years will hardly pay for it. You will stay where you are. And upstairs in my room, waiting for the police, is a detailed statement of your crimes—of the jewels which you sold me. And one or two letters which you were foolish enough to write to me, Lark, when you thought I could be—what is the word?—trusted.'

'Why, you——' Lark strained against the chains.

'Get on with your job!' snapped Bellamy.

Lark set to work again.

Now the only sound in the vaults came from the corner. The wailing grew worse. There was a scream and then a wild, hysterical sobbing.

Foss suddenly looked round.

'I tell you I can't stand that row!' His voice was shrill.

'I am afraid you will have to, son,' said Bellamy. 'I *like* it. I shall kill Ashton before we leave, but not yet—oh, not yet.'

'Put a bullet in his guts and finish him off,' growled Foss.

Bellamy said:

'No, Foss, I won't do that yet. Don't you know how much I dislike Ashton?'

'No, and I don't want to. He's getting on my nerves.'

'He once got on my nerves,' said Bellamy, without ceasing his work with the jewels. 'We were partners, years ago—partners in a small jewellery business. He wasn't "Ashton" then. We began to buy stolen gems, and were doing very nicely, when the police caught us. This was in Canada. I'm a Canadian—do you know that?'

Foss did not answer.

Mannering kept very still.

'Foss, you must listen,' said Bellamy. 'Ashton blamed it *all* on to me. And got away with it. He swore he knew nothing of the fencing. He escaped scot free, while I went to a penitentiary for five years—five years! And I was a hale and hearty man then, but undisciplined. I've learned better since then. I resented the brutal treatment of the warders, and struck one. I was battered into unconsciousness by the others, Foss, and flung into an unlit solitary cell. I was in a stupor there for a long time, and when I came round, I couldn't move my legs. I've never moved my legs since then. I was paralysed from a broken bone near the base of my spine. Paralysed . . . and Ashton——'

He stopped, and caught his breath.

The wailing grew louder.

'And now Ashton knows what solitary confinement is like. I always meant to make him understand what he'd done to me, but I couldn't find him. I met him by chance in the States last year. Wasn't that a lucky break?'

Foss said: 'You've had your revenge.'

'Yes, I've had that. I've ruined him. I've reduced his nieces to mental wrecks. And yet—he was a fighter. He struck back. He sent word to Mannering.'

Mannering's lips were set very tightly. He hadn't realised it until he'd learned the name of Stella's uncle, but he knew that this was true.

'I don't know how he managed it, but he sent word—and Mannering craftily advertised for the Lake emeralds,' said Bellamy, 'but didn't know I realised that Ashton had asked for help. That was where *I* outsmarted Mannering.'

'Well, he got away,' said Foss, 'And I don't give a damn. I can't stand that noise.'

Mannering stepped into the room, covering both men with the Luger. 'Nor can I,' he said to Foss. 'Go and unlock the door.'

Foss dropped his tools. Bellamy spun round in his chair. Lark pulled against his chains, and a case of jewels fell from his hands.

'Man—Mannering!' gasped Bellamy.

'A friend of Mannering's. Go and unlock that door.' He jerked the gun.

Lark began to laugh—a wild, hysterical sound.

Foss backed towards the door in the corner. When he reached it he turned the key in the lock. Bellamy was sitting like a carved figure in the chair. His lips were turned back; all the hatred, the bitterness, the viciousness of which he was capable, showed in his eyes. He kept his hands on the black rug, but the jewels fell to the floor, trickling down in a brilliant cascade.

Mannering said: 'Stay where you are, Foss. Shut up, Lark.'

He went slowly towards Bellamy.

The man seemed dumbstruck.

But as Mannering drew nearer, Bellamy moved his hands, gripped the wheels of his chair and propelled himself forward with a burst of speed which caught Mannering off his guard. There was no stopping the chair. Bellamy flashed his hand to his pocket, flinging the rug aside. A gun showed in his hand.

Mannering jumped to one side.

Bellamy fired; missed. As the chair passed, Mannering put out his arm and struck Bellamy on the side of the head. Bellamy gasped and sagged back; the gun dropped and the chair came slowly to a standstill. Mannering turned to Foss.

'Get inside with Ashton!'

Foss hesitated.

'*Get inside!*'

Foss backed into the room.

'You—you've made it,' Lark gasped incredulously.

Mannering said sharply:

'Where are the keys to that belt?'

With a quivering finger, Lark pointed to a ring of keys on a nearby bench. Mannering picked them up and handed them to the screwsman, while still watching the door.

'Get upstairs, find that dossier Bellamy's prepared, get an attaché case from the wardrobe in the room just beyond, and scram,' said Mannering.

Lark's fingers were unsteady as he unlocked the steel belt. 'Be careful, the police aren't far off,' Mannering went on. 'Keep off the Corwellin Road.'

'O-okay,' muttered Lark. The chain fell with a clinking noise. 'Mister, I——'

'Hurry!'

Lark hurried out of the vaults.

Bellamy was opening his eyes.

Blood was trickling down the side of his face, he was dazed and helpless. Mannering went to his side, made sure he had no other weapon, and backed away.

Through the doorway of the cell, he caught a glimpse of Ashton, sitting on the bed and rocking to and fro in awful despair.

Foss crouched against the far wall; he had no fight in him.

Mannering rasped: 'You're going to talk. What are the tricks with the lights?'

Foss said quickly: 'The petrol engine is doing the light tonight, the batteries, the burglar control, and—and there are one or two dry cell lights.'

'Why are the lights switched off when you come here?'

'To—to fox the men.'

'What will the men upstairs do if there's an alarm?'

'I——'

'Come on! What will they do?'

Foss said: 'If—if there's anyone coming, they'll—they'll telephone.'

'Here?'

'Yes, we—we've got a house-line.'

'Go on.'

'They'd be told to get out of the house, wait outside until—until they could see how things were shaping. If—if the police came and we were—were arrested, the men would rush the door, and get us away.'

'All right—now listen. You'll stay here with Ashton, and try to help him. When the police come, turn Queen's Evidence.'

Foss gasped: 'What—what are *you* going to do?'

'Never mind me. Foss, do you know who killed Holmes?'

'Y-yes.'

'Who?'

'Harrison. Bellamy told him to. Holmes suspected——'

'Don't forget your best line,' Mannering said.

He went out, closed the door of the cell and turned the key in the lock. Ashton had been there for so long that another hour or two would do no harm. Help would soon be here—it mustn't arrive until Mannering had escaped.

He went to Bellamy's side. The man seemed in a stupor. The blow had stunned him. He was only half conscious. He was shocked, numbed. Mannering looked at the jewels at his feet, saw the piles in the safe. He picked up a piece of wire and twisted it round the spokes of a wheel, to prevent the chair from moving.

He turned away.

A bell started to ring!

An old-fashioned candle-stick telephone stood on the bench, and he hurried towards it. The ringing sound was very loud, and Ashton began to wail again.

Mannering steeled himself, took off the receiver, and spoke in the deep, slightly nasal voice he remembered to be Bellamy's.

'Hallo?'

'Boss, there are three cars coming from Corwellin. They just stopped near the policemen—the two who——'

'I know who you mean. Well, son, call the others. Forget what I said before, put two on the drive and the rest near the garage. The two on the drive will tell you what's happening. Maybe I can bluff them. I'll be right up.'

'Okay.'

Mannering hung up the receiver.

Ten minutes later, crouching in the shadows near the wall, he saw Dando and Bristow enter the house, followed by several other men. They'd come because Mannering had asked Chittering to send them—and they'd nearly come too soon. They would find the secret entrance to the vaults and the doors of the Great Hall wide open; and he had thrown back the lid of the coffer in which Harrison lay.

Lorna lifted the telephone.

'Hallo.'

'Hallo, my sweet. I can't stop now; it's all over but the shouting.'

187

'John!'

''Bye!' cried Mannering.

The following morning rain was teeming from leaden skies, and Corwellin was drenched; the people were drenched; the prospect everywhere was dreary—yet Bristow, water streaming from the brim of his hat and from his raincoat, walked cheerfully into the police station and hurried up the stairs to Dando's office. It was now nine o'clock. He hadn't been in bed until after four, but he felt on top of the world.

Dando looked up with a scowl.

'Hallo, why the gloom?' inquired Bristow. 'Foss hasn't withdrawn his confession has he?'

'No, he hasn't done that,' said Dando, 'but I've been trying to get the people he named at the different pubs. They've all flown.'

'Flown?'

'Yes,' said Dando, sourly. 'They must have been warned. And although I can get a fair description of them, that won't help much to trace them. Perce Grey's gone—but that was an assumed name. That fair-haired man——'

'Yes,' said Bristow sharply.

'He must have warned them.'

'Possibly. He also warned us.'

'I know,' said Dando, 'but all the same, he shouldn't have —I say, d'you think he's Mannering?'

'*Mannering*?' exclaimed Bristow. 'Mannering's dark. And this fellow did a nice job for us, didn't he? He probably discovered the truth about Ashton, and turned against Bellamy. I'd be surprised if we ever catch that fellow. Will that worry you?'

'I suppose not. Still——'

'Let's be thankful for what we've got,' said Bristow warmly. 'We caught the whole mob at the house, and the two Frenchmen on that 'plane. We've uncovered a smuggling ring and a gang dealing in precious stones, priceless antiques, and what-have-you. It's one of the biggest hauls we've had for years, and it all happened near Corwellin.'

Dando rubbed his chin.

'Yes, that's very well, but——'

'We'll soon learn that Mannering's in London or Paris—I don't doubt he cleared out and left the job to us,' said

Bristow. 'It won't surprise me if he did, anyhow. And we don't need Mannering now. Unless you——'

'He's got to tell his story. His prints *were* on the door and the cabinet.'

'But Mrs. Dent's told you about that,' Bristow pointed out. 'He was allowed in the jewel-room, when the other stuff was there. I don't doubt Mannering recognised a lot of it as stolen stuff, and sent me that telegram. Bellamy discovered what he'd done, and Mannering had to fly. It'll all work out; Mannering will turn up soon, you'll see. He felt that he couldn't give himself up until he was cleared, as they were trying to frame him.'

'Fond of Mannering, aren't you?' demanded Dando.

Bristow looked surprised.

Much more came to light in the next twenty-four hours. It was discovered, for instance, that Victor Galliard's cousin had worked for Bellamy for years, and Bellamy had been blackmailing him; that explained the forced sale of the house at a ridiculously low price. Foss said the cousin had threatened disclosure; hence his murder.

Rundle, an ex-convict, also on Bellamy's pay-roll, had discovered Ashton was imprisoned somewhere in the house, and from then on tried to get help. Holmes had worked with him. Harrison and Emma Dent had managed the English side of Bellamy's business. He had been at the other end of the smuggling racket for years, sending the stuff to England.

The only thing the police learned about Lark was that Bellamy bought some jewellery from him; but there was no evidence against the little crook.

A month later, Lorna and John Mannering were in their Chelsea flat when there was a ring at the front door. The maid answered it, and soon the drawing-room door opened.

'Mr. Lark has called, by appointment,' announced the maid.

Mannering jumped up as Lark came perkily into the room.

'Hallo, Larky! I'm glad you've been able to make it.'

'I hope you are,' said Lark meaningly. 'I wondered how long you'd be in Paris, Mister! Pretty fine thing, going off like that. Some people have all the luck. If I'd gone to Paris and written a letter to the Press explaining what I'd done, I'd be extradited. That's what they'd do to me.'

'But you didn't go to Paris and you're as free as the air. What are you worrying about?'

Lark sniffed.

'I lost a good connection with Bellamy,' he remarked, casting a quick glance at Lorna. 'I dunno how much the missus knows, but——'

Mannering laughed.

'She knows as much as I do. That I sometimes have to use tools for opening locks and safes here and at Quinn's. That's all, Larky! You were wrong when you thought I was a screwsman.'

'Oh, was I!'

'You were. But all the same I owe you a great deal, and want to pay my debts. Remember the Lake Emeralds?'

Lark did not answer that superfluous question.

'I dunno about *owe* me anything. I won't forget them vaults in a n'urry, but a spot o' business now an' then——'

'You also remember I told you I'd paid Bellamy by cheque,' said Mannering. 'Well, apparently he destroyed the cheque—the police found a corner of it in a fireplace. As he didn't pay it in, I'm three thousand pounds to the good. I could have paid that into Bellamy's estate, but—why waste good money?' Mannering tapped a brown-paper parcel which was on the table by his side. 'There it is, in one-pound notes.'

Lark stared.

'For you,' said Mannering.

Lark sat down abruptly.

'Well, that's diff'rent,' he said slowly, and then beamed at Lorna. 'Yes, that's very diff'rent kettle o' fish! I know my onions. 'Ad any news of the girl?' he added, as an afterthought. 'The two of them I mean. There was two, wasn't there?'

'Yes,' said Mannering, his smile fading. 'The younger one is in a nursing home. She'll recover, but it will take time. Stella is getting on like a house on fire with young Vic Galliard. And their uncle—you've read about him, haven't you?'

Lark nodded, and said thoughtfully:

''Ow is he?'

'He'll recover, too. But he's a broken man. Business gone, reputation gone—and it was a good reputation; I did quite a lot of business with him. There'll be no case against him;

the police have only hearsay evidence, and he's pretty sick. Not a nice show, but he'll be all right. Did you know him well?'

Lark sniffed.

'Sold 'im a few sparklers now 'an then. On the side—*you* know.'

Mannering laughed.

'But I feel sorry for the old geezer,' said Lark. 'I wish——' His gaze travelled to the parcel of one-pound notes.

Lorna leaned forward.

'You needn't worry about Ashton, Mr. Lark. John has to arrange for the disposal of Bellamy's jewels and furniture, and the commission he draws will go to Ashton. It will be enough to see him through.'

'Oh,' said Lark, and looked at Mannering, his bright little eyes eager, approving. 'You're quite a guy, aren't you, Mr. M?'

'I'm making a special effort for Ashton,' Mannering said.

'Why?' demanded Lark.

Mannering took his cigarette-case from his pocket, and when they had lit up, poured out drinks. Not until he was sitting down again did he say:

'Because Ashton first put me on to Bellamy months ago, although I didn't realise it. It was Ashton who commissioned me to buy the Lake Emeralds. He knew I'd find out that Bellamy had them sooner or later. And Bellamy knew that Ashton had sent some kind of message to me; that's why Bellamy asked me to go down there, he wanted to cut my claws.'

'Now *what* do yer think of that?' cried Lark.

THE END

191

A SELECTED LIST OF CRIME STORIES FOR YOUR READING PLEASURE

☐	09297 5	CALL FOR THE BARON	*John Creasey* 30p
☐	09286 X	MURDER MOST FOUL	*John Creasey* 30p
☐	09384 X	DEATH IN HIGH PLACES	*John Creasey* 30p
☐	09385 3	DEATH IN FLAMES	*John Creasey* 30p
☐	09386 6	THE BARON COMES BACK	*John Creasey* 30p
☐	09189 8	FOUNDER MEMBER	*John Gardner* 30p
☐	08977 X	UNDERSTRIKE	*John Gardner* 25p
☐	09424 2	AN ACE UP MY SLEEVE	*James Hadley Chase* 35p
☐	09466 8	JUST ANOTHER SUCKER	*James Hadley Chase* 35p
☐	09491 9	I WOULD RATHER STAY POOR	*James Hadley Chase* 35p
☐	09550 8	DOUBLE SHUFFLE	*James Hadley Chase* 35p
☐	08640 1	RED FILE FOR CALLAN	*James Mitchell* 30p
☐	09325 4	THE EXECUTIONER: VEGAS VENDETTA	*Don Pendleton* 30p
☐	09326 2	THE EXECUTIONER: CARIBBEAN KILL	*Don Pendleton* 30p
☐	09443 9	THE EXECUTIONER: CALIFORNIA HIT	*Don Pendleton* 30p
☐	09262 2	THE EXECUTIONER: CHICAGO WIPEOUT	*Don Pendleton* 30p
☐	09206 1	THE EXECUTIONER: NIGHTMARE IN NEW YORK	*Don Pendleton* 30p
☐	09205 3	THE EXECUTIONER: ASSAULT ON SOHO	*Don Pendleton* 30p
☐	09204 5	THE EXECUTIONER: MIAMI MASSACRE	*Don Pendleton* 30p
☐	09261 4	NORSLAG	*Michael Sinclair* 30p
☐	09273 8	SHAFT HAS A BALL	*Ernest Tidyman* 30p
☐	09072 7	SHAFT'S BIG SCORE	*Ernest Tidyman* 30p
☐	09056 5	SHAFT	*Ernest Tidyman* 30p
☐	09309 2	SHAFT AMONG THE JEWS	*Ernest Tidyman* 35p
☐	09272 X	THE FLIER	*Mickey Spillane* 30p
☐	09111 1	THE ERECTION SET	*Mickey Spillane* 40p
☐	08769 6	I THE JURY	*Mickey Spillane* 25p
☐	08680 0	BLOODY SUNRISE	*Mickey Spillane* 25p
☐	08697 5	DAY OF THE GUNS	*Mickey Spillane* 25p
☐	09432 3	THE DEEP	*Mickey Spillane* 30p
☐	09335 1	KILLER MINE	*Mickey Spillane* 30p
☐	09336 X	THE GIRL HUNTERS	*Mickey Spillane* 30p
☐	09337 8	THE BY-PASS CONTROL	*Mickey Spillane* 35p
☐	09433 1	THE DELTA FACTOR	*Mickey Spillane* 30p
☐	09434 X	THE SNAKE	*Mickey Spillane* 30p

All these books are available at your bookshop or newsagents or can be ordered direct from the publisher. Just tick the titles you want and fill in the form below.

....

CORGI BOOKS, Cash Sales Department, P.O. Box 11, Falmouth, Cornwall.

Please send cheque or postal order. No currency, and allow 10p to cover the cost of postage and packing (plus 5p each for additional copies).

NAME (Block Letters) ....

ADDRESS ....

(NOV 74) ....